BAPTIS

BEASTS OF JÖTUNHEIMR

BOOK TWO OF THE ARMY OF ONE TRILOGY

Beasts of Jötunheimr

The Army of One (Book 2)

Copyright © 2024 by Baptiste Pinson Wu

All rights reserved.

No part of this book may be reproduced in any form or by any electronic or mechanical means, including information storage and retrieval systems, without written permission from the author, except for the use of brief quotations in a book review.

Cover art by Miblart

❀ Created with Vellum

To Artheo and Thorin

*When you're old enough to read this book,
let's also go for a beer.*

The fetters will burst, and the wolf run free.

Völuspá

PROLOGUE

Asgard, now

For each of my steps, three echoed back to me, yet of my breath, I heard nothing. Drops of water dripped from frozen stalactites after wriggling until they could hold no more, plopping onto a hard, unforgiving ground, and those I heard clearly. Just as I heard the groans and grumbles from the dark cells flanking the corridor dug into the mountain's rock. Sets of eyes, in various numbers, stared back at me through the uneven bars of the cells. They burned with hate, fear, and resignation. Only the gods knew what filthy creatures occupied those forgotten rooms. Nothing that could be killed, or they wouldn't be here.

Calling this place a prison would be an exaggeration. Æsir didn't keep prisoners. It was Asgard's pit of shame. A place where our so-called gods hid their mistakes and forgot their existence, like children hiding a broken plate under a rug. And I came to visit mine. I would find Muninn here, and if we needed another sign of Ragnarök's imminence, her occupying the last available cell would be it.

Chains rattled by my side, and four golden eyes blinked one by one as the creature they belonged to crept toward the bars. I stopped moving. The fear of being in Muninn's presence overpowered my thirst for it. The creature halted a step or two from the barred wall separating us and stretched a skeletal, spider-like limb ending in curved hooks. The beast squeaked plaintively for my attention. I doubted it still felt hunger at this point, but it would have taken anything I could give.

The hooked hand almost reached through the bars. A veil of pity draped my heart for a second, only to burn at the touch. The feeble, silverish light from the torches on the corridor's wall turned blood-red. Then, a flash of the same color erupted from the bars, striking the creature's hand and sending it whimpering back to a dark corner of its cell. I blocked a new pang of pity. Pity did not belong here, and I forsake the feeling, just as I had forsaken faith, joy, or love. I had given it all up to feed the only feeling that mattered, rage. Rage for the fallen. Rage for the betrayals. A rage I would need to save Odin.

Huginn passed through the bars of the last cell as if they did not exist. There were no doors to those rooms. The *seidr*-infused bars prevented anyone bearing the brand from passing them, but to the others, it was a mere illusion.

I waited for Huginn to come closer. I would have words with him before I spoke to his sister. He did not even pretend to be surprised by my presence. Even more than on that not-so-far-away day when he saved me from the cave, Huginn looked exhausted. The extreme paleness of his face accentuated the darkness of the pockets under his eyes, and the coldness of the prison had cracked his lips bloody. Since we had caught Muninn, my raven friend had not left her side.

"Anything new?" I asked, whispering.

"Nothing of importance." He sighed.

"What is it then?" The old raven had something on his heart; after so long with him, I could sense it.

"I believe—" he said. "I believe we might have misjudged her."

"How?" I asked, louder than I should have.

"I don't know, Drake." I heard his hand scratching the back of his head as he often did when in doubt. "She hasn't spoken much."

"So why do you think so?" Twice already, my lack of trust in Huginn had proven misplaced. I would not make the same mistake again.

"She's my sister," he replied. "I can feel a deeper motive behind her actions. Loki, Father, Heimdallr, she cared about none of them when I spoke. But when I used your name... She asked about you, Drake."

"What did she ask?"

"If you've recovered. If you intended to visit her. This kind of thing."

I had recovered. Physically, at least.

"She said anything else?" I coldly asked, killing any murmur of emotion as soon as they budded in my chest.

"She said she was happy to see me," Huginn replied, his teeth showing in the dark. "And that she would wait for her judgment and accept it."

"She does not plead?" I asked, surprised.

"She does not. She has resigned herself, I'd say."

"She did not even ask to wait for Odin's return?"

Everyone had assumed she would make this demand. Odin, when all was said and done, was a forgiving god, especially with his children. He had rarely condemned one of them and never to death. He would choose a form of exile or some sort of humiliation rather than a proper execution. He had created Huginn and Muninn from himself rather than with a woman, but he loved them as dearly as any of his progeny. If Odin were here, Muninn had a chance. That she did not ask to wait for his judgment meant only one thing.

"She does not expect him to come back," Huginn said, echoing my thoughts.

"Fuck."

Odin was dead then or would soon be. I loved Odin like a father, even after what he had put me through. Even after all the lies. I loved him, and a world without the All-Father... I could not picture it.

I was about to leave him and face his sister, but Huginn grabbed my arm.

"She's hurt you, I know," he said. "But I don't think that was her goal."

"So, what? I should forgive her?" I asked.

"No, I would not ask that. Just—" Once again, Huginn stumbled over his words. "Just listen to her, please."

I was to suppress my rage, my desire for vengeance, while I listened to the woman who had stomped on my heart. That's what he was asking. I was to keep three years chained to a rock and days of struggling through Jötunheimr bottled in my chest, and listen to Muninn as if she were still a friend rather than the betraying, lying, manipulative witch I knew her to be.

I could not do that. I could not be neutral with her.

"I will," I still said, for there was no point arguing with Huginn. He knew I was lying, but he nodded and smiled. I waited for him to vanish at the end of the corridor, then I waited a bit more.

Get her to speak, I told myself, *and then you can go back to just being Drake*. Ragnarök was near. Things would end. There was nothing to fear. *Just get her to speak.*

I found myself in the boots of a beardless fifteen-year-old boy about to embark on his first raid, palms sweaty and mouth dry. Facing Muninn, after so much time, was a battle I dreaded and longed for in equal measure.

"Drake?" she called. "Is that you?"

Her voice was weak and broken, but I would recognize it among any other. For years, it had made my heart jump. Today, too, it did the trick. I covered the dozen of steps separating us, then stopped just before reaching the bars of her cell. I sat against the wall, right under the light of a torch.

"It's me," I said.

She did not reply. All I heard was her constant sniffling.

"Why are you here?" she finally asked.

"Everyone is worried about Odin, and you know where he is."

"I meant, why are you on Asgard? You're not supposed to be here."

"And where am I supposed to be? In the cave where you left me to rot?" I asked, already struggling with my temper. Again, she let a long silence insinuate itself between us, one I was not willing to break.

"You were safe there," she said.

"Safe?"

I snatched the torch as I stood up, and before I could change my mind, I passed through the bars separating me from Muninn.

I felt her presence in the corner of the room. The silverish torch light barely reached her in the corner of her cell. I saw her ankles, dirty and bruised, then the jagged tip of a once-white dress. The Tyr rune-shaped brand glowed like lava on her shoulder, allowing me to guess the shape of her face, framed by her long, straight, black hair. She did not move, but the flames reflecting in the tears she yet held burned like melting silver.

"Do you know how *safe* I was? Three years I spent under that snake, with a mad Æsir by my side. Do you think safety was my concern? Did I ever ask for safety?"

"From Ragnarök," she pleaded. "Loki promised you were safe from Ragnarök."

"What is it to you?" I asked as I threw the torch so close to her that she recoiled even deeper into her corner. I finally saw her face, tired and dusty, except where tears had traced two furrows of clean skin. "I was born for Ragnarök!" I shouted. "You almost took it from me. *I* wasn't safe. *You* were safe from me. Safe to follow your real master's plan while I lost myself in that shitty cave." My anger was boiling. I wouldn't be able to keep my word to Huginn. "You have no idea of the dangers I faced to come back. You have no idea what I lost along the way. So let me tell you about my *safety*. Let me tell you, witch, of my time among the beasts of Jötunheimr."

1

Jötunheimr, a few days before

There was a time, before Ragnarök's shadow loomed on Asgard like the stench of a putrefied carcass, when the Wolves did more than recruit for the gods' army. We roamed the realms, accompanying the Æsir in their official—and sometimes unofficial—missions. Peacekeeping, investigations, and the eventual bit of head-bashing, we took part in all those quests now sung by our skalds in Valhöll with more or less accuracy. As the Wolves' Drake, their leader, I had visited several of the nine realms.

I was born on Midgard, as any folk, and reborn on Asgard, as any Einheri. I was the last Drake to visit Álfheimr and had once been to the border of Múspellsheimr, the land of fire and chaos. But if there was a place I hated more than any other, it was Jötunheimr.

Jötnar were not only our mortal enemies; they were vicious and violent beyond measure, just as their land was. Forests grew dark and hungry, mountains sharp and treacherous. Even the snow fell cunningly, always finding the perfect spot in your clothes to bother you, and sometimes it also burned your skin. The deeper you went into this land, the more its nature and its inhabitants tried to kill you, and from what I had gathered, we were deep into Jötunheimr. Plants and animals were deformed, ridiculous in size, and far more dangerous than their counterparts on Midgard. Just as was the hare we had been tracking for the past two days.

Its footprints were the size of a bear's, and the distance between them equaled three of our steps. We had spotted them while looking for shelter from the snowstorm. But the track led to the forest we had meant to avoid. The mountain in which I had been detained for three years had served as a landmark to measure our progress until it, too, disappeared behind the trees as we circled the forest. The storm was dangerous in the open, but at least it kept other dangers away. However, after four days of strolling through the white powder, we had nothing left to eat and were as cold as we were miserable. The forest looked safer by the minute as hunger weakened our common sense.

To say we were lost wouldn't be accurate. To lose oneself, one had to have an idea of where one was. We had none. We hoped to find a river, for rivers always lead somewhere. But we had failed to locate one. Only madmen could hope to see anything in this blizzard, and two of us were just that.

My body was still weak from years of being chained to a rock. Well, not my body, for I was stuck in Loki's. The trickster had stolen mine to free himself and gain access to Asgard. Getting it back was one of my priorities. My current vessel was handsome, tall, and lean, but it didn't belong to the warrior I was. I missed my beard. I missed my hands, rugged from hundreds of years wielding swords and shields, and my thick legs. I missed the scars and tattoos marring my skin and telling my story. And I missed... well, something else. If only being in Loki's body meant that I could use his power, it would be somewhat worth it. But as it was, I was just a regular man in a fairly puny vessel. And I was dangerously close to folly.

If Loki had stolen my flesh, you, Muninn, broke my heart. I had loved you for more years than I could count. For a short and beautiful moment, I thought that you and I could be happy. Then, you shattered my illusion when you drove my knife into my guts.

But I wasn't born to be your sacrifice, and by a strange twist of fate, Huginn was the one who freed me, helped by an old friend whom I had thought gone for good, Ulf.

Ulf was the only one with clear wits.

I drooled after my sweet revenge and used this thirst to empower each step across Jötunheimr, contenting myself in following Ulf and giving him no help whatsoever. Yet I was a great deal more dependable than Huginn.

The old man was a manifestation of the All-Father's thoughts and used to be able to shapeshift into a raven to carry messages or share thoughts from a distance. Twenty-three years on Midgard, however, had taken a toll on him. He hadn't been able to communicate with his father since his descent on Midgard, and his wings, following our way down from Loki's cave, possessed fewer feathers than Ulf's arrows.

I loved Odin like a father and counted several of his kind as my friends, Heimdallr and Tyr, most of all. But one thing had to be said about the Æsir; their minds were fragile. Æsir were capable of madness, and Huginn was deep into it. It was hard to describe what ailed him, but Huginn would suddenly drop to the ground, fearful of some invisible threat. He would talk to himself, debating our situation as if we were not there, usually to complain about his lack of trust in my sanity. Other times, he would be erratic and charge at some creation of his imagination.

Ulf, having spent the last three years with him, was used to it, but Jötunheimr was no place for this kind of behavior. There were beasts in those woods, Jötnar in those lands, and gods knew what was under the snow itself. So when we agreed to follow the hare's footprints into the forest, we left Huginn to rest at the bottom of a very large tree. He had been quiet enough to understand then and was shivering under a holed blanket when we penetrated the woods.

That was half a day ago.

The tracks led us to a small clearing, then to a hole lost between roots. Using our belts, some branches, and the very last piece of our hard bread, we improvised a snare in the clearing and flattened ourselves by its edge. There was no wind to carry our scent, so it was just a game of patience.

Ulf's breathing birthed steady clouds of steam, and his eyes never left the snare. An arrow waited at the ready against his bow in case the hare did not take the bait. He had spotted a regular-sized squirrel earlier and almost shot it, but it would have made a meager meal, so he let it go. I needed more than just meat; I needed the hare's skin. I wore Loki's thin tunic of linen, and neither Ulf nor Huginn had much to spare in terms of clothes besides the sorry blanket presently covering the mad raven.

So we waited, my friend behaving like a perfect hunter, and I trying hard not to fall asleep as the snow covered us in a slow, thickening layer of white.

I was proud of Ulf. As an Einheri, he had been fearful and short in bravery. That was when he had nothing. Now, he had a granddaughter waiting for him on Asgard. Odin had called her *a child of fate*, for our kind shouldn't be able to sire kids. Her name was Lif, and she gave him strength and courage.

"I hate hare meat," he whispered.

"Me too," I replied. Talking, even just a few words, kept us alive and awake. After two or three hours on the ground, we needed words nearly as much as we needed meat.

"But I'll suck that marrow as if it were ale," he said.

I was about to reply that hare meat beats any fish, but Ulf flattened his hand to make me quiet, and his eyes stabbed the horizon like daggers. The hare stepped into the clearing, its two long ears twisting left and right. It was as big as a Midgard wolf, which got me worried about the size of those beasts here. Apprehensively, it left the cover of the roots and moved its front legs, then the back, slowly advancing toward the bread.

Close to the ground, its nose twitched as it followed this unusual yet appetizing smell. I could already feel the juice on my lips and prayed that my belly did not make too much noise. My heart beat faster as the hare moved closer to the snare. It slowed down a couple of steps from it. It was hungry and curious, yet just as fearful as any of its kind.

Ulf nocked the arrow on the bowstring, ready to bolt into position and let it fly. It would take an amazing shot to kill the beast before it reacted, but Ulf was capable. And just as I thought the hare would decide the bread wasn't worth the risk, a shout echoed in the forest.

"Fuck," Ulf spat as he rose, spraying his blanket of snow and pulling the string to his cheek at the same time.

The arrow bolted, but the hare leaped randomly and away from its trajectory. I was about to swear, but the animal landed on the snare. Its front paw got stuck, and it squeaked when it failed to dart away.

Huginn, who had been the one yelling, stormed the clearing, bellowing like a berserker, and attacked the hare, panicking against the snare. The old raven wielded the blanket like a net trailing in his wake but otherwise charged the animal with nothing but a fist and two rows of teeth. Entranced by the sight of Huginn jumping on the back of the beast, I did not react, but Ulf did.

"Come on!" he yelled. I don't know if he meant it for me or as a curse to the Æsir, who was obviously taken by another bout of madness, but it stirred me from my torpor.

I ran after him, Huginn's long knife in hand.

The raven landed on his back, trapping the hare in his arms to show us its belly. This son of Odin appeared old and feeble, but he was still an Æsir. His legs wrapped around the hare's waist, and his arms coiled around its neck. The animal's chest rose up and down as fast as its heart and lungs allowed, and soon, it started trying to bite Huginn's face.

In its panicking thrashing, the hare kicked Ulf in the chest, and my friend flew backward as if taken by a door-breaking ram. I side-stepped to avoid him as he rolled in the snow, breathed out in relief when he cursed, and attacked the furious animal without him.

Huginn was biting the hare's neck when I reached them, and blood dripped along both their throats. The animal had all but given up the fight. It was done, and it knew it. But his eyes, white with fear, almost undid me. It looked more clever than his cousins on Midgard. Hel, I had met people with duller eyes than this hare. I took pity on it and hesitated. Then I remembered the pit in my stomach and that pity was a luxury I could no longer afford.

I jammed the knife into its throat and cut as well as I could with the rusty blade. The hare squeaked and kicked a couple more times nervously as its blood ran down Huginn's face. Then it became still.

"You crazy old goat," Ulf spat, massaging his chest. "You almost cost us our meal."

"I— I—" Huginn's eyes blinked rapidly, each time opening with more clarity.

"You nothing," Ulf said. "Even hounds know when to attack."

"Well, we can eat now," Huginn replied.

The laughter got all of us by surprise. It was a natural, heartfelt laughter, and I only realized it was mine when Ulf's frown vanished, and he, too, started laughing. I didn't know if it was the sight of Huginn hugging the unmoving hare, his face a mess of blood and conflicting emotions, or Ulf scolding an Æsir as if he were a slow-minded toddler, but I found the scene hilarious. My belly and my jaw hurt from laughing so hard, and it felt amazing. I hadn't laughed so naturally in years, and I was about to eat cooked meat for the first time in just as long. My vengeance could wait a little longer. Right now, I was about to feast.

ᚱ

I hated hare meat, but this meal was glorious. Waiting for the fire to roast the animal was torture, but that first bite... I can't explain in words the pleasure it filled me with. From the tip of my teeth to the bottom of my stomach, every part of me shivered in delight. Ulf and Huginn partook in the pleasure as well. No hare has ever been as appreciated as this giant one. It wouldn't care much about it, but I was grateful to this animal for its flesh. And for its skin. It felt raw and humid against my back but would keep me warm.

We built the fire at the bottom of a thick oak-looking tree

with a light-gray bark. The smell would attract predators, so we ate back-to-back, ready to bolt up the tree at the first sign of danger. But as juice spurted from the piece of leg I was chewing, I stopped seeing movements in the shadows and simply trusted my life to Ulf's senses, as I had so often in the past.

My appetite took a hit as I observed Huginn. The old raven, hair unbound and chin cacked in dry blood, held one of the hare's eyes at the tip of his fingers and inspected it with childlike curiosity. He then shrugged and gobbled the eye. The ball went down his throat whole, then he rubbed his hands in satisfaction.

Often, when I looked at him, I thought of you. Did you sometimes think of me? Of the brief moments we had shared and the feelings I used to have for you? Were you by a fire as well, on Asgard, wrapped in Loki's arms? Or were you alone and regretting your choices?

I felt pity for you.

Just like me, you had acted out of love, and just like me, it was misplaced. I persuaded myself that I hated you and would love to see the life vanish from your eyes, but in truth, what I desired was to know that you regretted your actions. I already feared then being alone with you someday, for I didn't know—and still don't—which temptation would be the strongest. Forgiving or killing you. Both would be a mistake. Both would leave a terrible taste.

"I will talk to her first," Huginn said just after a piece of burning wood popped.

"You can hear my thoughts as well?"

"I can read them on your face," he replied. When he wasn't as crazy as a blind horse, Huginn could be extremely perceptive.

"Why will you talk to her first?" Ulf asked before I did.

"She is my sister," he replied. "I know her better; I will see through her lies. If she lies." He rubbed some snow on his fingers to wash the blood, and Ulf gestured for him to wash his chin as well. "Besides," he went on, as pink snow crumbled from his fingers, "her attitude doesn't make sense. She was always the wild one, but still."

"What doesn't make sense?" I asked.

"Well," he said, "I never knew her to have a liking for Loki. Women have their secret gardens, but I thought I knew parts of hers. She was fond of you though, that I remember."

"She was?" I asked.

"She was," he confirmed. "But it's not just her behavior that I find strange."

"What do you mean?" I asked, recognizing his father's love for an active audience.

"Odin," he said. "Odin is extremely powerful, more than he pretends. I can't force his thoughts to reveal themselves to me, and I can't share mine if he doesn't want me to. I guess it's the same for Muninn's charms. She can't *just* erase his memory."

"Could she have become stronger?" Ulf asked.

"She could," Huginn agreed, nodding. "But not stronger than Odin. Even with some help from Loki. I just don't think it's possible."

"What are you saying?" I asked.

He shuffled the burning pieces of wood with a stick and sent some sparks to die in the night's air.

"I think Odin asked her to erase his memory," he said. The fire was undulating ominously in his eyes.

"Why the Hel would he do that?" Ulf asked.

"He knew this would happen," I replied for Huginn, who nodded again. Ulf snorted, clearly not buying it.

"He knew we would freeze our asses on Jötunheimr while eating some beast-size hare?"

"Probably not," I said. "But then again, it's also possible."

Huginn dropped his eyes back into the fire pensively and struggled, just as I did, with this idea that maybe all of this was part of a plan. Ulf's stare shifted from me to Huginn and back to me, his breathing betraying his frustration.

"Well, you two clearly know more than I do."

The archer was the sane one, but Huginn and I knew Odin and his twisted ways better, so I explained what I feared was true.

Odin had visions. His eye, which rested at the bottom of Mimir's well, could see things that were, are, or will be. Those visions were never clear, especially those of the future, and often left the All-Father more frustrated than wise, but he trusted them. Odin, I assumed, had peeked into the future and concluded that its current path was the best possible course. He had then sent Huginn to Midgard to protect this future against some threat, though the nature of this threat remained a mystery to us. Odin didn't know when his vision would come true and sent his raven right away with vague, prophetic instructions. That it took so long was just unfortunate for Huginn.

"Doesn't explain why he would have his memory cleansed," Ulf said after the explanation, which was true. But Huginn had a justification for that as well.

"Odin, like most living creatures, has weaknesses," he explained. "Whatever future he saw and acted on by sending me to Midgard was not going to be all golden and shiny. The temptation to stop it, or to alter it, would have been too strong, and Odin knew he would change his mind at some point."

"Never knew Odin to be the kind to doubt himself," Ulf said.

"Oh, but he is," Huginn replied. "And you would too if you were in his boots. Imagine, for example, that you knew with certainty that you could save your granddaughter but that to do so would cost Drake's life. You would ponder on it, hate the choice, but would ultimately accept the idea, wouldn't you?"

Ulf, his teeth pulling on a piece of roasted flesh, looked at me from the side, the weight of Huginn's question turning his face to granite. I chuckled, more at his reaction than his hesitation.

"Don't worry," I replied. "Theoretical me would understand."

"But then," Huginn went on, "as the plan unfolds, you would remember your three hundred years of friendships, all the times Drake saved you, all the laughter and tears you shared, and a piece of you would wonder if saving a child you barely knew was worth it. Now imagine that your granddaughter is the fate of the nine realms and Drake is something you love above all else, and you might start understanding Odin."

Ulf frowned, sighed, and tossed the now meatless piece of bone into the fire.

"I like you more when you're crazy," he said.

"It's just a guess, really," Huginn said, "but I believe Father asked Muninn to wipe his memory so that he would not be tempted to tamper with his own plan. He would thus not know where he sent me, why he sent me, or that he sent me at all."

It sounded crazy, as Ulf then not so respectfully commented, but it made sense. It was reassuring in a way. Odin's plans did not always work out, but at least there was a reason for all of this. As usual with fate, the logic behind my lord's scheme would only reveal itself once it was too late to do anything about it. Until then, all we could do was follow the path Odin had dug for us.

Of course, there was also the possibility that another force altered the future—Loki or Surtr, the King of Múspellsheimr, maybe. But until proven otherwise, I would assume our current situation was the best-case scenario. Not a very optimistic thought, but it was all we had to keep us hoping.

"So," Ulf said, "Odin purposefully let Drake rot in a cave for three years, his own son to mold in Midgard's asshole, and me to struggle across the land through Fimbulvetr. Starting to wonder if another god is hiring because our leader isn't very caring with his crew."

It was meant to make us laugh, and it did, but Ulf had a point. Odin had been cruel, even if it was for the greater good.

"You folks," Huginn said with a head shake and a sneer. "You've been on Asgard for a few centuries but still think like regular humans. Twenty-three years is a long time while it goes, but the moment we are back in Asgard, it will start washing away. A few meals of our food, a few baths, some time by my father's side, and I will be as I was. Even my rancor for Father will disappear fast enough."

"You might not have the chance," I said before finally throwing the meatless bone I had been holding for a couple of minutes into the fire. "We're dealing with Ragnarök this time."

"True," Huginn replied. Æsir had a hard time dealing with the notion of their final death, but Huginn had spent enough time on Midgard to accept his. He was, however, no longer interested in this conversation and lay down on his spot. His eyes closed, he turned around, and his chest heaved more slowly after a few seconds.

"All of this," Ulf said, "doesn't help us with our current problems."

"In a way, it does," I told him. "If it's fate, we just need to continue and wait for the next twist."

Despite my best efforts not to, I yawned. My stomach wasn't used to so much meat, and days treading through Jötunheimr had depleted me of whatever energy I possessed. I gave half a thought to the skewered, roasted hare, wondering if we should cover it with snow to mask the smell, but Ulf spoke before I could ask him to do it.

"In that case, let's hope fate won't eat one of us in the process."

I cursed him and his mother, for I could recognize an omen when I heard one.

"You take the first watch," I told him as I, too, lay down and covered myself with my freshly skinned blanket. He groaned, but I barely heard it, for sleep was already embracing me into a sweet slumber.

"I am not saying that Asgard is worse for their presence, no. But I am not saying the opposite either."

Lofn of the Vanir, about the Einherjar

2

"Drake," Ulf whispered, "Drake."

I swore, thinking that my turn to keep watch had come, but Ulf's hand dropped on my mouth, keeping me quiet. Something was wrong. It was almost dawn.

"We're surrounded," the archer whispered in my ear.

I dared not move and slowly nodded. The fire was fuming; Ulf had fallen asleep during his watch. I could not see Huginn's face, but he was snoring. It had stopped snowing during the night, there was no wind, and the sun greeted us with a timid light unbothered by clouds. I could not distinguish them, but I could sense it too – we were surrounded.

"What do we do?" Ulf asked, lying against me like a lover. "Do we climb?"

I was tempted to say yes, but we had no clue what had us trapped. They might be able to jump, fly, or maybe uproot a tree.

"We run," I said. "Take the hare, I'll wake Huginn."

But Huginn did not need to be awakened, for in the next instant, he leaned on his elbows and realized, too, that something lurked in the forest. I prayed that he had his wits about him this morning, but my hope proved vain.

Huginn sprang up, his breathing betraying his growing panic. I saw a large and dark shadow sway between two shrubs and heard a low growl from the other side. Huginn turned his head very slowly to me, eyes wide and mouth agape.

"Wolves," he said, and sure enough, one of them howled.

"Run!" I yelled.

We all moved at once. Ulf grabbed the branch on which remained half a cooked hare while I grabbed Huginn's wrist and pulled him into a run.

Trusting my instincts, I ran toward the young light of dawn. The forest edge, if I remembered it well, would be there too. Not caring about stealth, the wolves engaged in the pursuit. Their paws crunched the thick layer of snow in our wake. A group of shrubs trembled ahead.

"The hare!" I shouted, urging Ulf to toss our meal in the direction I pointed at. The archer swung the carcass, which fell at the center of a leafy group of shrubs. Two beasts growled and started fighting for the meat, uncaring for our passage.

"What do we do?" Huginn asked, searching for his breath.

"Don't you see," Ulf replied, right hand fondling the quiver on his back, "we run."

"We can't outrun wolves," Huginn said.

He was right. Wolves were formidable runners who never tired. If they behaved like those on Midgard, they would chase us until we exhausted ourselves to the doors of death, then would go for the kill. It wouldn't give us much time.

One of them ran past us, but I only saw its silhouette before it disappeared deeper behind a line of trees. Ulf did not even shoot. It had felt big, much bigger than Midgard wolves.

The forest broke to a plain rich with snow, and we veered left, following the forest's edge. We couldn't run in the snow, so we remained close to the trees, right at the border between the forest and the plain.

Huginn swore instead of keeping his breath, so Ulf told him to shut his beak. The archer was running with his head turned left, ready to let an arrow loose. He had a dozen of them, and from what I had gathered, we faced at least as many beasts. Their growls and barks accompanied us, but they never came in sight. They were toying with us. I, too, cursed, for if I had been in my own body, things would have gone differently. I would not have been so out of breath, at least.

Two wolves emerged from the forest behind us, and my heart sank. They were much, much bigger than Midgard's wolves. Those beasts dwarfed their cousins from the middle realm. They flashed yellow fangs the size of my hand, thick as my thumb, and their eyes, just like that of the hare, gleamed with cleverness and cunning at the center of long, dark faces. They put the fear of death right in my gut. They first moved farther from us, then parallel to us. Their thin bodies were knotted with hard muscles. If they reached us, we were dead meat. But they did not reach us and contented themselves in matching our speed.

"The fuckers are playing with us," Ulf said.

I hate Jötunheimr.

Ulf released his first arrow between the trees unrolling on our left. The missile was followed by a whimper. I had seen nothing.

Huginn was struggling to keep up the pace. His fatigue would not go unnoticed, so I slowed down a notch. Even then, his breathing was ragged.

"Drake," Ulf said, "what do we do?"

I had no fucking clue and told him so. *Waiting for the next twist of fate, my ass.* The pressure from the forest side grew, fed by the killing instinct of the beasts as they neared us. The two on our back responded to a bark by increasing their pace. Within a minute, they would be on us.

"Keep them away," I told Ulf.

He stopped in his tracks, twisted on his ankles, and released another shaft in less time than it takes to say *Tanngnjóstr*. The arrow whistled through the drizzle of snow and ended its course at the base of the closest wolf's ear.

The beast rolled in the snow and shook its head as Ulf resumed his run. The second one stopped as well, unsure whether to help its sibling or resume the pursuit. They shrunk from our sight, and I thought to run farther from the forest now that they had interrupted the chase. There was a low hill that way, and maybe we could find some cover there.

But once again, my hope died with its first breath.

Another beast jumped out of the forest and ran after the two wolves. They must have belonged to the same pack, but the difference in size was so great that I suddenly understood that we had been running from training pups so far. She was white, dirty white, with massive shoulders and a long muzzle ending in lethal rows of fangs. It headbutted the one who had stopped running in the flanks, and the young one resumed its chase, though it kept looking back, terrified of its leader. The white one caught the fallen one's neck between its jaws, and I stopped looking there. Even from a distance, we heard the wounded wolf's plaintive whimper end when its neck snapped. The game was over now. They would move to kill.

"Back into the woods," I said. On the plain, without any cover, we would be easy prey to this monster. Well, *easier* prey.

We stormed back between the trees and startled one of the wolves, who leaped away from us.

Huginn's legs seemed to grow wings, and I guessed his mind was coming back as well, for he led us on a path only he saw. Maybe his preservation instinct was calling him back, or maybe his fear did the work. Or, more likely, the wolves were driving us to a spot of their choosing. We went unopposed until we reached another clearing, much like the one where we had killed the hare.

Besides the frozen stream splitting the clearing in two, it was an unremarkable place. Yet the second we stepped into it, I knew this was the killing ground of their choosing. Three males burst from the trees facing us, and half a dozen of their comrades barged in from the sides. They groaned and snarled, heads low, shoulders high, clouds of steam rising from red maws as they slowed to a prowl.

"Fuck," I said, "that's a lot more than twelve."

I stopped counting when I reached twenty.

"You think Odin saw this?" Ulf asked as we backed each other.

"If he did," Huginn said, "he'll have a word with me."

Huginn is back at least, I thought.

As the circle of wolves tightened around us, I could not prevent a chuckle. The irony was too good. Two of Odin's famed Wolves, one of whose name actually meant "wolf," would be eaten by the real beasts.

The big white one, the mother of this pack, stepped into the circle, just a bit farther than the others, her fangs red and dripping. Her upper lip was broken, and a fang stood down without cover even when her maw was closed. She was old and strong and merciless. She snapped, and the pack got quiet. Her eyes darted to one of her children, the last of the two running behind us on the plain. It bolted toward us, kicking a flurry of snow with each step.

I was about to call for Ulf, but Huginn reacted first. He ran at the beast, fist raised behind him, screaming as Thor would to welcome a battle. I ran after him, sure that he had once more lost his mind.

Ulf's arrow fizzed between Huginn and me and finished its course in the tip of the wolf's muzzle. It did not wound him, but the beast winced, and that's when Huginn hit. A punch, a very clumsy one, but full of his Æsir strength. It caught the wolf right on the upper jaw. It toppled like a tree, tongue lolling pitifully. I was on it next. Not wanting to test if the beast was dead, I stabbed the blunt knife in its ear several times until I was sure it would never get up.

The circle of wolves yapped and barked, but none dared step closer.

I punched the pommel of the knife into the beast's mouth to break a tooth and tore it free with a painful effort. It was the length of my hand and would make for a good weapon. With it, I planned, or hoped, to take at least one more of the animals with me.

The white wolf left the pack then and paced toward us. She had recognized our strength and would finish the work herself. Her gait was regal, and her eyes bestial. Black and golden and full of blood they were.

I raised my improvised weapon, feeling the futility of my gesture as I did. The beast snarled, baring her teeth the way we unsheathed our swords.

Come, I thought, *let's see if you can take the three of us.*

Her pack was tensing up. Some skipped on their spots, eager to partake in the killing but not daring to disobey their leader; others howled themselves into a frenzy. She did not quiet them this time, as if she fed on their bloodlust. She chose me. Her stance lowered. Her shoulder blades looked as if they were growing from her back. The pack leader was on the prowl.

"Fuck," was all I said.

Then fate intervened. And it did in the shape of a spear.

The white wolf tilted her head instinctively, but her muzzle was punched backward, taken by the spear that stabbed deep into her eye. One moment, she was facing me, threatening and lethal; the next, she was dead on the ground.

I call it a spear, but it was the length and thickness of a *Knarr's* oar. The pack and us froze in our spots. A roaring Jötunn trailed the spear, breaking into the clearing like a fox in a coop. The giant kicked the closest wolf so hard that the beast left the ground and ran away as soon as it found it again. Many others did as much, but a few remained, and it took the Jötunn to raise a second spear above his head for them to depart. They ran for the protection of the forest as one, yapping like a litter of pups.

Our savior roared still as he reached the center of the clearing. He raised the spear higher, looked at the sky, and ended his roar with a victorious shout. Then, as the echo of his feral shout faded, he looked down at us, a wide grin splitting his massive hay-colored beard. I kept a tight grip on my two weapons, and Ulf readied an arrow in his bow though we lowered them. This could go wrong in many different ways, but it didn't have to.

"Thank you, my friends," the giant said as he passed between us, legs spraying snow with each step. "I had been wanting this one's pelt for a long time. Never found the bait for her until this morning." He yanked the spear out of the wolf's head, and blood oozed out of her eye. If he had meant to keep the pelt intact, it was an incredible throw.

I looked at Ulf, feeling the knot forming in his throat. Huginn stood behind me, but I guessed he was more or less feeling the same, not sure if we should be thankful or desperate.

In my childhood, I reveled in the stories of the Jötnar. They were always big and strong and dumb. In reality, Jötnar could be as small as a human or as big as a hall; some were indeed slow-minded, but many were cunning. Loki was one, after all, and Odin was half Jötunn, too. You never knew what you got with Jötnar. Most I have met were violent, but I have also befriended a few.

This one was on the tall side, about two men's height. His skin was brown, almost black, beautifully contrasting with the nature surrounding us. I had seen men of the same color when the Wolves went on missions in big trading towns. I had never seen one with blond hair, though. He was wearing boots of thick fur, breeches of dark brown leather, and a sleeveless shirt made from white wool. A heavy golden chain hung around his neck, carrying a symbol I did not know, a rune-looking thing shaped like a boat's anchor.

"Now," he said, shifting his massive body to face us. "Care to tell me what an Æsir and two Einherjar are doing in my forest?"

Nothing in him looked threatening; he even seemed genuinely curious, and my hands dropped. His voice was deep and gentle. And he could see I was an Einheri despite my current body. In truth, I probably looked far from the Loki who had roamed the world free, but I was even further from looking like an Einheri.

"*Your* forest?" Huginn asked.

"Do I know you?" the giant asked Huginn, scanning the Æsir from head to toe.

"I know you, Eggther," Huginn said, using a name I had heard at some point.

The frown on Eggther's forehead deepened as he searched through his memory, then released like a bowstring.

"Odin's raven! Ah, that can't be!" He slapped his belly, producing a sound like a drum, and went with a burst of rich, heartfelt laughter. What was funny, I did not know, but Eggther enjoyed it. "You got old," he then said, wiping a tear from the corner of his eye.

"For now," Huginn replied.

"Your father has a message for me or something?"

"We are not here for you," Huginn said. "But we could use your help."

The Jötunn produced a long hum from his throat and went to scratch his beard apprehensively. "Helping the Æsir," he said, "not sure I like the sound of that."

"You know our gratitude is generous," Huginn replied, pointing at the golden chain hanging from the Jötunn's neck.

"And even more generous with the problems you bring," Eggther said, opening his arms to the clearing as if the wolves infesting *his* forest were our fault.

"We need to talk about that too," Huginn said.

"Aye, we do, and when you see your clan's lord, you'll tell him what I think of his *gift*." He pointed his thumb behind him as he spoke, to the north. "You are, of course, welcome to my little home. You folks look like you could use a bath and a bed."

"That we do," Ulf said, "and ale."

"Oh, I have much better than ale, my little friend," Eggther replied with a mischievous look in his eyes. Fate had chosen an interesting character in this Jötunn, and meeting him so deep in those woods made me all the more certain that we were on the right track.

"Drake," Huginn whispered as Eggther moved to the white wolf's body. "Don't be fooled, Eggther is friendly, but he is not a friend."

"Noted," I whispered back. "Why do I know his name?" I asked.

Eggther puffed when lifting the beast on his shoulder. Huginn lowered his crow-like eyes, and again, I saw his father in him.

"This forest is Járnviðr," he simply said, and the dots connected in my mind.

Ironwood. We were in Ironwood. A dark place at the center of which lived the only thing Odin feared; Fenrir, the beast fated to kill him. And Eggther, also known as the Herder, was the guardian of the forest. As Jötunn, Eggther was a mortal enemy of the Æsir. Still, for some reason, the gods had trusted him with the guardianship of the domain surrounding Fenrir's prison. I did not know the details of this arrangement except for one clause. On the day when Fenrir manages to free himself from Gleipnir, the Dwarven-made chain binding him, Eggther is to send a signal to Asgard.

"We're near Fenrir?" Ulf whispered. Huginn nodded.

"We are also close to some gate to Asgard," I guessed.

"Crossing it will cost us, though," he said as we resumed our crossing of the forest toward our host's "little home."

Huginn was right; it would cost us, more than he could have known.

3

"So," Eggther asked an hour later, "how, by his daughter, did you end up with Loki's body, and where is the trickster now?" He asked those questions as if they were the most banal topics in the world. Not only had he guessed that I was an Einheri, but he had also recognized Loki and reached the perfect conclusion as to what it meant.

"He tricked me, stole my body, and went back to Asgard with it," I answered truthfully. Huginn clicked his tongue, not liking my honesty. We needed this giant's help; secrecy was not a priority.

"That must itch you in the wrong place," he said.

"I intend to scratch it as soon as possible," I replied.

Eggther chuckled, and it was a pleasant, friendly sound. "Poor Loki then. He's in trouble."

I don't know if he was being sarcastic, but he was right. Loki would deserve what was coming for him. I didn't know how, but he would pay, or I was no Drake.

The forest felt different. I could sense no threat; shadows were just shadows, and trees seemed to keep a distance.

Ironwood wasn't such a bad place when you walked through it with its guardian.

"How is Fenrir behaving?" Huginn asked, once again the good little messenger of the All-Father.

"As usual," Eggther replied. "Loki's son can't move much. You guys made sure of it, but he's active all right. Sires pups as if his life depended on it."

"Those were Fenrir's?" Ulf asked.

"Of course they are. Did you see the size of those things? Mean as Hel, those bastards, and clever too. Aye, they are Fenrir's."

"They bother you?" I asked.

"I'm a herder; of course they bother me. But I get by. They take a kid; I kill one of them. It's a form of trade. Some meat for some fur. But the other day, they took something precious to me, and something has to be done about it."

"Ah," Huginn said, for me as much as for Eggther.

"Don't *ah* me, you little scarecrow. You bloody well know I have something to ask of you, and that's not new feathers for my pillow." Eggther was honest, too, at least. "You want a way to Asgard? I have one. You get something for me, and you will. A trade of some sort, everything's a trade."

"So what did they take from you?" Huginn asked. Even I did not like his tone. We needed Eggther. I would have to ask Huginn to keep his feelings to himself.

"A bird," Eggther answered with a smug grin. "*You* should feel sympathetic. My most beautiful bird."

"Why can't you get it back yourself?" I asked, trying hard to sound more curious than reproachful.

"There are some places I cannot go to," he said. "And my role in this forest prevents me from doing certain things."

"Guarding Fenrir?" I asked.

"That's my mission for the Æsir; though I am not

guarding the beast, I'm just waiting for it to break his bonds. No, I am talking about my role as a herder."

"I don't follow," I said. How could being a herder prevent Eggther from getting his bird back?

"Eggther, among other things, herds wolves for the Jötunn army," Huginn answered for the giant. "Those who will attack us during Ragnarök."

My mouth clamped shut. I wasn't talking to a new friend but to a proper enemy. He could not get his bird back because to do so meant killing too many of those wolves. Which meant we would have to, somehow.

"Little birdy is right. I herd those beasts. That's a full-time activity, let me tell you that. If they multiply too fast, I reduce the herd. Not enough; I release some of my livestock. I keep the forest healthy for their hunt and not too big so they don't disperse. This one," he said, bumping the white wolf on his shoulder, "was getting her pack too strong. Though, had I known Ragnarök was so close, I would have kept her alive. Now that I know, I can't risk killing more of them."

"Fenrir was put here even though this is where the Jötnar raise their beasts?" I asked.

"Why do you think we agreed to keep the ugly mutt? We did not cheat the Æsir; they knew they were giving us a weapon, but they could not kill it, so they preferred us to have it."

Back then, long before I became an Einheri, the gods had grown fearful of Loki's three children, those he had sire on a female Jötunn. They threw the snake one into the ocean of Midgard, sent Hel, the daughter, to rule the land of the dead, and chained the last one to a mountain in the middle of Ironwood. To do so, the gods pretended to challenge Fenrir to a contest of strength and bound him with several chains, which the Wolf King broke easily. But when they brought the real chain, the one made especially for Fenrir, a solid charm-forged thing called Gleipnir, the wolf bristled and refused to be bound with it. Tyr, who had been Fenrir's friend, offered to put his right arm in the beast's maw to prove this was no trick, and the Wolf King agreed. When he realized he'd been cheated and could no longer free himself, Fenrir snapped his jaws, maiming his friend forever. I heard Fenrir had been crying then, not out of rage but because of Tyr's betrayal. I also heard Tyr had enough time to remove his hand but accepted the punishment.

For Loki's sake, who was still a part of the clan back then, they did not kill any of his children but made sure to send them as far away as possible. That was long before we heard the prophecy of the world's end, and the gods tried to forget about them. But fate did not forget, and their names resurfaced with the prophecy. Jörmungandr, the giant snake, and Thor would slay each other. Hel would unleash her armies of the dead on Asgard. And Fenrir would kill Odin, as well as many of my brothers. Jörmungandr, Fenrir, Hel, and Surtr from Múspellsheimr were the four leaders who would bring an end to the Æsir's rule.

"I can't believe the gods are fine with it," Ulf said, meaning Fenrir living where wolves were being herded.

"The gods," Eggther said, puffing scornfully. "They are just a clan of us. They thought they were better, so they split and called themselves the Æsir, or the Vanir, that's all. Pompous asses." He spat, and I had to step over a puddle-sized gob of saliva.

"Can't argue with the last part," I said, and Eggther smiled at my remark. Despite Huginn's warning, the giant was growing on me. He was no friend, but he was easy to appreciate.

"They made us," Ulf continued, "so, of course, they are our gods."

Eggther ducked a branch from a venerable oak just as I heard the first sounds of life, bleating sheep.

"Should I instruct my own shit to call me god, then? I made it after all?" he asked.

"Are you calling me shit?" my friend asked, not liking the comparison.

"I meant no offense," the Jötunn replied. "You do smell like it, though. Not to worry, you will wash soon."

The sounds grew louder and more diverse. I heard neighs, moos, bells, and clucks. The smell of freshly cut wool came to my nose. And, finally, after we passed a sturdy fence separating a long, curved palisade of spiked wood, we entered Eggther's land. His "little home" was the biggest farm I had ever seen and one of the most beautiful places in the nine realms.

ᚱ

According to Titus, we Norsemen were a dirty people. A man, he claimed, especially a warrior, should wash as often as time allowed him. He claimed his countrymen bathed at least once a week, but I did not believe his words, for surely no one needed to wash so often. They soaked themselves in man-made baths of hot water, and we did as well, though in water made hotter by the world below. I was born in southern Sweden, where we did not have the luxury of those natural hot springs, but I have visited such places and agreed that few things soothed a man better. Asgard boasted a few as well, but only within the limits of the gods' private lands.

So, when Eggther offered us three to share a hot bath, I did not complain.

His farm owned a spring of hot, blanched, and fuming water not far from the goats' enclosure, but we were not allowed to bathe in it. It took five or six trips for our host to fill a gigantic barrel with the spring's fuming water. Eggther did not explain why we could not simply bathe in the spring, but as he placed the barrel to face a most picturesque view of his farm, it was fine by me. This barrel, he told us, used to be his father's tankard, and he waited for a long time before laughing at his own joke. I had seen Jötunn who could use this bath as a tankard, so I had believed him. He then left us to our steaming moment of bliss to attend to some of the dozens of tasks that kept a herder like him busy.

Animals lived in the hundreds in Eggther's place, but nowhere they lacked space. We were still in the forest, but it had been so well wasted it could be in another country. The snow did not seem to touch the ground, and a lush layer of grass grew here and there. Enclosures the size of a hamlet welcomed beasts of two or three species, each of them living in a harmonious and noisy back-and-forth.

I remembered the constant struggle I faced with my handful of goats and the two cows given to me by marriage. But Eggther single-handedly managed this huge farm while taking care of the forest and its inhabitants. I was in awe. And he was doing a great job of it, too.

The palisade surrounding the farm appeared solid and well-maintained. Eggther had rooted stakes at its bottom, and a series of chimes and bells alerted him whenever the palisade shook too strongly. Yet the stakes remained hidden and did not temper this land's beauty, and the chimes produced a soothing sound.

Trees of many kinds dotted the farm in a mosaic of fruits and flowers. I knew very few of those species, but their aroma calmed whatever anxiety I yet harbored as I soaked in the barrel. The sweetness of something resembling mulberries mixed with the freshness of exotic firs caressed my skin and filled my nose, and all those days struggling in snowstorms and running from giant wolves were momentarily forgiven.

A particular silver-barked tree producing purple fruits caught my attention when Eggther introduced us to his domain. I had seen trees of the sort in Asgard and in Asgard alone. It piqued my curiosity so I told him as much.

"Ah, this pretty one?" Eggther had replied after a raucous giggle. "A gift from the only Vanir I can tolerate." He did not say more, but I knew he was talking about Freyja. Only our goddess of love and war could make a Jötunn giggle.

The sun was drawing behind the horizon, and yet the water kept its warmth. For the hundredth time that afternoon, I sighed with delight and let myself sink deeper, knocking Ulf's ankle in the process.

"Sorry," I said without opening my eyes.

"A bit cramped," he replied.

"You can go," I said.

"You first," he replied, and though I did not see it, I could picture the satisfied grin on his face.

We had been soaking for a couple of hours, and by then the water had gained a thick layer of dirt. I couldn't care less. This was my first moment of peace in three years. Even if this bath had been filled with Heidrun's piss, I would take it. Huginn puffed when I said so, but he, too, enjoyed this moment too much to complain.

A young goat bleated nearby, drawing my attention. It

stood against the barrel, calling for us. I don't know what it wanted, but all it got was a pat on the head between its two small horns. It was a cute, brown-spotted animal with two common, wide pupils gleaming with youth. Eggther's herd contained regular-sized animals, like those we had on Midgard. Cows had longer horns and more fur, pigs were dark-skinned, and his goats could climb trees, but besides this kind of detail, it was like back home. Life was simple for those animals, and they seemed happy enough.

"That's because they don't know of their fate," Huginn commented.

"Wisdom," I replied, chuckling. "You took this thirst from your father, didn't you?"

"What kind of being would scorn knowledge?"

I had poked a sensitive topic, it seemed. Ulf's kick warned me of it as well. Still, I was feeling better and could not resist. "Doesn't seem to bring happiness," I said.

"Happiness," Huginn said, snorting. "The ambition of simpletons and farm animals."

"Eggther seems happy," I replied and again received a kick from my archer. "And I don't think he is a simpleton." Just as I said so, the giant came out of a wide, flat building that could have been the place where he milked his cows. He was transporting two buckets on his shoulders, and I shivered at the thought that our dinner would include some thick butter or possibly even some creamy cheese. The taste invaded my mouth in the next second and jabbed invisible daggers in my belly.

"Eggther is many things," Huginn said, "but no, he isn't stupid. I warn you again, Drake, do not trust him."

I turned around to my two friends, and as I suspected, Huginn was staring at me with his dark, Odin-like eyes.

"I won't," I said. And yet, despite his warning and

knowing of Eggther's role in the upcoming end of the world, I could not stop myself from liking the giant. After what Muninn had done, I would never trust anyone again, let alone a Jötunn like Loki, but I would count Eggther as a good person until proven otherwise.

"I know he doesn't like your people," I said, insisting on the word *your,* "but he doesn't seem belligerent."

"He is a Jötunn," Huginn said, "it's in his nature. When Ragnarök comes, one of you might have to kill him. He won't hesitate to do the same. And seeing how he throws a spear, I dare say he will be a tough one to take down."

He was right. In the chaos of what Ragnarök promised to be, I did not like my odds against an Eggther.

"Why would he fight?" Ulf asked. "I mean, look at this place. Why would someone risk all of this?"

"As far as I know, he's been here for a good five hundred years, at least. Wouldn't you be bored?" Huginn asked.

Of course, it was more than this. Eggther would fight because it is what we do. Belligerence is not exclusive to Jötnar. In every people, there is violence, war, and aggression. The purpose is often secondary to the desire to fight. Thank the gods for fear. Without it, our race would have gone extinct a long time ago. Eggther would fight because it was his role in the great scheme of things, and I would fight for the same reason.

"So," Ulf asked when no one pursued the point, "what do you think he will ask of us?"

"As he said," Huginn answered, "get his bird back." He spat on the side, nearly hitting the pile of clean clothes the giant had prepared for us. I preferred not thinking about how he got them. They looked clean, warm, and free of fleas; that's all I wanted. "What kind of bird it is and why he wants it back so bad, though, is a mystery."

What kind of bird mattered little, and I said so, but the reason for Eggther's demand also got me curious. He would not tell us where to find the gate to Asgard until we completed our task. It could be the hot spring, a pond, or even an underground river, for all we knew. Huginn could not find it, not even with his Æsir senses, which, he claimed, were slowly coming back since we entered the forest. Finding the source of the passage would do little good anyway. Without the guardian's key, we could not open it.

We could either agree to Eggther's demand, make a new bargain, or force him to open the damn thing. I did not think the last option was possible and could not see what we could bargain with. In any case, as I told them, we would first listen to his request.

Huginn, not liking the thought, stood and climbed over the side of the barrel, moaning as he let go on the other side. I stretched my legs and enjoyed the extra space in our filthy bath.

I was about to close my eyes again and let the late afternoon light grow weaker by the minute when the door of Eggther's longhouse opened, and its owner walked out of it again. Our host carried a harp, and his steps were loud as if he meant to scare a snake.

The whole farm got agitated. The animals who were not stuck inside pens and enclosures came to the giant like ducklings to their mom. They followed him up to a mound stuck between two ponds in which floated ducks, geese, and swans. I, too, followed each of his gestures with my eyes, already sensing the compression in my heart when someone used *seidr*.

Eggther sat on the moss-covered ground of the mound, right under the shadow of an overgrown oak, and the farm got silent in the next few seconds. The change was sudden, but the animals showed no fear. They mixed and stared in the same direction toward the giant tuning his harp.

Ulf knelt next to me, arms dropped over the barrel as well.

Eggther pinched the strings of the harp, slowly at first. Each note was allowed to live and die before the next took its place. Then, the pace increased slightly. Every eye in the farm observed him; every ear was hanging on to the sounds of the instrument.

The melody forming under the giant's fingers was melancholic and happy at the same time, like a beautiful day coming to an end. I had never heard Jötnar music before, but if Eggther was a good emissary of it, their art shamed any other of the kind in the nine realms. There was nothing fancy about his performance, certainly nothing astonishing in technique. And yet I was trapped in the soothing rhythm of the harp, as were all the creatures listening to it, including Huginn.

Eggther paused in his music, and the whole farm held its breath. When the next string rang, it was accompanied by his voice. It was a deep, soft, clear voice in low tones, and it was a voice I would never forget. The Jötunn, contrary to everything we had seen of him suggested, was a brilliant skald.

He sang in his people's tongue, and even if the meaning was lost to us, the emotions could not be clearer. Eggther was grateful, full of joy for being alive, and sad beyond words that it would one day end. I cannot tell how I understood, but I did in my heart. Clear like the rain and thin as a needle, Eggther's music will stay with me until the end of time.

It stopped naturally as the sun vanished behind the tallest trees on the horizon, the last few notes being like murmurs to the hundreds of ears thirsting for them. When Eggther stood again, the animals dispersed quietly, each of them walking to its enclosure in good order. There was *seidr* in this sight. *Seidr* and the habits put in place by a great herder.

"I don't know if we can trust him," Ulf said after a long sigh. "But I could listen to him singing until Ragnarök."

I nodded, then left the bath. It would get cold and dark.

I was getting dressed, still awakening from Eggther's music, when the giant approached us, a white and gray gander quietly resting in his arms. The Jötunn was petting the bird from head to back as if it were a small dog, and it seemed to genuinely appreciate the feeling.

"I hope you're hungry," Eggther said before I could tell him what I thought of his skaldic art. "We dine soon."

His right hand, resting on top of the geese's head, twisted on itself, breaking the bird's neck in a violent sound of bones and flesh. It woke me out of my torpor.

Poultry was on the menu.

ᚱ

We had eaten the hare a mere day ago, and yet its taste was washed away by the bounty of Eggther's table: roasted gander, steaming wolf meat, vegetables of all shapes and sizes, some crunchy, some earthy, freshly baked bread covered with thick, melting butter and liquid honey, a rich and creamy, white-crusted cheese. This was a feast worthy of kings and jarls.

Huginn, so prompt in distrusting our host, showed no manners when it came to eating his food. The old bird gobbled the content of his plate with the appetite of a bear at the end of winter but kept his gratitude deep and hidden. At least the meal kept him quiet.

Ulf could not drink enough of Eggther's cider. While it did not warm a man as ale or mead would, cider was a delicacy for the senses. I knew my archer favored this beverage above all, but according to him, this was the best cider he'd ever tasted.

The honey nearly got me to faint with pleasure. Such a taste, produced in the middle of Ironwood, was a miracle.

Eggther's smile grew with each moan that escaped us, but he, surprisingly, ate lightly. He left the gander's meat untouched and made quick work of his share of the wolf's meat. He ate a couple of onions and a large soup of peas and turnips, to which he added some of the juice from the roasted poultry. He removed a small leathery bag from his belt and fished a pinch of herbs from it, which he dropped in his soup.

I was just wondering what they might be when I smelled an aroma close to juniper, and I recognized this plant. A wild celery, the likes of which grew abundantly around my village. We used it for everything, from medicine to cooking. Our seers used it as well for their trance-inducing fumes. This plant could make those with the knowledge of *seidr* dream-walk or shapeshift. Eggther used it to flavor his soup, his alcohol, and, from what he showed us next, to smoke in a pipe.

His longhouse was a comfy place kept warm thanks to a wide hearth. His table was high and long, the ground made of solid earth, and a few beds covered with blankets bloated with feathers littered the back wall. To think that I would sleep in one filled me with joy. After three years lying on a sharp rock, even a plank of wood would feel like a cloud, but this... I was afraid I would never wake up.

"I trust you are reviewing your views on Jötnar hospitality?" Eggther asked after letting a rich cloud of smoke float from his lips.

"I would not go that far," Huginn replied, lips greasy with the gander's juice. "But you have my thanks for all of this."

Eggther nodded and took his small victory.

"So," Ulf said while he filled his fifth cup of cider, "how are we to repay you for your generosity and our passage to Asgard?"

If the table hadn't been so wide, I would have kicked him in the shin.

Eggther grunted. He too, I believe, would have preferred to let the pleasant atmosphere linger a little longer. His chair creaked with relief as he stood, then he walked toward the hearth behind and crouched. He stirred a pan of chestnuts over the embers, and the idea of their taste opened the hole I thought I had filled in my stomach.

"Those wolves," he said, pointing at the flat white pelt drying from a beam, "no matter how many traps I put around my farm, they always find a way in. They snatch one of my animals or two and vanish back into the woods. I don't mind so much, seeing that it is my role to keep them fed anyway. But lately, they have entered my land more regularly and their appetite has grown. They feel Ragnarök coming and are making themselves strong."

"*Their* appetite?" Huginn asked as Eggther came back to us and dropped a large pan filled with roasted chestnuts in the middle of the table.

"Aye, you're right, old bird," Eggther said. The chair winced with pain when its maker sat back on it. "*Fenrir's* appetite is growing."

The Wolf King could not venture far from his mountain,

so he sent his children to bring him food, and his hunger forced them to Eggther's farm, where a bounty awaited them.

"Any idea how he will free himself?" Ulf asked.

"I don't share words with the big bad wolf," Eggther answered as another cloud of smoke rose from his nose. "And I don't care. When it happens, I will know and will tell your people, as agreed, then will rejoin my comrades and lay waste to your land." The last was said to Huginn, who stopped slurping his soup at last and returned the stare.

"I don't enjoy the idea," I said, "but if I see you during our great battle, I will honor you myself."

"It will bring me no joy either, but I promise to end you quickly," Eggther replied. On those words, he picked up his cup and held it up for me to knock. It was a promise from warrior to warrior, a sign of respect.

"You might have bargained for more than you can chew, herder," Huginn said. "This one is our Drake." Why Huginn said so, I had no clue, but our host's reaction filled me with pride.

Eggther's eyes rounded up with surprise, and an appreciative whistle passed from his lips.

"Odin's dragon? You don't say."

"You've heard of me?" I asked, genuinely surprised that a Jötunn living in the middle of Ironwood would know of my existence.

"You've killed a couple too many of my kind to remain anonymous in our realm. And I have a few cousins who would pay good silver for your head. Don't look at me like that; I won't do anything of the sort." The last was to Huginn, who was already clutching his knife. "I would never harm guests; that's against our laws."

I hadn't fought with a Jötunn for ages, but it wasn't a

merry memory. Ulf had been there too, but he kept this information to himself. He had, after all, offed a Jötunn prince back then, and if my head promised a reward in silver, his guaranteed gold.

"So, a dragon is going to get me my bird back from the wolves. Ah, that's some good material for a poem right there."

"Tell us what we are supposed to do," I asked, bending over the table to reach one of those fuming chestnuts. Eggther hummed to himself while I peeled it off, searching for his words.

"The wolves don't always kill their prey. More often than not, they snatch one of my animals and take it alive to their master. Fenrir likes to play with his food and keep it alive for many days, selecting his meal as a king would, depending on his mood. He will have kept my bird for a special occasion, like getting free of his bonds, for example. Or so I hope."

"What kind of bird is it?" Huginn asked.

"A purple one," the giant replied de facto. "That's how you'll recognize it."

"Why do you think we can get it back?" I asked.

"Because you have to," he replied. "Despite all my Jötunn grace, I am not as discreet as you smaller folks. Plus, your passage back to Asgard depends on you bringing me my bird back, and I believe it is your fate to return to your realm. You have got to have faith in fate, it is always right in the end."

His mention of fate is what convinced me; it had driven us this far after all.

Contrary to many of my people, I hated the idea of fate. Yet, I had to admit it had controlled my every movement. What it had in store for us, I didn't know, but all we could do was believe in its wisdom. Arrogance it may have been, but I did not think fate had brought us here to be eaten by Fenrir or his pups. It had something else for me; hopefully, revenge. I would get Eggther his bird back, even if it meant facing Fenrir. We would get back home, I would get my body back, kill Loki, get my men ready for the great battle, and play my part in it.

"So," I asked, "how are we supposed to get your bird back?"

4

I could have used more rest at Eggther's farm before putting our plan into motion. I needed it. The plan involved talents I lacked, acting among them, and if something went wrong, I would need talents I did possess but which required a rested body. Time, though, was of the essence. If the bird died before I could get my hands on it, Eggther would, at best, kick us out, at worst, sell us to his cousins.

So, I left the farm, our host, and my friends behind. I had to do this alone. Eggther and Huginn had for once agreed that it was pure folly. Ulf and the old raven threatened to follow me even if I refused, but my mind was made. Fenrir, according to the stories, was the fearsome image of his father, a cunning bastard and a bloodthirsty trickster. He would try to trick me, and I wanted to have nothing to give him. I had suffered enough at the hands of fate to know its mind. It was always a question of sacrifice. Well, fuck fate. I would meet Fenrir with nothing to bargain. I would get that bird without giving a thing. Of course, I first needed to reach the Wolf King. Easier said than done.

And with the hope of a fool who believes he knows the world, I left for Fenrir and Eggther's prized purple bird.

It was a two-day walk to Fenrir's lair. Eggther had been generous in gifts for the journey. On top of the clothes from the day before, made from good Danish fabric, he had armored me with a supple lamellar of leather, well-crafted boots, and an improvised cloak tailored from the white wolf that had so nearly ended my saga. He filled a bundle with some hard bread and dry meat, and a skin of ale hung from my shoulder. But more importantly, Eggther had armed me with a brutish short axe and a remarkable sword.

A Dwarfish blade, light and solid, wide and sharp. It had no sheath, and its pommel of robust iron had been scratched repeatedly, but it was a magnificent weapon. I waved it in the air a couple of times to get a feel of its balance and once more marveled at the craft of the Dwarves. It sang as it slashed the air. A melody of death and a promise of worse for those who dared face it. I guessed it had served its previous owner poorly, but I would make it mine. Eggther did not seem to realize the value of his gift, so I kept my emotions from showing, for I was beaming inside.

"Come back with my bird in one piece, and it is yours, on top of a safe passage to Asgard for the three of you," Eggther had declared.

I took no cumbersome shield, no noisy helmet, and no smelly cheese. I was going silent. Even the lamellar was more of a nuisance, but I felt naked without some kind of armor, and the bands of leather on my chest gave me the confidence I so sorely needed.

I left the farm without a second look at my friends and stepped back into the darkness of Ironwood. The sounds of the animals living their life accompanied me for a short time, and then it was back to the heavy silence of the forest.

North, I was to keep going north. We Norsemen hated going north and only did so when returning home from a raid south. *There is nothing but blizzards, dark magic, and death in the far north*, I recalled my uncle saying.

But Fenrir was north.

The Wolf King's prison was a small, hollowed mountain, though Eggther believed it to be a dormant volcano. The mountain, and the stretch of land around it, was bare of trees and would appear naked after days in Ironwood. Eggther called the place "Angrboda's Tit," but I would not call it as such, for Angrboda was Fenrir's mother, and I dared not use her name in such a place.

"Just keep going north," Eggther had said. "You won't miss the Tit. And if you have walked for three days without seeing it, it means you've missed it." He had laughed in a booming, thunder-like guffaw and left me none the wiser.

The weather remained gentle on the first day, and I made good progress, at least it seemed like it, for I had no real way of knowing how much distance I had traveled. Using the moss of the trees to guide me north, I penetrated deeper and deeper into a forest most of my kind knew only from stories.

It only occurred to me late in the afternoon, as the sun disappeared behind the tips of the tallest trees, that I had no idea how I was supposed to bring the bird all the way back to the farm. I had marked the path here and there, so I assumed I could find the way. But how I was to carry the bird, preventing it from flying away while keeping it alive, I didn't know.

"If a stupid wolf can do it, so can I," I said, speaking to myself.

I used the last of the sun's light to find a thick tree to climb on. A family of red squirrels fled its trunk when I made it to the third branch, which was solid enough to hold me for the night. I hated sleeping in trees, but it was the only way I would get some sleep. I tied myself to it around the waist with a rope, arranged the white fur under my ass for comfort, and used the rest of my focus to chase the image of Ulf and Huggin sleeping comfortably on Eggther's beds. Two hours later, I welcomed the night with a full belly and the tension of the prey growing in my chest.

The forest sounds chilled my blood. Something *whooshed* behind me, and the last squeak of a rodent soon followed on the floor. Gnarls and grunts sailed the shadows. Creatures sniffed the ground when they passed by the tree I sat on. A pair of eyes glimmered when they looked up. A fox or something of the kind. I kicked the trunk with my heel, and it scampered away. I was still a threat to many things in this forest. But to others, I was a fine meal.

Sleep came in bouts of five or ten minutes, vanishing with a sudden yap. No, I did not like sleeping in trees.

Mani, the moon god, whom I have never met in person, was strong and unbothered by clouds that night. I was tempted to climb down and use his light to keep on moving. But traveling at night was too much of a gamble, so I stayed put, stealing a few minutes of rest here, another few there, until Sol took over from her brother in the sky, feeble as she was during Fimbulvetr.

It snowed on the second day.

Heavy flakes showered the land and shortened my sight. There was no wind, but my progress slowed nonetheless. Once in a while, I had to brush the white from the moss clothing the base of trees to make sure I still traveled in the right direction. And it was on such an occasion, as I crouched by the knotted roots of an ash tree, that I heard a growl.

I stood as if I had not heard it and walked away, softening the fear rising in me to the best of my capabilities. My heart pounded like a drum, but I kept my face of stone and my breathing slow. For a while, the wolves, for there were several of them, kept their distance. They studied me. If they were from the pack I had encountered, they had lost their leader and would not know how to act.

I counted five, three on my left, two on my right, each of them of a size close to those we had run from. One approached me more directly. Keeping my pace, I stared at it, telling the beast I knew of its presence and did not fear it. It went back to its siblings, puzzled.

Then, as one, they darted farther ahead, and sure enough, a minute later, one of them charged from the front. It took all the mental strength of the Drake I used to be not to run away, which would have meant my death. Instead, following Eggther's advice, I kept walking as if the beast meant nothing, stabbing my gaze in his golden eyes and trying not to notice the length of the fangs gleaming in the beast's snarl.

The wolf stopped an arm's length from me, and though it kept snarling, its confidence vanished. I stood motionless, bile in the back of my mouth. The wolf suddenly put those fangs back behind its lips and waved its head left and right in search of its brethren. I then followed the next step of the plan.

"*Jag ar Loki, furen til Fenrir,*" I said, repeating the sentence taught to me by Eggther. I said it again, louder this time. *I am Loki, father to Fenrir.* If those beasts were Fenrir's children, they would understand my words. Such was Eggther's theory, and my hope.

The wolf's gigantic head froze, and his ears turned toward me. His menacing features vanished and were replaced by a mask of curiosity. I took another step, making myself threatening, and the wolf sat back. Another step, and the wolf rolled on its back, offering me its belly in a submissive gesture. The other wolves stepped closer, heads low and tails tucked between their legs.

"*Tag me til dun furen*," I told them, using the last of my Jötunn knowledge. They looked at each other, not knowing what to do of my command.

"*Tag me til dun furen!*" I repeated louder and stronger this time, and at once, they moved.

It turned out we were not far from the sleeping volcano. Half an hour of walking with my canine guides later, we stepped out of Ironwood and into the empty plain. Empty of vegetation, at least, for more wolves than I could count spotted the snowy plain in gray, black, and red. I nearly gasped at the sight and forced my next step over a frozen heartbeat. My presence came as no surprise, and just as we penetrated this furry sea, it seemed to come alive, and like a murder of crows smelling a corpse, the wolves started moving in my direction.

Small packs of five to ten individuals approached from every direction, muzzles raised to sniff my scent and ears twisted at the sound of my boots crunching the snow. A hundred giant wolves soon formed an impenetrable circle to which I was the center, and my progress slowed almost to a halt. My guides bared their fangs to any beast coming too close and barked threateningly when it wasn't enough. They were replied in kind by what I assumed to be pack leaders. They must have claimed to be leading Loki to their father; otherwise, some older, stronger wolves would have torn them to pieces.

It chilled my sweat to imagine the same beasts attacking

the citadel of Asgard. The press was getting more dense, and my guides pained to keep their brethren at bay. They slithered one after the other, like a school of fish stuck in the fishing net. Some came closer, if only to smell the white pelt on my shoulders. If they recognized her, they showed nothing of it. I prayed that wearing the fur of a pack leader improved my standing among them and would not be taken as an insult.

Through the mass of wolfish heads, the "Tit" appeared clearer and clearer, though no longer seemed to gain in size. An old mountain, no bigger than a hill really, with its summit chopped flat. Trees of yellowish fumes grew from the cracks, and it was indeed barren of vegetation. More wolves climbed down the mountain. Fenrir would be in the crater.

An old gray wolf shouldered his way to the center of the mass. All the others, even those bigger and stronger than him, took a step back and lowered their heads. If there was a more complex hierarchy than leader and followers among those creatures, this one would be at the top. He was lean and mean and quiet and reminded me of those venerable jarls whose life stories alone commanded respect. His left eye was snow-white, split in two by an old scar. I was given more space, too, when he reached me.

The wolf jarl would not let me pass, so I stopped walking and met him head-on. I looked up into his good eye, adopting a Loki-like, snobbish pose. He smiled, or at least it looked like he did, and approached even closer. The black leather of his wet snout came so close to my face that I could feel its heat. He sniffed me, then tensed. A sudden tension rose among the beasts surrounding me. Whimpers multiplied, growls too. Loki, the real one, would have reacted there and then. He would have slapped the beast dead or something of the sort. I shouldn't have let that old wolf do as he pleased; it was a sign of weakness. The old beast was testing me, and I failed.

His sniffs turned to growls. He shoved his nose under my armpits to strengthen the insult, and the beast's white eye met mine.

He knew.

I was a dead man if I did not react. So I did.

I lunged under the belly of the closest wolf, drew my sword in the same movement, and cut at the beast above me. My new blade was razor-sharp; it opened the skin as if it were butter. Warm entrails dropped on my back as the wolf they belonged to pitifully yapped. The maw of the wolf jarl snapped right behind me, but his fallen comrade fell on him just as I slipped away.

Confusion spread within the wolves' ranks as fast as I did. One of them was dying noisily, the smell of blood was flooding their senses, and a creature was running between their legs like a mouse fleeing for its life. Confusion turned to panic; wolves snarled and barked at other wolves, and soon they did as humans would have done; they drew blood.

Lost in a labyrinth of fur and legs, I cut and slashed with each step, then slipped away to spread the confusion. I could no longer spot the mountain and moved by instinct more than logic. Bony legs kicked me unknowingly, shoulders bumped me into their neighbor's flanks. I was trapped, unable to do more than stab randomly. This was a world I knew well. This was a shield wall of fur rather than wood, of fangs rather than blades. It stank like a kennel, but the smell of blood was overpowering the canine stench. A wolf stepped on my foot, and I thrust through its eye. I was lost, as confused as the beasts were, and feared I would never step out of this maze.

Then I saw a light between two rear legs and darted in this direction. Rolling on my shoulder, I back-slashed behind the knee of the last wolf and ran, breathless and sweating.

I had veered from the mountain and corrected my course as soon as I regained my senses. Snow came halfway up my shins, making my steps clumsy, but the mountain was growing bigger by the second, and I noticed a path cutting through it, like the scar from a gigantic axe's blade. It appeared narrow and uneven but widened with every step.

Not fast enough, though.

A powerful bark echoed on the plain like the crack of thunder, and when I dared a look behind, I saw the old jarl wolf slithering out of the pack and engaging in pursuit. The shield wall was my world, the open plain his. He devoured the distance on lighter feet, unbothered by the thickness of the snow. Two, then four more followed his lead, and I stopped looking. The whole pack would be on my tail.

For the first time in ages, I prayed. I prayed to Tyr, Heimdallr, then Odin. I called their name for a miracle, for the distance to the mountain shrunk slower than that of the pursuit. If there was ever a time for them to hear me, it was now.

They did not, of course.

Snow crunched under soft paws right behind me, but the wolf's panting and snarling betrayed his presence more surely. The warmth from his breath told me of his proximity. The mountain was not closing fast enough.

I grabbed the short axe from my belt, twisted on my heel, and hacked the weapon with all my strength. I thought the old male would be on the receiving end, but a younger, bigger one stood in his place, and my blow lost its aim. The wolf twisted its head to avoid the axe, and my weapon bounced from its skull and from my grasp, doing little more than scraping a bit of blood. The beast, either from pain or surprise, tumbled, and I left it kicking the snow as if life was abandoning it. Two more wolves jumped over their fallen brother, one of them being the old leader from before.

The snow was getting thinner as we got closer to the sleeping volcano, and my pace increased. Theirs too, but I could still make it, I hoped. More beasts were dashing from the summit, though, and would cut me from the path I was aiming for. I cursed Loki for his useless body. The real me could run faster, and I wouldn't have been so out of breath.

But then, just as the wolves climbing down the mountain were about to cut my only path to safety, just as hope gave up on me, a pleasant heat ran down my legs. The air I breathed filled my lungs and my senses with a burning liquid-like sensation. The distance with the wolf behind increased, and those in front moved slower. My knees were rising higher, my feet barely touched the ground, the blade in my hand weighed nothing, and my sight tunneled, darkening at the edges and sharpening at the center. Fluffy flakes of snow plopped against my cheeks, and the wind began to howl around me. The world turned silver-gray, and those barely moving beast's barks stretched through several of my steps.

I burst through the crack a second before the old wolf snapped at me.

My sight lost its edge, and my limbs felt suddenly heavy. Taken by my momentum, I fell on my ass and, after resisting for a couple of heartbeats, threw up a bucket-load of bile. The wolf jarl's head fit through the crack, but nothing else did, and his frustration revealed his fangs as they closed on nothing. He tried to get in again and again, but I was out of reach, and he soon gave up and threatened me with nothing more than growls. Then, my breathing still ragged, I laughed. I laughed like a madman. I had tasted the power of the gods, and it was intoxicating. Loki's body still contained power, and I had tapped into it. My legs shook, and my mind buzzed, but for the time of a few heartbeats, I had been as powerful as an Æsir.

I felt the old wolf's eye on me, and behind him, a swarm of beasts gathered. I wondered if their younger ones could fit through the crack and did not wish to find out, so I resumed my path and left them to growl in frustration.

The narrow canyon path went on, hopefully, all the way to the crater, snaking through the mountain as if carved by a lightning bolt. The rock was sharp and pointy and dry, thorny bushes made it their life's purpose to grip the white fur on my shoulders. Eggther's gifts of fur and clothing suffered several tears, but my skin remained untouched.

Even without the power surge from before, I was glad for Loki's body at the moment. Mine would have been cumbersome in such a narrow place. But even with the slender vessel of the trickster, it took agility and some climbing to make my way through the sleeping volcano. The yellow fumes smelled like wet farts and burned my eyes, but they did not seem toxic, at least.

A patch of snow fell on my back. That's when I noticed the wolves were following my progress from above. Like shadows lurking in the sky, they moved when I did. Fat drops of drool fell from their maws, but the beasts were powerless, the distance between us increasing with each step. The walls grew so tall that soon the sky became a thin line of white and gray, and the wolves barely more than blurry shapes.

I stopped thinking about the beasts above and wondered about the one in front, and, as if he had heard my thoughts, a malevolent *seidr* suddenly compressed my heart. Fenrir was welcoming me. His power felt like Loki's, but where the trickster's vibrated with a quiet, vicious anger, the wolf's bubbled with a wild rage.

I had hoped to sneak into Fenrir's lair, but this thin hope had faded as soon as the wolves found me in the forest. If discretion was off the table, things would have to go down with a face-to-face, somehow. I don't know what I hoped for. A miracle, another twist of fate, a compromise, maybe. We needed that bird, and Fenrir would give it to me. Not for nothing. No, I wasn't so naive. I had nothing to give, but now I had power, and maybe this could interest him. I tried to summon Loki's power once more, but either the previous attempt had depleted me of *seidr,* or I did not know how to control it, and nothing happened. I would meet Fenrir as an Einheri soul using a Jötunn body.

Fenrir's power was great, threatening, and foul. There was anger in his *seidr*, so much anger I thought my chest would explode. And there was sadness, too. I recognized those emotions; they felt familiar. I had been chained to a rock for three years and had almost gone mad. Fenrir had been chained here for more than four centuries. He was me, but worse.

The air suddenly felt different, fresher and hotter at the same time, and still the *seidr* grew in intensity. It was like pushing against the current of a river. The corridor widened a little, soon giving me enough space to walk normally. It turned one last time to the right, and then, through an erupting cloud of fumes, I saw the king. I saw *him* who was destined to kill the All-Father. Fenrir, son of Loki.

An unmoving pitch-black shape the size of a hall, peacefully lying like a hound by the hearth in winter. Even with the distance separating us, I could spot his two honey-colored eyes watching me. His right front leg rested on top of the left, and his long maw quietly lay on them. He looked at peace, but the violence evaporating from the Wolf King was suffocating. Dozens of giant wolves, looking ridiculously small in comparison, walked to their father's side, forming an arch of gray, white, and brown facing me.

As I stepped out of the path, more of them came down from the inside slope of the volcano. They jumped down, quiet and obedient, guarding my sides and accompanying me to their lord. Those beasts who had been ready to tear me apart a few minutes earlier were now guiding me again. I had passed their test and would now face their king as my prize.

I sheathed the Dwarven sword in my belt to show I meant no more harm. For some reason, I thought the blade would need a name when all of this was over. A geyser popped close to me, but I managed to control my startling. The inside of the volcano resembled a beehive with all the caves dug into its rock. Hundreds of beasts watched me walk to my fate from those alcoves. The pups seemed curious, but their mothers appeared unbothered. Fenrir was siring an army. Some of the younger ones yapped. It quickly riled the others, and soon the noise grew louder. Full-grown wolves barked, growled, and howled until the whole place rang with a mad racket. Only the wolves at my sides kept their composure—and only because their father was watching us. The madness still got to them; their muscles trembled, and their desire to partake in the chaos reached their lips and throats.

Fenrir barked, just once. A low, echoing bark with enough power to make all his children cower at once, and my heart froze on its beat. He slowly sat up. The sun, feeble behind the thick, perpetual layer of gray clouds, hid behind his head and left me in his shadow. He looked down on me, and I thought my neck would snap with the effort of looking up.

Gleipnir, the famous chain forged by the Dwarves to keep Fenrir bound, protruded from the black fur at the base of his neck. It was a common-looking chain, except for the size of its links. I could fit through them. The chain clanked with each of the king's movements and trembled from his body to the ground. The links were marked by claws and fangs, some of those scratches so wide they had to have been inflicted by the Wolf King himself. He and his children had dug the ground around the chain, but Gleipnir must have reached deep below the mountain. In truth, I felt some sympathy for the beast.

"What do we have here?" Fenrir asked. His voice, booming from deep within, was pleasant and smooth. "I see my father, but I do not sense him."

"I am Drake of the Einherjar," I replied. "Your father has tricked me and stolen my body."

Fenrir showed no reaction. His frightening eyes were scanning my soul, and the gentle wind made his fur move like a field of black wheat. He cocked his head to the side, as a dog would have, and finally, mercifully, lowered it back on top of his legs.

"So, my father is free. And soon, I will be too."

"Your father is unchained, but he won't enjoy his freedom for long. Next time I meet him, I will kill Loki." I had decided to bet on Fenrir's probable hate for his father. Loki had done nothing to prevent his son's captivity. How could the wolf love him?

My bet paid off, and I was rewarded with a booming chuckle.

"If you believe you can kill Loki, you are either bold or stupid," Fenrir said after his chuckle died down. "Many have tried and failed. What makes you think you will succeed?"

"I already killed his wife," I said. Fenrir's ears turned to face me. I had his attention now. "And I have allies in Asgard. Your father's death is coming; it has already been decided. He will die, painfully and slowly, I should say. You don't know me, Hrodvitnir, but do not underestimate me." I had to sound boastful and confident, as all proper warriors were, and I had used Fenrir's nickname, *famous wolf,* to pat him the right way. I was looking for an ally here.

"But will you leave my lair alive?" Fenrir asked. Some of his children became agitated and shifted their gaze from me to their father, waiting for the signal to put me down. I had not realized until then that my guides had stopped a good dozen steps behind, but they, too, reacted to their father's threat with a series of growls.

"You're right," I replied, dropping my hands on my hips, "this depends on you. I have no quarrel with you and wish you no harm, but I will defend my life dearly. I will die if you so wish, but I will take many of your children with me, and as you probably know, Ragnarök is near; you will need your army."

My argument was feeble, and he knew it. He had enough of the bastards that losing even a dozen would make no difference. Maybe he had sensed my surge of power earlier, or maybe I amused him, and Fenrir decided to play along.

"If you know you are to die, why did you come to me, Drake of the Einherjar?"

"I need something from you. Or rather, Eggther needs something back from you," I answered. "Your father tricked me and got me jailed in a cave for three years. I escaped and found myself in this wretched place. My way back to Asgard and to my vengeance goes through Eggther's bridge, but the herder asked for a favor, and here I am."

I was taking a risk in mentioning Eggther's bridge. Fenrir would be tempted to send his army through it. The herder had mentioned that nothing bigger than a human could pass through it, but Huginn had warned me not to believe him.

"And what does the herder need so badly that he would send Odin's dragon to his death?" Fenrir asked while yawning. I froze at the sight of those immense, blood-stained fangs and the depth of his maw. The smell of death, when he closed it, proved impossible to ignore.

"A bird. A purple bird, that's all I know."

"And what makes you think I haven't eaten this bird?"

"Fate," I replied.

"Ah," he simply said. "Fate would have kept a bird alive so that you could get your vengeance on the trickster. Interesting concept, Drake ill-lucky. And you claim to have no quarrel with me, but I am to swallow your lord, so how could you have no quarrel? Do you hate Odin? If it is so, then maybe we could come to an agreement."

"I love Odin like a father," I replied. Fenrir pursed his upper lip just enough for me to see the tip of his longest fangs. "And when the day comes, I will do my duty and prevent you from fulfilling the prophecy. Until then, no, I have no quarrel with you."

The chain bidding Fenrir ruffled, and I sensed his *seidr*

boiling, or maybe it was the sensation of my bowels twisting on themselves.

"Why," he said, letting word stretch, "would you adore a being as vicious as Odin? Why would you worship this clan of liars and manipulators?"

My heart hurt; Fenrir was getting angry.

"Some of them are heartless bastards, I grant you that, but not all of them."

"All of them!" he barked. "Not *one* is worthy of your sacrifice, Drake."

Fenrir shook himself up, and I took a step backward. The chain made a noise like a shield wall hitting another shield wall, and his bones cracked as he stood on all four legs.

"How did *he* trick you? What did he use?" Fenrir asked. "No, don't tell me, let me guess."

From the king's monstrous form emanated a translucent fume, like heat over a fire. Shapes blurred and undulated around his silhouette as if I had been in an induced dream. Yet, the king's eyes remained on me, unmoving and lethal. Then, his whole body seemed to evaporate. The darkness of his fur turned grayer, then mist-like, and then nothing more than the memory of his massive body.

From the fading cloud came a man. A naked man with the chiseled body of a warrior, minus the scars. His dark hair hung loose and wild down to his hips. His beardless chin was angular, like his father's, and his eyebrows were thin and sharp. His muscles were lean and dry, but I could sense the strength of an oarsman in his arms. You did not need to love men to find this one handsome; he just was. The collar remained around his neck, linked to a now regular size chain binding him to the ground. Fenrir's eyes stayed golden, sad, and breaming with rage.

The mist glided off him as he stepped right in front of me. We were of the same height, but he stood more muscular than my current body, and I felt no less intimidated than before. My fear, though, was second to my sympathy. Those eyes... They did not belong to a beast but to a victim.

"He used love, didn't he?" he then asked in a pristine, cunning, princely voice.

I nodded, a lump forming in my throat.

"That's what they do," Fenrir went on. "They use what is most precious to you, your weakness. Æsir, Vanir, Jötnar, it does not matter. They would do anything to get what they want. You may trust them, Drake; you may worship them, but they are not worthy. They call my father *the god of mischief*, and he is one, maybe the worst, but at least he is honest about it. Tell me, Drake truth-teller, when did you last hear a so-called god admit one of his flaws or own their mistakes? Not recently, I assume. And yet, they are flawed. Loki is a trickster, but so are the others. And you, fool, do their bidding, hoping for some scraps of attention, a hint of respect from them. Like a good dog at the corner of the dining table."

Fenrir had to halt his walk, for the chain tensed to its maximum. I stepped closer and found myself face-to-face with a being who had suffered more than any other I had met.

"Respect," he went on before spitting. "As if their arrogance allowed them such a thing. They *need* your strength but desire your devotion and your sacrifices above all. Tell me, Drake, do you consider some to be your friends?"

"Very few of them," I said, careful not to name Tyr, who had betrayed Fenrir the most.

"Fool," he gently replied. "I, too, thought the same when

I lived among them. And do you love some of them? Not just like a father or a brother, do you truly love some of them?"

"I did," I replied, having to swallow hard.

"Look where it got you," Fenrir said, looking me up and down with a hint of disgust. "Look where it got us."

The air fled from my lungs, and my hands, so tightly shut into fists, opened like the petals of wildflowers in the morning. I would never be able to hate Fenrir anymore. I could only sympathize. We had suffered the same betrayal and paid the same price for it.

I also knew that my friendship with Tyr would never be the same.

Tyr had told me Fenrir and he used to be friends, but he was lying. They had been more than friends or brothers; they had been in love, and Tyr had used the trust born of their feelings to trick Fenrir. The reasoning behind the act didn't matter to me; Tyr had committed the worst kind of betrayal. And if Tyr, the Æsir I respected the most, was capable of such a thing, then what about the others?

Tyr was Fenrir's Muninn, and he had been chained because of the same weakness. *Love*.

Telling another person you shared his pain was futile because pain is unique to its bearer. Yet, I did and wanted him to know. Tears of rage pearled in his eyes. How many times had Fenrir felt those words stuck in his rib cage, unable to share them with his children?

I offered my hand, a mark of respect from one wounded man to another.

He observed it for a long time with curiosity. I pushed back the memory of what he had done the last time a hand had been offered to him. Now that I knew the truth, or a bigger part of it, I thought Tyr had deserved to lose his arm.

"Then, you understand my thirst for revenge," I said.

His eyes met mine again.

He took my hand with a firm and powerful grip.

"May we both exert it," he replied. "I, too, have no quarrel with you, Drake love-wounded. For now."

The tension vanished as if chased by a summer breeze, and we both took a step back. Fenrir shot a look over his shoulder, and in the next second, a wolf left its spot in the ranks and moved toward the back of the pack, slithering through its siblings with haste.

"You will kill him slowly," he said, an order, not a question.

"Very," I said.

"And when my turn comes, I will do the same. Do not interfere then." I wondered if he was talking about Odin or Tyr.

I had planned to trick Fenrir into believing we could be allies, but somehow, we had become just that. An understanding was born between us, and it did not fill me with joy to imagine that someday soon, we would face each other in the last battle of our age.

The wolf came back, a lidded basket held between his jaws. It stopped just next to his father and dropped the basket delicately on the ground. The king gave him a pat between the eyes, and the wolf remained there.

"Here is Eggther's *purple bird*," Fenrir said. "It wouldn't have made a great meal anyway."

I scooped the basket and was comforted to feel some movement in it. Then I heard a clunk, and curiosity got the better of me. I opened the lid. I wouldn't have called its color purple, more like red or something in between. And really, who called a rooster a bird?

"Now you see," Fenrir said, a satisfied smug on his handsome face. "Not even Jötnar can be trusted."

The prophecy struck the back of my mind in Odin's voice, and I understood what I now held. This was no simple rooster, and I had been played by the herder. His *purple bird* was one of the three roosters whose crowing would announce the beginning of Ragnarök, the one who would announce to the beasts of Jötunheimr that their time to invade Asgard had come. Fenrir had just given me the mother of all poisoned gifts.

5

Asgard's prison, now

"I lost my faith in Ironwood."

Muninn remained quiet during my tale, peppering it sparingly with gasps and moans, mostly when I almost lost my head or mentioned her. She listened with care, but I could no longer trust her. For all I knew, her focus was aimed at surviving the prison and her coming trial. Fenrir's warning remained as clear in my mind as the day he offered it along with the rooster. None of the beings I used to call gods were worth my sacrifice or my trust.

"But you made it back," she said. I must have let the silence go on for too long, and she took it as an invitation to speak. "Safe and whole."

"Whole? I just told you, I lost my faith in your people and everything that went with it."

Muninn could not understand my meaning, and why would she? She was born an Æsir, a part of Odin himself.

Serving her father, then Loki, was as natural as the air she breathed.

"I have been at the All-Father's service for three hundred years," I said, readjusting my posture against the opposite wall of the cell. "I have killed and died, over and over again, because I believed in your people. I disliked many of you and knew from experience you wouldn't lift a finger to save your worshippers, but at least you had a certain sense of morality. I believed we were fighting to keep chaos from spreading on Midgard and that the nine realms without the Æsir would be worse. But you're no better than any other creature of Jötunheimr. You betray, you cheat, you abuse those inferior to you. What you did to me is what you've been doing for eons to all those fool enough to worship you. I don't know about the other realms, but Midgard and its people would fare better if you ceased to exist. I am not whole, Muninn. You took my heart when you stabbed me, and Fenrir took my faith and rendered my whole life pointless when he showed me the truth."

"I am sorry," she whispered.

"I bet you are."

"You suffered when you realized the truth about my people," she said, rattling her chains as she padded a little closer, though the whole cell separated us. "And I can't grasp all that it meant to you. But, Drake, I must ask you, what did you do with the rooster?"

"The rooster?" I asked, baffled by this change in the conversation.

"The purple rooster," she said as if the specification was needed.

"Worried that I might have twisted its neck and toyed with the prophecy?" The face she made told me she was.

"The idea rattled my mind from the moment I stepped out of the crater. In fact, it was all I could think of."

Ironwood, then

The prophecy was generous with signs announcing it and little else. The great winter, brothers killing brothers, Loki's escape, Fenrir's escape. We didn't know much about the battle itself, but we would know when it was about to start. And of all the signs, the most precise and yet confusing one was the three roosters.

Three roosters would crow to announce Ragnarök, thus signaling to the three great armies the end of the world was near.

A golden one would warn Asgard. No golden rooster had been seen in ages on Asgard, and since the prophecy, every hatchling had been inspected with great care.

A dark rooster in the underworld. The land governed by Hel and named after her had been off-limit to us for longer than I existed, and thousands of dark damn roosters could be roaming it for all I knew.

And finally, a crimson rooster in Jötunheimr would call the Jötnar to gather for the Great War. A crimson rooster, not a purple one.

"Crimson," I told the basket as if its resident could understand. "You're fucking crimson, not purple. Stupid Jötunn." A blizzard had stormed the land soon after I left the volcano, accompanying me deep into the woods. It did not help my mood. "And you're a rooster, not a *bird*. Yes, I know, roosters are technically birds, but who calls them birds? Stupid, tree-humping, dirt-sniffing Jötunn."

I was angry and cared nothing that I was talking to a rooster. Eggther had tricked me. He hadn't just asked me to fetch his animal back. He had asked me to get him the key to Ragnarök.

Fenrir had not eaten the bird for this exact reason. There was no possible confusion; this was the crimson rooster from the prophecy. On my shoulder hung the very thing that would send the armies of Jötunheimr to Asgard, and I was taking it back to our enemies. I cursed Eggther, I cursed fate, and I cursed this moronic bird, their mothers, and grandmothers until I had no more insults available and could only repeat myself.

Fenrir's grin when I departed his lair reminded me of his father. A wolf-like smile of victory. He had given me what I wanted, a means to stop Ragnarök before it happened, yet it was no gift.

"I can kill it for you," the Wolf King had offered as I closed the basket lid.

I had been tempted. Just as I was now tempted to twist the bird's neck and be done with it. But I refused his offer, and that's when he grinned and resumed his giant wolf form. Fenrir knew I would not hurt the bird, just as Eggther knew. They had left it in their enemy's care, the key to the nine realm's destiny, betting that I would do nothing about it. And it pissed me off.

Alone, I had climbed the volcano up and down, then crossed the plain where the red spots from my escape slowly vanished under a new layer of snow. The rooster was mostly silent as if it knew how precarious its life was under my care. It only replied when I shook the basket in spasms meant to bother it. But when I spoke like a madman, the rooster said nothing.

I walked faster on the way back, not bothered with

trying to be discreet. Fenrir's children would be escorting me back to Eggther with my precious cargo from a distance and would remain clear from my path. And despite the weather making the way back more difficult, I moved faster, recognizing the marks I had left on trees a few hours before.

I was physically safe but mentally on the brink of collapse.

I tore the last piece of dry meat with my teeth, removing a long chunk of it to chew my anger on. I readjusted the basket on my back, and the rooster made a little, plaintive cluck.

"Shut up," I said. "You're not allowed to complain. All cozy and warm in your cocoon while I dig the snow like a plowing cow."

The rooster clucked again as if replying.

"Oh, and you're not the one carrying the bird announcing the end of the world; you're the damn bird! So just shut your beak."

And the rooster did. It pissed me off even more. I needed an outlet for my rage, and speaking, even to a bird, was a way to let it go a little.

"I should turn you into a stew. You know when was the last time I ate some poultry? Yes, a couple of days ago, I know, shut up. Still, I haven't had some capon meat in forever, and I am getting very curious to see if purple roosters taste different. Yes, crimson, not purple, I know!"

If Fenrir's wolves were indeed following me, I wondered what they thought of this scene. This wasn't my finest moment, but I needed it.

"Why don't I, you ask? It would be so much simpler indeed. One quick twist, one stroke of my blade, and *poof,* no more Ragnarök. I get my belly full, Jötnar don't invade

Asgard, Odin lives, my men live, even fucking Thor lives. Not bad for the life of a chicken, is it? So why don't I?"

I asked the last question to myself. *Why not?* For years, I had scorned the indecisiveness of the gods toward Ragnarök. Of course, back then, all I wanted was to prevent Ragnarök to save the woman I loved. Like the Æsir, I had accepted my fate, but I would have done anything to preserve my precious raven from her own. I no longer cared for it now, so why, by the nine realms, was I still considering killing or not killing the rooster?

"Because it could be worse? Worse than Ragnarök?" I asked, snorting. Heimdallr had said as much. Preventing Ragnarök, he had said, could bring something far worse than the end of our time. At least, with Ragnarök, we knew some gods would survive, as well as a few humans. I hated this argument. I still did. The prophecy had everyone trembling in their boots. Acting could trigger Ragnarök; not acting could do the same.

"How about we take a chance? How about we let fate surprise us, huh? Æsir and Vanir are so hung up on their prophecies and known future that they would not take chances. Worse than Ragnarök, my ass. So why don't I just turn you into my next meal? What do you say?"

I was tempted. I did not care about preventing Ragnarök as much as I used to, but it would still be a win if my brothers survived it. And just picturing the faces Odin, Heimdallr, and all the others would make when I told them that I, Drake, a simple Einheri, canceled Ragnarök, was worth the risk. I, a punny human, with one swing of my new blade, altered their future irrevocably. That would give us a good laugh in Valhöll for sure.

And maybe this was Odin's plan after all.

Maybe Odin had foreseen all of this and put his plan in

motion for this very moment. The All-Father, from the eye he cast in the well of wisdom, had divined that sending Huginn to Midgard and asking Muninn to erase his memory would trigger a chain of events leading to me cutting the throat of the rooster. This was his plan, I knew it, felt it in my bones. Odin had given me the means to end the end of the world.

I stopped in my tracks and stood mouth agape like a fool. There was a small frozen pond on my right. We were in a part of the forest where trees did not grow as much and where water had formed a flat and thick layer of ice.

This is where the crimson rooster is to die.

I dropped the basket, the bird clucked unhappily, and I got on my knees. I lifted the latch, seized the rooster by the neck, and laid it on its back, just at the edge of the frozen pond.

The bird racked my arm with its claws but did little damage. It tried to peck my hands, but my grip was solid, and after a time, its chest, rising in quick motions and its heart even faster, calmed down. It cocked its head and looked me straight in the eyes, its round pupil dark as Fenrir's pelt. My sword rested next to the rooster, and the reflection of the bird on the blade turned it crimson as well. And so would my sword be named from now on, Crimson.

The blade remained still for a long time, the rooster too, for neither of my hands dared move.

"Why don't I kill you? Why?" I shouted.

Its chest rose faster a couple of times and got quiet once more. It was not worried, just as Fenrir hadn't been worried, just as Eggther hadn't been either.

They could see something in me that even I couldn't. But I was getting a taste of it in the back of my mouth. A thirst.

There was something I wanted more than saving my brothers or the gods. I thirsted for revenge. I wanted to make Loki and his pet pay. I was mad at Odin for the ordeal he had put me through, and if his goal had been to get me here to kill the bird, then fuck him, I would do the opposite.

I needed to let Tyr know how much of an asshole he had been to Fenrir. I wanted to punch Eggther in the face, behead Magnus Stone-fist once more for being a pain in my ass, and kick Thor in the balls just for the sake of it. I had killed a man named Halfdan, even though he had won the honor of becoming an Einheri, just for the sake of revenge, and did not regret it. It felt like justice. The Æsir and the Vanir deserved what Ragnarök promised them, just as I deserved my revenge. I was vengeance, and vengeance was all I had left.

Killing the rooster meant that I would have none of it. And if the price for vengeance was Ragnarök, so be it. I would deal with that in due time.

I roared at the rooster just to get it out of my chest.

Once that was out, I stuffed the bird back in the basket and resumed my journey back to Eggther's farm.

My steps were lighter, the bad taste in my mouth was gone, I had Crimson in my belt, and I knew who I was. Vengeance. I was vengeance in the flesh, and this is what I would have.

ᚱ

With a clear head on my shoulders, I realized how futile killing the bird would have been. Nothing guaranteed this was the rooster of the prophecy. For all I knew, crimson roosters were common in some parts of Jötunheimr. That a big part of me believed it and that Fenrir believed it as well didn't mean it was the right bird. I could have killed a regular rooster, and it would have cost me my passage back to Asgard. Even if it was the rooster crowing for Ragnarök, it did not mean only this one could be it. Fate would have hatched another one somewhere. I could no more control fate than I could control the weather, as it had proven again and again. And since the army from Jötunheimr was going to join that of Hel and Múspellsheimr on their invasion of Asgard, the Jötnar were bound to hear about Ragnarök another way.

At least, by following the path traced for me, I would get my vengeance, Huginn would rejoin his clan, and Ulf his granddaughter. *For the price of a chicken.*

On the long walk back to the farm, I hesitated a couple of times, wondering if I should prepare to spend the night in the woods, but I kept on walking and arrived late in the night.

And, as if Eggther had guessed how everything would go, he had lit dozens of torches by the entrance of his farm to guide me. Like a king coming back to his hall, I was welcomed with fires. I passed the fence, and my two friends, along with the herder, came out of the longhouse.

"What took you so long?" Eggther asked with greasy lips from the meal I had interrupted.

I dropped the basket, then walked the two steps separating me from the giant. I slightly crouched with the last step, then soared, grabbed his right shoulder for support, and punched him in the face just as I hit the highest point of my leap. Eggther toppled face-first into a puddle of mud.

One thing to cross from my shit list.

The burning sensation of Loki's power ran through my bones and cooled down again.

"Drake, what the Hel?" Ulf asked as he knelt to check the giant.

Eggther shook his head with disbelief, but I saw no anger in his eyes, just confusion.

"Didn't know folks could hit so hard," he said after making his lower jaw work a couple of times.

"That was for tricking me," I told him. "And this is for our passage home, as well as for the blade." I kicked the basket, which landed against his chest.

Eggther nodded, his face now marred by a rapidly darkening bruise. We understood each other, but Ulf did not follow. Huginn, who may have guessed some of it, stood motionless, arms crossed.

"I owe you an apology, old raven. You were right about Jötnar."

"I am glad you are back," Huginn said.

"So," Eggther said as he towered over us again, "I guess you'll leave in the morning."

ᚱ

As I had assumed, the hot spring of Eggther's farm was the gate to Asgard. A spring of hot fuming water stuck between some coop pen and an enclosure where domesticated boars lived, bubbling from the ground, just big enough for Eggther to bathe.

"I don't like this," Ulf said as we listened to the bubbles popping continuously.

"I know," I said. Ulf had never liked crossing the Bifröst. We had to die to pass the rainbow bridge upward, courtesy of Odin's failure in its making. Other passages didn't require such extreme measures but were more random in their crossing. Some worked only one way, like the one on Eggther's farm. Others could be used both ways, but those were rare. Some led to dead-ends, under the ground, or in the middle of the sea surrounding Asgard. Using a bridge for the first time was a hazardous adventure at best, a death sentence at worst.

The Wolves, my warband, needed an Æsir token to make sure they could ride the Bifröst back to Asgard, so the All-Father gave us the ten nails from his hands so that my men could accomplish his will and come back. We ate those disgusting things before dying to avoid ending up in Hel instead of Asgard. I would have preferred Ulf to get one before using Eggther's gate, just for good measure. Thankfully, Huginn had another way, or at least he hoped.

Ulf held a black feather between two fingers, studying it with care, but I knew that he had his doubts. First, by his own words, Huginn had lost most of his power after having spent more than twenty years on Midgard. Our confidence in his feathers' potency was limited. Second, if a feather was enough, how come Odin had never thought about it? Plucking his son's feathers was far less painful than pulling his own nails.

"Maybe their effect doesn't last as long," Huginn had replied when Ulf made this point.

Ulf rolled the feather on itself, making its shaft snap, and then shoved it in his mouth. He took a few unpleasant gulps of cider to help its passage down.

That I did not need it was the funniest part of the joke played on Ulf.

I had a Jötunn body, and so was my blood. I was now more than an Einheri, as Eggther's face showed. The Loki part of me was gaining in strength. And if I could do none of the incredible things the god of mischief could, I was by far stronger than any other of my kind and capable of crossing a bridge between the realms.

"Drake, a word," Eggther said as Ulf finally gulped the thing down.

"I won't apologize," I said.

He waved my comment off as if it were nothing, though his jaw bothered him. "I wouldn't have it anyway," he replied. "And I won't apologize either. We all do what we have to do for our own reasons. No need to be sorry. I have my people, and—"

"—and I have my vengeance," I finished for him. "What is it, Herder?"

"Once you cross that bridge, you and I will be enemies," he said, arms bulging as he crossed them over his chest. "Should I see you on the field, I won't hesitate."

"Neither will I," I replied, my tone harsher than intended. I was mad at Eggther, but I still liked the giant.

"This being said, should you survive Ragnarök, you are welcome here," he said, uncrossing his arms. "If I, too, survive the end of the world, then we will be comrades again in this place. I enjoyed your company, little man, and hope we will share many more meals and cups as friends."

I did not understand his words and said so. Ragnarök would engulf the world, not just Asgard, so why should I come here, or survive, for that matter?

"This place is special," Eggther said. "You could say it is blessed. Winter is never harsh, summer never too dry, and it will know no end. Only a few parts of the nine realms have been so blessed."

Sigyn had said the same about Loki's cave. Those places would survive the end of the world, and this one was far more welcoming than my prison. Why Eggther owned such a place was a mystery, but his generosity was touching. He was offering hope where there was none and to his enemy nonetheless.

"May we both survive then," I said, extending my hand as I had with Fenrir. "And may enough time pass before so that I can digest you tricking me."

Eggther smirked, accepted my hand, and squeezed harder than needed.

Ulf was still struggling with the next step when the giant and I faced the hot spring again. Eggther held his harp and pinched a string, just one, and the water's bubbles popped stronger in greater number. The colors of the rainbow rippled over the surface. The bridge was open. As far as incantations went, it was rather low-key.

"Who goes first?" I asked Ulf, enjoying his misery a little while longer.

"I don't know, maybe Huginn could—"

We never heard the end of his sentence. Eggther dropped his massive hand on Ulf's back and sent him flat in the water. His body vanished as if he had fallen down a cliff.

"It's faster this way," he replied. "Goodbye, old crow," Eggther said as Huginn stepped into the water.

Huginn did not even bother replying to our host, but I assumed it was because the pull from home was too strong. He most likely did not even hear the Jötunn's words. Twenty-three years he had been away. One more minute might have been too much for his sanity.

I, too, stepped into the water, wincing at the sudden warmth. Crimson was at my side, my prize for the last three years of suffering. That and the powers I was learning to control. If I ever got my hands on Wedge again, I would have a collection to rival the best in Asgard.

"Wait," I said as Eggther was turning back. "Do you actually know where it goes?"

"Oh," he replied. "That will be the best part of your journey. Believe me."

The spring swallowed me.

I was going home.

6

I had missed the crossing between realms.

The light, the movement, the coldness, the colors, and the rebirth, I had missed it more than I knew. It always went too fast, but it was a worthy experience. That, for once, I did not suffer the trauma of death only added to the pleasure of the crossing. Of course, this was not Bifröst per se, just a backdoor path to Asgard, but the feelings remained the same. And, as with the rainbow bridge, the dreamlike state it put me in meant that, for a few seconds, I forgot about everything.

I gasped for air before I knew it was over, and immediately, a hand covered my mouth to keep me quiet. Panic seized me, but Ulf shushed me discreetly, and I remembered what was happening.

The water was just as hot as the one we had dived in, and the smell was stronger than what I was used to upon arriving on Asgard. A mix of incense and herbs, like in the cabin of an old seer, but pleasant. I blinked the water from my eyes, and the shapes formed.

We were in a room, a large one. The walls were of solid

stone, dark and chiseled with care. Candles had been lit as if we had been expected, but their light was dim and only revealed the closest objects. Cushions, mirrors, cups, and a good number of trinkets made of gold and silver were randomly arranged around the pool we came from. This was a bath, but not just for one person.

I joined Ulf by the side of the pool, and Huginn, who I had not even noticed, hid behind a pillar. His eyes stared at the only entrance of the room. An arched-shaped hole with only a thin piece of purple linen to mark its limit. The light from the hallway, dimmed by the drape, bathed the room in a similar color. It was all very soothing, and this, in turn, made me nervous.

There was no sound, but people lived here and used this bath regularly. Some cups still contained liquid.

"Where the Hel are we?" Ulf whispered once we joined Huginn.

"No idea," I replied.

"Sessrúmnir," the old raven said with a look over his shoulder. I could not see it clearly, but I think I saw the corner of his lip rising.

Sessrúmnir was Freyja's domain. A place held as a legend by Einherjar, where Valkyries were said to live naked. The idea of visiting this domain kept many of my brothers sane and motivated. How many had challenged the brawl to gain access here? But only a few lucky ones ever got their wish granted.

I had never been inside Sessrúmnir, but I knew this place was it. It had Freyja written all over it.

"Why do we hide then?" Ulf asked, still whispering.

"We don't know how Freyja or her Valkyries might take our intrusion," I replied. "You remember how she slap-killed you?"

"How could I forget, with all of you reminding me all the time." His hand moved by itself to his neck, and I chuckled at the memory.

"We have no idea what the situation is on Asgard," Huginn, who had kept his seriousness, said. "She might not be an ally."

"She won't be one to Loki, that's for sure," Ulf replied.

He was right. The goddess of love allying herself to the trickster was as likely as Thor becoming abstinent of anything. Freyja hated Loki more than anyone.

"And you want to show up with this one looking like that?" Huginn said with a thumb pointed at me.

"Fair enough," Ulf replied. "So what do we—"

Huginn shushed him with a raised finger.

Voices. Feminine voices, laughing heartily and chatting without care. Their shadows cast themselves on the piece of linen, dancing with the flames of the closest torches. Ulf and I crouched behind Huginn, making ourselves as small as possible. Our cover would not last long if they stepped in.

They took their time to pass the piece of fabric, first exchanging pleasantries about one of their comrades having fallen for an odd-looking Einheri. They giggled and then entered the bathroom.

And for once, gods be praised, the legends were true, or very nearly.

Two young-looking, red-headed, and athletic women entered the bathroom, only covered by a thin towel of linen tightly wrapped around their waist. Those two being naked meant nothing for the rest of the domain, of course. This was a bathroom, after all. But their beauty was astonishing, naked or not.

As we had heard, Freyja kept her most beautiful specimens in Sessrúmnir's hall, while the others lived in the outer wings, making the very room I crouched in the stuff of legends.

The one with the heaviest breasts dropped a pitcher of some kind by the side of the pool while the other removed her towel and sat, dipping her well-defined legs in the water. I can honestly say that my focus wasn't at its best.

The first frowned in our direction, looking at the floor, where marks of our wet feet showed.

"What is that?" she asked before walking around the pool toward us.

Huginn acted when she was but an arm's length from him. He grabbed her by the wrist and pushed her against the pillar in one quick motion, then seized her by the neck. Ulf and I rushed to the entrance to block the second Valkyrie's path. She, now standing, dashed in the same direction, but we were faster, and she stopped in her tracks. She saw me, recognized Loki, and terror drew itself in her eyes.

She screamed.

Not for help, not as a signal; she just screamed loud and high.

"Scream again, and she dies," Huginn barked, the first Valkyrie now kneeling in front of him while his knife found her throat.

"Why would you say that?" I asked him. "We won't hurt you," I said, this time to the Valkyrie in front of me. She had grabbed a pitcher and was holding it as she would an axe. What she hoped to do against Ulf and I, armed to the teeth, I do not know and did not mean to find out. Some Valkyries were amazing fighters.

"Like I would trust you, snake," she said before spitting at me.

Ulf dropped his blade and held his hands high, which

was the first clever thought we've had since we came back to Asgard. She barely noticed it, though, for her eyes never left me for more than a blink.

"I am not Loki," I said, tucking Crimson back in my belt.

"That's exactly what Loki would say," she replied, which was probably true.

Steps came rushing in the hallway, ruining any chance I had to resolve the situation quietly.

"Over here!" the Valkyrie shouted.

I rushed her and dropped her on the ground. She fought and tried to knee me in the ribs, but Ulf's blade kept her from trying more than once.

"So much for not hurting her," he said, enjoying the situation more than he should have.

"Step in, and they die," I yelled at the shadows forming behind the screen. A man with a feathered helmet and a large shield. One of Freyja's pretty boys. We liked to make fun of them for their oiled chest and loincloths, but they, too, were peerless warriors, and I preferred this one to remain at a good distance from us. "I am not Loki," I told the Valkyrie again, using the last of my cool.

"What now?" Huginn asked as he approached with his hostage while Ulf helped the other up. The two women exchanged a rebellious look, and I wondered how long we could keep them obedient. Probably not very long.

"Who are you?" the guard asked in a clear, sharp voice. He was probably thinking we were just some Einherjar who had managed to sneak in.

"We need an audience with your leader," Huginn said. "No need to ask her— We'll do it ourselves. Drake, let's move before more show up."

"It's Loki!" the first Valkyrie yelled at the guard. "Tell Freyja!"

His curse lost itself in the noise of his running steps.

"I am not Loki."

"Let's go," Hugin said, moving his knife from her throat to her lower back. She followed his command and passed the purple screen. Ulf followed with his hostage, and I closed the march.

"The best part of my journey, my ass."

I hoped someone would recognize Huginn before things turned uglier, though there wasn't much left of Odin's Thoughts in this old-looking creature.

The hallway was dug in the rock of the mountain, for this is where we were, under the sacred mountain at the center of Asgard. The stone was dark and roughly shaped in an arch reaching just above our heads, giving a pressure I did not particularly like at this instant. We barely made fifty steps in the corridor before more people joined us from both sides.

"Don't walk any farther," said a woman in front, just as a group of three guards lined up in a tight shield wall behind us. They were fearsome, but their eyes betrayed their fear. I could use it, I thought.

I adopted the most Loki-like smile of my repertoire and raised a hand, two fingers pointed at them. Then, using what I thought was an ominous voice, I used the only Vanir sentence I knew.

"*Mane vid un vaohi!*"

If they knew what it meant, we were screwed, but the growing white in their eyes suggested they did not.

"One more step, and I finish this incantation. Then not even Njord will accept you in his hall; I guarantee it." It did the trick. They looked at each other, but none of them stepped any farther.

"Did you just tell them to hump a goat?" Ulf asked.

"That's the extent of my Vanir," I whispered back.

Huginn was doing his best to sound threatening as well, but I could hear the voice of the female leader growing impatient. I knew this voice, or at least the flow of curses she was throwing at the old crow. I had been at the receiving end of both a long time ago, but my memory failed to remember who she was.

"We are not who you think we are," I yelled above my shoulders.

"Give us your weapons, and I might believe you," the woman said.

"We are not that stupid either!"

"Freyja will kill you," the Valkyrie held by Ulf said. "She has wanted it for centuries."

"She will want to hear us first," Ulf replied. "It looks bad, but we are not your enemies."

"I know you," she then said, this time to Ulf. "I've seen you before."

"You might if you ever served in Valhöll," Ulf replied, just as I raised my hands again to keep the small shield wall, now two men deep, at its spot.

"One more step!" the woman in front of us said, "and I won't care about those two!" But we pushed farther still, one tiny step after another. Huginn's hostage cursed.

"You're an Einheri," Ulf's Valkyrie said, "I know you."

"Final warning!" the woman barked. I knew this voice.

"Drake," Huginn called, his resolve mostly gone. I feared that the madness would take him again. I could picture the woman facing him with a sword raised above her head and a group of armed Valkyries by her side. In my mind, she appeared tall and strong, ugly, with red hair and a face splattered with dark freckles.

"You're the girl's grandfather," the Valkyrie said after a

short gasp. Then I felt Ulf's back against mine. He had stopped moving.

"Iona, Tove, I'm sorry," the woman in front said.

"Gunhild, wait," both the Valkyrie who had recognized Ulf and I said.

Gunhild, the strongest shield-maiden in Valhöll. I had not recognized her because I did not think an Einheri, even a woman, would live here. Furthermore, Freyja only accepted the most beautiful creatures in Sessrúmnir, and Gunhild was everything but. An ox of a woman Gunhild was. She had red hair close to the color of tainted copper, freckles spread on her face as if the sun had sneezed them there, and a square jaw that could bite a tree in half. Gunhild was ugly, but she was a brutal and efficient fighter. For some reason, she kept to the second square of the brawl, where she and Titus were often locked in some of the fiercest battles I had ever seen. According to Titus, she was as strong as she was clever in the way she fought.

"You know my name, snake?" she barked.

"He isn't Loki," the Valkyrie, who was either Iona or Tove, said before I could.

No one spoke for a time, but we had stopped moving, and I did not like it. "I am Odin's Drake," I said, "leader of the Wolves. You were a member of the pack once; you know me. I am not Loki."

"That's the cheapest trick you've ever come up with, trickster," Gunhild said.

"Then do you recognize me, shield-maiden?" Ulf said.

"He's Lif's grandfather," the Valkyrie said.

"Go," I told Ulf as I took his knife. "I am not Loki," I told the Valkyrie now in my care.

"Freyja will tell," she said.

"Ulf!" I heard Gunhild call. "The trickster got you out of Hel?"

"Never went there," he said, "too cold for me, I hear. And this is not Loki; this is Drake. Let us pass, and we will explain all of it to Freyja."

"Sorry, archer, I can't let you pass," Gunhild replied. "And if that is truly Drake, then one more reason for my sword to split his skull." I had forgotten that Gunhild blamed me for kicking her out of the pack, though the decision had been forced on me. Her grudge was one of the many I should have resolved many years ago but never managed to.

"She won't let you," my hostage said, "but I can get you to Freyja."

"How?" I asked.

"Give me your knife."

R

I felt pretty stupid as we passed the door leading to Freyja's throne room, a knife pointed under my chin. Huginn had refused to let his hostage go, so it was a weird group that stepped into the goddess's hall. We had almost reached it, but the unit of Valkyries and guards facing us would not have been breached. Gunhild's presence alone would have prevented us from going any closer. So when Iona walked to the shield-maiden, pushing me as her hostage, I could see a rainbow of emotions on Gunhild's face. She walked backward as we moved on, never keeping more than an arm's length between my heart and the tip of her sword.

The massive rune-covered door creaked open, and I went to meet my fate.

The room bathed in purple light as well, though this

time it came from the flames themselves. Eight pillars of massive rock supported a natural hall of dark stones at the end of which, on a narrow and high throne of silver, sat Freyja, goddess of love and war, leader of the Vanir on Asgard.

Even though she sat far and deep in the darkness of the room, I could see she was still the beauty of legends. I could also guess the hatred in her eyes, for here I was, her arch-enemy in the flesh.

Freyja stood and climbed down the three stairs of the dais; then I blinked, and here she was. Like an arrow, she had crossed the distance of her hall and did not stop there. Her elbow hammered me in the stomach and made me gasp in pain. Iona screamed as her lord pinned me against the wall.

No need to guess any longer; Freyja's mask of hatred was right in my face. Her pristine beauty turned to a mask of pure hatred in the blink of an eye. I meant to say, for what seemed the hundredth time, that I was not Loki, but her grasp on my throat was too strong.

"What are you doing here, trickster?" she asked.

I had counted on Freyja to be able to see through me, as Eggther had, believing that some gods could recognize the essence of my being rather than what my flesh showed. I was wrong. Extremely wrong, I thought as her nails pierced the skin of my neck. Stupidly, a part of my mind could only think about Bjorn and how he would love to be in my stead.

"Wait, Freyja," Iona said as she sat up. "He is not Loki."

"You stupid girl," Freyja spat without taking her eyes from me. "He tricked you. That's what he does."

Iona opened her mouth, but nothing came out. Of course, she would assume her goddess was right. She was probably remembering the stories of Loki's tricks as Freyja meant to crush my windpipe.

"What about me then? Do you recognize me?" Huginn asked, his head barely reaching over Tove's shoulder, who he still kept at knife's point.

Freyja dared a glance at him, and her frown grew even deeper, revealing wrinkles I had never noticed on her forehead. She was searching.

"How about like this?" Huginn went on. He closed one eye to look more like Odin, his father.

Her grasp loosened just a little. Not enough for me to breathe.

"Huginn?" she said. "We thought you dead."

"You thought a lot of things wrong," Huginn replied. "Loki has tricked you all. And this is not Loki, as you will see if you calm down a second."

The whole room, now half-filled by guards and armed Valkyries, was holding its breath. I felt the tension from Freyja's *seidr* as she looked through me, making me feel naked. Her eyes were gleaming with the color of the torches, and even with all the hatred pooled in them, those were amazingly beautiful eyes darkened at their corners to extend their line. Her long and curly eyelashes flapped like butterfly wings, and her full lips tightened. Yes, Bjorn would have loved to be in my place, I thought, as oxygen became a rarity in my body.

She dropped me, and I coughed, the sting of her nails feeling stronger now that she had removed them.

"Even if you are Loki," she said, "you are weaker than I am. One wrong move, and I crush you." I trusted her and said so.

"Thank you, Freyja," Huginn said as he finally let go of

Tove, who then joined Iona. Two more of their kind wrapped them with pelts, for they were still naked.

"So," Freyja said, "if you are not Loki. Who, by Frigg's flappy tits, are you?"

"I am Drake, leader of Odin's Wolves."

Freyja's tongue clicked in her mouth, which I guessed happened only once every other minute.

"Well, that explains a lot," she said. "You have much to tell me, privately."

"Yes, we do, goddess," I replied, remembering how much she adored to be worshipped. "Can you first make sure that no one leaves your domain?"

"I assume you have been away for about three years, correct?" she asked, tilting her head.

"Yes." Loki had probably made a poor enough impression of me that even Freyja had realized a change.

"Don't worry about my people leaving my domain. Few of them ever do nowadays. I guess I, too, have a lot to tell you after you bathed and changed. You stink of Jötunheimr."

"The water we serve the victors of the brawl comes from the source that fills Mimir's well. We take it from a spring above the well. If one of them drank the well's water, they would surely die or turn mad. Not that we get many thanks for it. More often than not, all we receive is a tap on the butt. Except for Titus. This one is always respectful. But Titus is already taken. Astrid has been shrewd in her choice of man. Not that I envy her, of course not."

Brune, Valkyrie.

7

Comfort isn't something I have known much in my very long life. It makes a man weak and crushes his resolve to act. But as I lay half-naked on one of Freyja's beds, alone and washed, I thought I might give it a shot.

We would eat soon, invited to the table of the goddess herself. The room would be filled with guards, and I can't imagine there would be music and dances. Yet, it was a great improvement from a couple of hours ago. We had washed, the three of us together, in the bath reserved for the male guards, which was smaller, colder, and altogether less enjoyable than the other one. Gunhild had stayed in the room with us, her eyes never missing a gesture, her ear fully focused on our conversation. I was glad to see the shield-maiden and said so. Her reply came in the form of a grunt.

Ages ago, I had forbidden women within the Wolves. In general, they were as capable, if not more so, than men, more focused, and less prone to going off-plan. The problem wasn't with them but with the men. A woman in the pack had a way of creating problems I did not want to lose time with. Even in me, I noticed a change. I would care more about a woman than a man, whether her well-being, her health, or her impressions, just so slightly more. My last mission including a shield-maiden had been a disaster, ending with the execution of an Einheri and this rule about our female fighters. Gunhild never liked me much since.

"Do you want to know the whole story?" I asked her as, for the third time, I rubbed some hard soap on my chest.

"Don't talk to me, trickster," she replied. Gunhild was a harder buyer than her lord.

"Tell me then," I said, "why are you here?"

"Wouldn't you like to know?"

"Yes, I would. I can't imagine the All-Father parting with his second square champion just like that. Did Freyja ask for you?"

There was a silence during which I assumed Gunhild debated the danger of telling us her story. She saw none.

"Odin has been different since Baldur's death, but for the last three years, he has barely been there at all. Thor presides over the Brawls most of the time, but not as often as before, and no one watches the Einherjar. And men," there she stopped to shoot an accusing glance at us, "when not restrained, turn to dogs."

I knew what she meant. Fearing Odin kept the men behaving well enough. Without him or another to leash them, the men would go from warriors to scoundrels. I did not envy the shield-maidens living in that environment.

"I guess the current Drake did nothing to help?" I asked, thinking to use the way the conversation was drifting to get some information, but Gunhild wasn't fooled and just snorted.

"He's been different too," she said after a long time. "He's always been an asshole, but at least he used to crack some heads when needed. Shield-maidens fought hard to be among the front square, where men behaved better for his presence and mine. But because he was an arrogant prick, he never cared past the twentieth square, and things were always ugly beyond that."

I did not like her accusation and told her so, to which she replied with a rich, green gob that landed at the center of the bath. She was right, though; since I became a Drake, I never really cared about the lower squares.

"And now?" Ulf asked.

"Now it's all over the place like that. So I did what I had to do."

Gunhild had fought the brawl in the first square and won, then asked whoever granted the wishes to let the shield-maidens join Freyja's domain. I was amazed that she won. She was capable, but I did not know she was that good.

"Well, there are a few good men in Valhöll still," she said, a shy smile on her lips.

"Bjorn?" I asked, guessing that my champion, at least, had not succumbed to any bestial second nature.

"And the one with the weird eyes," she said, talking about Sven Cross-Eyes. "Couldn't have made it without them. That fucker of Magnus Stone-fists and a few of his minions have completely taken over the first square, but the three of us managed. Aye, I owe two Wolves dearly for their help. From what I heard, they paid the price soon after."

"What do you mean?" I asked, too abruptly, maybe, because she looked as if she suddenly woke up and realized who she was talking to, as if I had tricked her into speaking. "Gunhild, for fuck sake, tell me if the Wolves are all right."

"They, too, have changed," she said. "After that fight, Drake made Magnus his champion and kicked some of them out of the pack. Don't look at me like that; I don't know the details. But as far as I know, they're alive, if that's what you ask."

I sighed in relief. This was old news, but it was better than nothing.

"What about my granddaughter?" Ulf asked, his wet hair stuck pitifully on the sides of his face.

"Ah," Gunhild said, a wide grin suddenly appearing on her lips. If Lif had one power, it was to get this kind of reaction from anyone. "I think I owe her some, too. The day I won, Frigg was there. The old queen never joins the brawl without her new daughter, and when I made my wish, I saw the little mouse whispering into Frigg's ear, then Frigg said something to Thor, then Thor granted the wish."

I looked at my friend and marveled at the stars in his eyes. He barely knew his granddaughter, yet he was as proud as if he'd raised her.

"Don't you worry about her," Gunhild said. "As long as Frigg is there, Lif is doing well."

I wanted to ask about you. I needed to know about you, but this topic was for later, no matter how much it burned my lips to ask.

"Do you often leave Sessrúmnir?" I asked instead.

"Less and less," she replied. "As often as Freyja does, which is getting rare."

"So that's all old news then," Huginn said.

"Well, that's all you'll get," Gunhild replied before spitting in the bath once more. We would have no more from this conversation, but the fatigue from the bath was settling in, anyway, and I thought that we had learned a great deal already.

We were accompanied to three separate rooms, and my eyes struggled to remain open as I stepped into the chamber. Clothes of light linen and silk waited, folded by the huge cushions, but I shoved them aside and tumbled like a bag of turnips on the mat. This is how I imagined clouds felt like. So soft and warm, so welcoming. I fought a conquering slumber but knew I would lose this battle. If dinner wasn't ready soon, they'd have to wake me up.

Small candles flickered here and there, atop stools, on the single table, and inside the walls where small holes welcomed them. They smelled of honey and pine. I felt as if the mat was slowly, very slowly, swallowing me down. I did not want to resist anymore. I remained bare chest, my hair still wet, and the towel tucked around my waist not covering much, but I couldn't care less. Sleep was winning.

The door opened just as I was conceding my defeat, and I cursed, for I was more tired than hungry.

"So much for gratitude," Freyja said as she closed the door behind her.

I snapped out of it, her voice stirring me like a bucket of cold water. I turned and leaned on my elbow in the next second. Freyja wore a thin dress of beige silk, revealing her thighs as well as her arms.

"Lovely view," she joked, looking down at my towel and what it no longer shielded. I meant to rearrange it, but Freyja removed the pin from her hair, and her tightly wrapped bun unfurled in a blond cascade of silky hair. I was confused, and she used it. She was on me in the next second, the tip of her pin right under my chin and her knee so close to my balls that I did not know which threat to fear the most. She made me look up into her eyes, and I knew I had to fear the whole of her.

"You almost had me, trickster," she spat, using her free hand to pull me by the back of my hair. "But I told you I would kill you one day. And today, I intend to keep that promise."

She pressed the pin against my throat. I felt it penetrate the skin.

"Not Loki," I babbled, which changed nothing. There was murder in her eyes. She just wanted to kill something that looked like Loki. "But I'll get him for you," I said. The pin did not move. The skin of her thigh against mine was soft and warm.

"You won't trick me this time," she said, pulling so hard that I was now watching the ceiling, where our shadows mixed in many shades.

"I would be dead by now if you truly believed I was Loki." It made her angrier.

"And why should I believe you? How many times will you betray me, Loki? If I kill you now, I will know you were honest."

"Not sure I like this plan. Doesn't help me much."

"I will kill the real Loki as well; you have my word," she said as her elbow raised higher, ready to stab. I grabbed her wrist with my left hand and let the heat from my lungs take me.

"Loki isn't the only one on my list," I said as I sat up, forcing her hand back. Frowning, she let go of my hair and tried to push the pin with both her hands, but I was getting stronger with each heartbeat.

"I don't care about your list," she grunted.

"That's your problem," I said, rage bubbling in my chest. The Æsir and the Vanir, I could see them clearly now, and I'd had enough. "You all like to be treated like gods, but you only help when it serves you too." I pressed on her wrist until she let go of the pin. She did not scream, but I had hurt her. I slapped the pin against the wall and heard it plant itself in the rock. I was strong, and she got scared.

She meant to scream, but I did not let her. I grabbed her

by the throat and pushed her as we stood. The towel fell at my feet. I pushed her until she bumped against the door. Freyja did not panic, but her anger was rising again. She scratched my arm to the blood.

"Listen to me," I barked so close to her face that I could smell the berries she had eaten. She stopped struggling and shot her most defiant look in my face. "I am not Loki, but I am not weak. I will get him, and he will die painfully; you have my word, for I have given it to a more worthy being than you." Thinking of Fenrir rekindled a bit of my hatred for her kind, but this was not the place.

"And then?" she asked, fighting for air as she spoke.

"And then I will avenge myself on Muninn."

The room became quiet. I did not need to say more. Freyja was the goddess of love; she could read my emotions. Her eyes changed. I recognized pity in them, and I did not like that. I wanted her ire, I realized. I wanted the fight she was offering me. I wanted to yell at her and curse her kind for all they had put me through. I was a pawn in their game, and my pain, and that of thousands upon thousands of folk, was of no concern to them. I wanted some vengeance right now. Not tomorrow, not whenever Loki would be at my mercy; I wanted it now, and Freyja was stealing it away with her pity.

She moved her hand from my arm to my face gently, like a caress.

"Stop it!" I said, slapping it aside. But she brought it back, and I could feel my will withering away. Freyja was using kindness on me, and I did not like it. I needed more.

"They used love against you," she said, a voice full of compassion. She used no magic, I felt no *seidr*, but she was bending my will with her power.

"Stop it," I said again. The fire was growing colder in my chest, replaced by a sadness I did not want to feel.

"I would never—"

"Stop what you're doing!" I shouted, using the last of my resolve. "I don't want your pity!"

"So what are you going to do about it?" she asked, furious once more.

I pushed her once more against the wall, but this time I accompanied her. I needed her to stop talking, and I had a knot of rage to release. My lips found hers, and my tongue found hers. If she was surprised, she did not show it.

She caressed me with her thigh and wrapped it behind mine so that we were close enough to be one. Freyja meant to put her hand on my cheek again, but I wouldn't let her. I grabbed her by the wrist once more and raised her hand above her head. I did not want her love; I wanted her lust.

She got the message, and when our faces broke apart, I saw the side of Freyja all men dreamt of seeing once in their lives. She was desire in the flesh. She bit her lip as our hips moved together, and her free hand went down my belly until she took me in her long, graceful fingers. I gasped with pleasure at the touch, and she smiled a cunning, victorious, and provocative smile. She was winning again, putting me under another kind of spell.

I refused it once more.

I took her hand away and, grabbing her by the hips, forced her to turn the other way around. I felt no resistance. Still holding one of her hands above, I reached for her dress with the other hand and pulled it up slowly, using this moment to feel the smoothness of her thighs.

She giggled, then moaned, when my fingers reached between her legs. But her pleasure wasn't my purpose. Only mine mattered.

And pleasure is what I got when Freyja and I became one. She tried to look at me once our back-and-forth began, but I did not let her. Grabbing her by the hair as she had done, I pulled on it so she would keep looking straight ahead. It only increased her moans. She put her two hands against the wall, for I could no longer control my strength, and the fire was back. It was burning, heating up with each thrust, with each moan from Freyja.

Then, the heat became sharper, more focused. It left my limbs to gather in my groin. No longer able to control myself, I let go. Pleasure, more intense than I had ever felt, shook me to the core.

Freyja did not move as the last of my rage rushed from me.

When I opened my eyes again, Freyja, panting and sweating, had recovered her victorious smile, but I no longer cared.

We broke apart, and she gracefully put a strand of hair back behind her ears.

"At least now I know you are not Loki," she said, recovering her breath before I did.

"What do you mean?" I asked as she traced a line on my sweaty chest with her nail.

"He would have made it last longer."

We looked at each other, me judging the seriousness of her insult and her expecting my reaction. And as if the spell keeping the tension between us had just shattered, we laughed together. It was a heartfelt, almost friendly laugh, and it felt amazing.

I will never know how much of this moment she had planned, but she cured me. And no matter what I was willing to admit, she won me over during our exchange. I had spent a good part of my Einheri life disliking Freyja, but I could see now that she was the only honest god on Asgard.

ᛉ

Asgard's prison, now

Muninn's ragged breathing betrayed her frustration, and I could not hide a grin of pleasure for her reaction. Her eyes shone darker in the corner of the room, slanted and sharp as daggers. Free of her chains, she would have ripped my head off; I could feel it in the air. The story wasn't over, but I would remain quiet until she gave me some reaction. An absence of reaction would be fine, too; at least I would know how little I meant to her. I was short on time, but so help me Odin, I needed to know that I hurt her by sleeping with Freyja. My patience, however, proved useless.

"Why?" she asked in a broken, coarse voice.

"Why?" I asked, playing dumb.

"Why did you have to tell me of you and Freyja?" Muninn was shivering; her chains rattled. I saw her, in my mind's eye, bursting forward and testing the strength of her bonds.

No one knew how strong Muninn truly was. She might break the links, tear them from the wall, or shapeshift to her raven form. Her *seidr* had been sealed by Tyr's mark, but if she was, in fact, stronger than him, she could overcome the rune. Any second now, she would let her rage explode and come for my head. She had cared enough for jealousy to fill her ire, but she had betrayed me, and I was ready for her. My hand dropped to Crimson's hilt. Muninn gathered herself. She tensed.

And sobbed.

All the pleasure I was sipping in this conversation turned to ice. Muninn sobbed, her chain clinked when she wiped her tears, and guilt squeezed the heart in my chest. Her body was taken by spasms, and soon she wailed through tight lips. I did not know where to put myself.

"No!" I shouted. It cut her sobbing. I stood, fuming. She almost had me again. "You won't fool me! You don't care that I plowed Freyja. You never cared about me, witch. All that mattered to you was Loki."

I needed this to be true.

I paced my side of the room, foam coming to the corner of my lips. The silverish, dull light of the torch would not grow weaker, but I wished it did so that I could consume my anger in peace. Instead, Muninn witnessed the pain veiling me as it had three years ago when she stabbed me in the guts. Even the scar suddenly felt fresh and burning. I kicked the torch and sent it flying against the wall on her side. It was a clumsy kick, and the light did little more than graze her tear-smeared face.

"Loki? Why him, Muninn? Why not me, huh? *I* loved you. *I* would have kept you safe. You knew of my feelings; you even gave me hope. That last night on Midgard, was it just a game to you? Did it mean anything to you?"

I made no sense. I could no longer think straight. Instead, I spilled all I had kept in my chest over the last few years. My voice rang louder with my rising anger. I did not care about keeping face or that I was here with a purpose. I wanted her to know how much she hurt me. I needed her to acknowledge all she had done and that she had done it knowingly.

She sobbed and gasped again, and when I was done and could barely articulate, so strong was my wrath, she stood up as well. Her hands closed into fists. She stepped into the light, and I leaned backward. Muninn was not pretty at this moment; she was in pain, and she was serious.

"It meant everything to me," she said.

The knot in my throat formed in a heartbeat. I opened my mouth, but no sound came out.

"You're lying again," I forced myself to say.

"I knew you loved me," she said as if I had not spoken. "The way you looked at me when I stood next to my father, no one ever looked at me this way. That you even saw me when I was in the shadow of the All-Father meant everything to me. And the way your eyes searched for me as soon as the battles ended gave me purpose where I had none. I am the lowest of my kind, but in your heart, I was the grandest."

I prayed for her to stop. She was bringing all those emotions back to the surface as if they had just been hibernating. I saw myself on the battlefield, expecting the short moments I would share with her before the Bifröst. In those days, I fought to survive, not for the glory, not for victory, but for those fleeting moments in her company. Her words were summoning my lost love, and I was weak to it.

"I knew you loved me for more years than you can remember. But do you know I have loved you for much longer? Do you know how long I have loved you, Drake?"

"You lie," I said, though my voice was breaking like that of a teenager. She took a step forward, and I one backward.

"I've loved you since I first saw you on the field of battle, a mortal man. When you died that day, I prayed for you to be picked by a Valkyrie. Æsir don't love humans, but your image would not leave my mind. And when you rose through Valhöll and found yourself in front of Odin, fighting in the first square, I thought my heart would burst, for I had found you again. And later, when Odin made you his Drake, I was proud of you as if you were my husband."

"Stop it, Muninn."

"Odin gave you your title, along with a *brynja* of good steel, which you lost on a mission ten years later. You spent the night polishing it in your new house. I know because I came to you. I wanted to know you, wanted to spend the night speaking with you. I am the one who first called you after the battle so that you could give me your report, you remember? I never did that with your predecessors. I even remember your real name while you don't."

"Of course you do," I said accusingly, "you are Odin's memory; you remember everything. This is how he made you."

"He made me to remember the things that mattered to him," she replied. Strength had come back to her voice during our short exchange, and I was now facing Muninn as I remembered her. "Do you think he cared about your name?"

Of course Odin did not care about such a detail. Even I did not care.

"What's my name?" I asked. I wanted to believe her. The love I thought extinct needed to believe her.

"Sune," she said, "Your name is Sune."

And Sune was my name.

My first life came back in a flash with its name. The two daughters I had left under the care of a woman whom I had married for her father's farm. The first shield I had assembled, the ring given to me by my jarl as I became a man, my uncle taking me hunting in the forest. My mother had died when I was a child, and I had no father, so he had been as such to me. The people I had been raised to hate and those I had raided summer after summer until one of them managed to put an end to it.

Yes, my name had been Sune.

And none of it mattered anymore.

I snuffed the flame of her charms, using the strength given to me by those who died for me to stand in that cell. Muninn had cared after all, but her twisted love—if love it truly was—had just caused the death of a good friend. For him and for all the suffering Loki's plan had brought, I had to remember why I was here.

"My name," I said as I stepped back against my wall, "and my love for you belongs in the past. They both belonged to someone who's no longer. I am not the Drake you knew, either. He was stupid and easily tricked. But I came back from Jötunheimr with a purpose, and with Freyja's help, vengeance was mine."

Sessrúmnir, then

Huginn and Ulf were seated at a wide table of silverwood when I entered the dining room. It was half the size of the throne room. Tapestries hung from the walls, each of them depicting Freyja at the service of her worshippers. The presence of the guards standing around the table and Gunhild, sitting on the other side from my two companions, made it clear that we were hardly guests. They had touched no food or drink and sat straight as a mast when we joined them, Freyja and I.

"You took your time," Ulf said when I pulled the chair next to him.

"Not enough, no," Freyja replied, hinting once again at her disappointment.

A Valkyrie, seemingly younger than the others, appeared from the shadow behind Freyja's larger chair and pulled on it so that her mistress could sit. Freyja waved her guards away with a soft hand gesture as the chair was pushed in a very synchronized manner, and they left, turning their shields and feathered helmets with as much efficiency.

"So he's really who he says he is?" Gunhild asked, munching on a big chunk of bread.

"Well, he is not Loki, that's for sure," Freyja answered.

The young Valkyrie filled Freyja's silver cup. Surprisingly enough, it was mead. I always assumed her tastes were more exotic.

"At least you managed to convince her of that," Ulf said, and I had to suppress a chuckle under a cough.

The goddess invited us to fill our plates, which we did without being offered twice. Fruits I had never seen overfilled bowls of silver encrusted with precious stones, meat fumed from a thick broth, bread, fresh from the oven, crisped under our touch. This would be a great meal. Freyja touched none of it except for a few of those small, round, and green fruits full of water.

The servant, whom I had not even seen leaving the place, came back carrying a basket of red and green apples. She stopped by Freyja, who examined the content with care before picking what she judged as the best of the lot. Without a word, she gestured for the servant to bring the basket to Huginn, whose eyes turned white with envy at the sight of those fruits.

"These are not for your kind," Freyja said when I frowned at the basket passing behind me.

Huginn's hands were shaking like autumn leaves when he reached for the closest of the fruits. He closed his eyes with pleasure when his teeth snatched a piece of it, and a single tear dropped from his eyelids when he swallowed. Huginn was home, and things would get better for him from now on. If anything, we had saved the old raven.

"So," Freyja said, catching our attention, "how is sweet Eggther?"

"He fares well," I replied before Huginn could sour the mood with a remark about the giant. "Your tree grows well on his farm."

Freyja blushed, just as Eggther had, and I had to stop my imagination from working out the details of their relationship.

"But he's getting ready for the war," I said

"Ah," Freyja replied absently before tearing another piece of her apple.

"Are we ready for it here?" Ulf asked.

"Not more than before," Gunhild replied, chewing on a fat and juicy piece of meat. "Nothing has been done for the past few years. Nothing has changed."

"Not true, my dear Gunhild," Freyja said. "One thing changed: the Wolves don't go down anymore."

"How come?" I asked.

"It is *Fimbulvetr* in most realms," Freyja replied. "You know, *brothers killing brothers for a piece of bread*. Einherjar join Asgard without needing a push; as such, the Wolves remain here. At least as far as I know."

"When did you last see Father?" Huginn asked. His voice had changed, and his hair had darkened from light-gray to silver.

I felt Freyja's foot against my ankle just as I was about to swallow a spoonful of green peas. I almost choked on them.

"Half a year," Freyja answered. She then sipped some of her mead and smacked her lips. I must admit, it wasn't a bad beverage, though a bit too fruity for my taste. "You would hardly recognize him. He's old. Well, he's been old for a while, but now, he is worn out, almost senile. It pains me to see him like that, so I stopped seeing him altogether."

"How about Queen Frigg?" I asked. I got a kick in the shin from my use of the title.

"The old goat is doing better than her husband," Freyja answered. Though a hint of respect existed in this old rivalry, Freyja and Frigg hated each other as much as they hated Loki. The origin of his feud was blurry but of course, involved Odin's lust. "I hear her new pet is doing her a lot of good."

"Lif is well, then?" Ulf asked

As I looked toward both my friends, I witnessed Huginn's youth regaining him. His wrinkles were vanishing, his fingers were gaining some meat, and his darkening hair was thickening.

"She is well," Freyja answered, a motherly tone to her voice I did not know she possessed.

Ulf dropped deeper in his chair.

"Haven't I killed you once?" Freyja asked, staring more strongly at Ulf.

"You did," Ulf replied, his hands reaching for his face, where she had slapped him dead. "Not my fondest memory, I must say."

"Well, you were a poor suitor. But you sired an amazing girl," Freyja said.

"She's not the only one who's thriving, by the way," Gunhild said, munching louder as the meal went. "Some bastard who pretends to be the Drake is having a great time making himself the little lord of Valhöll while no one is watching."

I did not like this and said again that Loki would pay.

"How?" Gunhild asked.

"Not sure yet," I replied. "I need more information, but I have the beginning of a plan."

"A beginning of a plan?" Gunhild scoffed. "How reassuring. Surely you also have a *tidbit of an idea* on how to stop Ragnarök as well?"

I tried to mask my discomfort at her comment, thinking about the rooster I had not butchered. And the irony was that I did have a tidbit of an idea concerning Ragnarök. But that would be a topic to breach later; when Loki was out of the picture.

"Don't be so harsh," Freyja told Gunhild. "Drake just escaped Loki's cave after three years in chains, then survived a journey through Jötunheimr." She had used my name for the first time; we were going somewhere. "And if my intuition is right, he even survived a meeting with Fenrir, didn't you?"

It sucked the air out of me. How much more had she guessed?

"Drake, is that true?" Gunhild asked. I nodded, and she whistled, impressed.

Freyja's foot came back to mine, and now she caressed my leg with it. It was impossible to notice from above the table, so perfect was her act, but anyone looking at me could guess that something was off.

"Everything's all right?" Ulf asked, and, of course, he had been the one to notice my face reddening.

"It's the mead," I said, coughing. "Treacherous this fruity taste, it packs a mean punch."

Ulf looked into his cup and pursed his lips in disagreement.

"Ah, now I recognize you," Freyja said with satisfaction, bringing our attention to Huginn, who looked exactly as when he had left Asgard some twenty-three years ago. His hair was dark, his eyes alive and brown, his chin narrow, and his skin white as bones. He looked like his sister, I told myself as a hole grew in my heart.

"You have my gratitude, Freyja," Huginn said in a strong and clear voice I had forgotten. She waved it off as if it were nothing, but I guessed those apples, for it could only come from them, did not grow from any tree.

"Just a small favor for a friend, that is all," Freyja said.

"Can you connect with Odin now?" I asked Huginn. We knew too little about Odin and whether we could count on him.

"Not while in Sessrúmnir," he answered.

"This is Vanir's land," Freyja said, "given to us at the end of the war between our two clans. Odin's power does not reach here."

"So much for that," Ulf said.

"So," Gunhild said, smacking her lips. I made myself ready for another of her remarks. "Besides putting some feathers back on your bird and reassuring this one about his little girl, what else can we do to help you and your *beginning of a plan*?"

I needed to know more about Valhöll and Loki's whereabouts. I also needed information on Odin's mindset and the status of the Æsir and Vanir, who might offer some help, Tyr and Heimdallr among them. I would also later ask Freyja about her brother Freyr, the one they claimed to be Thor's only rival. He had exiled himself in Álfheimr out of shame for a couple of centuries, but we would need him.

But first, I needed to know about my men and whether they would stand with me or with Loki. Bjorn and Titus would remain loyal to me, but for the others, especially Rune and Snekke, I wasn't as confident. For this beginning of a plan to become a real thing, I needed as many of them as possible. Getting in touch with the Wolves was my priority, but the how escaped me.

"Freyja," I called, taking her from her cup as her foot kept its incessant up and down. "Is Astrid still living here?"

Astrid, I thought, glad that I had remembered a name for once, was the key to contacting my men. Her relationship with Titus was a secret to no one, and she was probably the only person who could get to one of my men without raising suspicion.

"Tell Astrid to join us," Freyja asked her servant, who had been standing right behind me.

Titus. I would see Titus soon. Things were shaping up better than they had started.

8

Odin had been generous with Freyja when he gave her Sessrúmnir and Folkvangr, the land surrounding it. The war between the Æsir and the Vanir, which had happened many centuries before I was born, had been bloody, bitter, and chaotic. Members of the two clans had died, some forever. But in the end, they made peace, and Freyja, her brother Freyr, and their father Njord came to Asgard as honored guests and equals.

Njord had regained his watery realm since, while Freyr had been given Álfheimr, the Elven realm, as his personal kingdom. Odin made sure that only Freyja remained in the citadel and gave her the hall in the mountain, Sessrúmnir, and the rich and luxurious land facing it, Folkvangr.

Anything could grow here, but Freyja had turned it into a meadow of wildflowers with colors of every kind. From the main gate of the hall, Folkvangr stretched as far as the eye could see. A palisade of polished stone protected the goddess's domain in a semicircle starting three hundred steps from the hall, and hundreds of shield-maidens guarded it professionally while more trained in the courtyard. I pitied any man or Æsir willing to face their blades. This was the maidens' realm, a small, awe-inspiring land ruled by a strong, unforgiving Vanir, and her daughters, whether human or Valkyries, would fight like Jötnar to defend it.

Shallow buildings with no front walls lined the inside part of the palisade. This was where the lesser-looking Valkyries and shield-maidens slept. There was perhaps one shield-maiden for thirty Einherjar, but seeing them practicing in good order, shouting and slashing as one, I could not help but feel jealous.

The sun was about to reach the wall for the fifth time since we had come back. I sat on the upper step of the stairs leading to the hall, using the last of Sol's warmth while enjoying some light ale, when my foreign friend passed the gate of the palisade.

Titus had not changed: straight as an oak, wide of shoulders, hair cropped, and eyes unwavering. He was and always would be a leader of men and a perfect soldier, and so said his gait. Titus was my brother, and despite his southerner's features, we looked alike. Or he looked like the real me, at least. As I was now, I paled in comparison.

He passed between the ranks of warriors, his eyes never wavering from my position. I had to admire his self-control. Very few men could walk through Freyja's domain without scanning it with curiosity. Or maybe it was the presence of Astrid by his side that kept him from his most basic instincts.

Astrid was one of the Valkyries who crossed the realms to choose the new Einherjar among the slain and guide them to Asgard. A sacred role among her kind. She had kept it a secret even from Titus. If Einherjar knew which of those women went down to Midgard, there would be a great deal of bribery. Sons and brothers would be picked over worthy warriors for a price in silver. Astrid was a serious woman, but her smile, as discreet as it was, could melt hearts as it had done Titus's. According to my friend, she could boil like a pool of lava, but it was hard to picture. She had dark, long, undulating hair with hints of red, beautiful freckles on her nose, and lips full of life that remained shut more often than not.

Astrid had become a friend in the last few days as we shaped a plan to get Titus here. As it turned out, it had not been so difficult. Titus and Astrid were seeing each other once a week, on Freyja's day. Even during the current period of isolation, Astrid, being one of the few ghost-Valkyries, as we called them, had more freedom than others. They met by the cliff, halfway between Folkvangr and the citadel, which, by my estimation, put them somewhere within Bragi's land, and spent the night under the stars. Last they met, Astrid told him I was here and looked different. As she described it, Titus had been doubtful, but Titus was never one for trust, anyway.

He stopped before the first step, his left hand never leaving the handle of his short sword. His eyes searched through mine as if he could read my mind. I stood and gave him the time he needed. I was Loki. Even his lover's words would not be enough.

"How many nights in your house have I won in bets?" Titus asked.

I smiled, seeing where this was going.

"Three nights," I answered. "Every time over a game of *tafl*. Though, if I am right, you used it a good dozen other times when I wasn't around." Astrid's blush told me I was far from the count.

Titus climbed one step, his face like marble. There were three left.

"What was my wife's name?" Now, that was an awful question. My memory of names has always been atrocious. I closed my eyes and tried to remember the first time he had mentioned her. We had built a fire camp in the wilderness of Rügen in the middle of summer. Titus had fought the people living there in his lifetime, and it had made him nostalgic. He had spoken of his life, of his land, his emperor, and his wife, who was named after some kind of fruit his people loved.

"Olivia," I blurted out.

Titus climbed the second step.

"What is the stupidest thing Eigil ever did?" he asked then.

"Besides being born?" I said, which got me no reaction whatsoever. "Trying to drink himself to death with Cross-Eyes?" Titus tilted his head. He had probably thought of something else but found my answer acceptable. One more step.

He was so close now that I suspected he did not feel very comfortable. He was never a man for proximity, and neither was I. But it was his game, and he would play it to the end. I guessed he had kept the worst for last, and I was right.

"*Mars pater, ego pro vestra sapientia—*" The prayer for his people's god of war.

"If you expect me to remember the rest, you can shove your prayer up your ass, you *cunnus*. Not only don't I remember the words, but I would never pray to one of your false gods." That I had used his word for a woman's private part as an insult may have convinced him, for he climbed the last step and faced me.

"It is you then?" he asked, still expressionless.

"Aye, it's me," I said. I only thought then that Ulf's presence would have been helpful, but the archer was too busy chasing a shield-maiden he had once been intimate with.

Titus's shoulders slumped a little, his face untensed, and then he embraced me. I was pulled into his arms before I could react and felt all the scales of his lamellar armor against my chest. The last three years had been hard on him, too, I assumed, and now it made sense to him. It didn't last longer than the time it takes to say Múspellsheimr, and then he went back to his proud warrior self. We both looked away rather than facing the shame of what had just happened.

"Men," Freyja scoffed from behind, a cup in hand. I had not even felt her presence despite having grown used to it. Freyja had not given me much alone time since our first moment of intimacy. Not that I complained about it.

"Goddess," Titus said, fist on the chest, "thank you for inviting me."

She opened her arms and bowed her head in a show of politeness.

"You are welcome to my hall," she said. "Though I assume you cannot stay long."

"Indeed. I need to be back before dawn, or it will raise some *people*'s suspicions."

"Come then, let's talk," Freyja said before stepping back into her hall.

I was about to follow her, but Titus grabbed my arm.

"Is it true?" he asked. "Ulf's alive?"

"Very much so," I said. "He's after some old lover right now, but you should see him soon." Titus smiled at last, and it was a sight. Yet, his relief was a sign of how things had gone since I had left. And as he was about to tell us, the situation was far more desperate than we had thought.

Loki had been busy.

ᚱ

Titus's presence in Sessrúmnir, while an occasion for some rejoicing, had soured my mood. It had not changed Freyja's appetite, though. As I lay in my bed, spent and panting from trying to fill it, my mind went back to the dinner we had shared and the information Titus had given us.

Valhöll, according to him, was now Loki's kingdom.

The trickster had used Odin's absence to strengthen his power over the Einherjar. He regularly visited the lower squares and exchanged words with warriors I had never bothered knowing, sharing stories and jokes the way I never could.

"The men love him," Titus said. "He doesn't make them practice as much, lets them play and fight, and fills their cups with mead and their ears with honey. They even stopped washing." Knowing him, this last bit bothered him the most. "Thousands of men, shaped year after year into a formidable army, now turning into a mob of lazy asses that wouldn't hold their shield against my grandmother."

"He is weakening us," Ulf said, voicing my thoughts.

Loki was gathering a flock of supporters and was making things easier for his army when they showed up.

But as it turned out, not every man loved him.

Before Odin had ordered the Bifröst to be closed, the Wolves still handled some missions on Asgard. Those were, by Titus's own words, piss and shit missions. Loki-Drake had cared very little about gathering men, preferring to enjoy his time among men and women. Battles did happen on his watch, but rather than involving warriors, they engulfed villages in flames and chaos. Besides my last mission's outcome, I usually managed to keep our battles away from peaceful folks. Loki did not make it a priority.

"More children and women died than warriors," Titus explained, "and the warriors who died did so without proving their worth. We gained very few brothers during those missions, but Drake—sorry, Loki came back with a shitload of silver."

More to share with the men, I thought. "Surely Odin wasn't happy about it?" I asked, wondering how this could have happened several times without Odin turning this Drake into a pile of ash.

"That's the thing," Titus replied. "Odin barely flinched at our results. Loki would report to him in private and come back with praises from the All-Father."

Now, I was feeling positively jealous. I could never find the words with Odin, but Loki knew exactly what to say to shift a failure into a song-worthy tale.

He had Odin's ear and would whisper all the right words in the right order. This always had been his greatest talent. Odin's absence was Loki's doing, I assumed. And with Odin's Memory on his side, weaving a web of lies would be the simplest matter.

"Nevertheless," Titus said, "most of us were unhappy at those trips down." And by "most of us," Titus meant that the Wolves had complained enough to make Loki's life a bit more complicated, for which I was grateful.

This, in turn, forced him to make some changes within the pack.

Magnus had become the champion; this we knew. The big bastard might even have been aware of Loki's identity. Bjorn had to step down and, according to Titus, was turning fatter by the day.

"No doubt he also misses someone's presence at the

brawl," I had said for Freyja's benefit, who acknowledged it with a discreet smile.

Einar was the first to be kicked out of the group and was soon followed by Karl. The old man had turned even more bitter after Loki's return, which I took as proof of loyalty, and the trickster found some excuse to remove him from the pack. And finally, Snekke had been pushed away. I did not understand why. Snekke was corruptible, after all. But as Titus explained, this new Drake possessed a sudden and unique talent for words; thus, Snekke became redundant.

The three of them were replaced by Magnus's men.

"How about Rune?" I asked. This was the one topic I could not make up my mind about. Rune had either been Loki's minion all along or just a young man with a disposition for bad luck.

"Rune is quiet," Titus said.

The two of them had formed a teacher-student bond forced on the youngest by Titus. He knew the lad better than anyone. Quiet was not an adjective that suited Rune, and Titus had used it unhappily. Rune's quietness worried Titus, and since he loved the boy like a son, I did not pursue the point. Titus, however, wanted to.

"He will be glad to know the truth," my friend said.

"I doubt he will care so much. Let's not include him in our plan," I replied, preferring to keep Rune from any information Loki could use.

Titus and Ulf shot me a curious glance as if I had told them that ale was made from onions. But we had bigger things to discuss, and Titus moved on at last.

"What are the Wolves doing since they don't descend anymore?" Ulf asked as Titus gulped another of those fruits Freyja loved so much, which he called an *uva*.

"Honestly, nothing worth mentioning. Certainly nothing saga-worthy."

The Wolves' stillness did not bother me as much as Loki's grasp on Odin. Changing the members of the pack was one thing, but keeping the All-Father in the dark was another. Every day he played his game with Odin was a step closer to his victory and a step further from my vengeance.

"What are you thinking?" Freyja suddenly asked me, taking me away from my recollection of the evening. We had both regained our breath and my sweat had cooled as well. She lay above the blanket, the light of the candles bouncing on her perfect skin.

"That we need to act fast," I said. The tip of her finger followed the line separating my abdomen until she reached my chest.

"You have such dark thoughts after sex with me?" she asked maliciously. "I leave you too much energy, it seems." She kissed me on the shoulder, then on the throat, and finally, one more time on the left nipple.

She did not leave me much energy, I thought, but it was fine. I had yet to see her bedroom. I wasn't ready for that, she had declared. Her appetite was incredible, and the fact that she enjoyed Loki's body so much was fairly disturbing. But I longed for her enough to keep quiet on this point.

"Why did he leave Heimdallr in charge of Bifröst?" I asked.

Freyja bit my nipple, not happy at her lack of result. She looked up, and the anger in her eyes woke my lust for her as well. I almost gave in.

"Only Heimdallr can open the Bifröst," she said. "Well, he and Odin. It would make no sense to remove him. At least not until the last moment."

We were lucky here. Heimdallr was an ally, and his presence would help. Tyr wasn't in the citadel, but I preferred it that way. His betrayal of Fenrir still lingered in the back of my mind. There were other gods to count on, but if Loki truly had some power over Odin, how many of them would join us when the time came? We needed allies, and we needed to act fast.

"I think that's not what disturbs you the most, though," Freyja said as she dropped her head on the pillow next to me.

"What do you mean?"

"What your man said about Loki's behavior with him specifically."

"Oh, that," I said. It did disturb me.

Titus had been eager to believe Astrid when she told him about Loki's presence, and the reason why wasn't to my liking.

"He is quite...tactile," is how Titus had phrased it.

"Tactile?" I had asked.

"Let's say that he seems to have an interest in exotic matters." This was the first time I ever saw him blush.

"Oh," I simply replied.

"I never gave in, of course." I trusted him for that, but it made me wonder how many men had resisted Loki and how many had not.

"Yes," I told Freyja. "It does bother me."

She giggled, then kissed me on the cheek.

"It's not such a big deal, and if you want to, you are welcome to use your real body with me once you get it back to wash Loki's deeds from it."

I never thought she would accept me once I was myself again, but rather than telling her, I showed her my gratitude. It did bother me to imagine what Loki was doing with my body, so I took my revenge by kissing with passion the body of a woman he hated. I took my time, savoring her sweat as I traced my way down her belly.

Those dark thoughts would wait for the morrow. Titus was on his way back to the citadel and would soon send as many reliable men as he could find.

Freyja's gasps and moans grew in intensity, which in turn only increased my desire for her. Then I remembered a question I had meant to ask her for some time.

"Why did you never accept Bjorn?" I asked, looking up at her through the blond hair between her legs.

"Now you think of Bjorn? I am really losing my touch," she said. She grabbed me by the back of the head and forced me to perform my duty. "What do you think?" she asked between two gasps.

I thought about it, but I knew Freyja enough by now. The answer was simple.

"Because he asks," I said. She could not speak; she just nodded. "Should I tell him?" I asked as I pulled her closer to me.

"Yes," she said with a moan.

I did not ask anything else that night. I simply acted as I wanted, knowing that Freyja and I agreed on many things when it came to lovemaking. And yet, as we enjoyed each other, her facing the other way, me closing my eyes for a second, my thoughts went to another night, three years and some ago. A night of passion and lies. A night of illusion when I thought you loved me as I loved you. I opened my eyes again, and your image replaced Freyja's. Her hair was dark, her bosom smaller, her skin whiter. It was you when you had betrayed me the most.

"What of Muninn?" I had asked Titus just as he was about to leave on the very steps where I had welcomed him.

The question had burned my lips for the greater part of the evening, and I could not hold it any longer.

"What of Muninn?" he asked back. Gods, I hated it when he did that.

"Do you see her?"

"As often as I see Odin," he replied, which meant *not much*. I would not pursue the point further, for I knew Titus would not have paid Muninn too much attention. He would be more careful now.

"But, Drake," he said, "don't hesitate with her, all right?"

I knew what he meant. And he was right; my anger toward you was only slightly stronger than my curiosity. I wanted to know why you had used me the way you did. I wanted to hear it from you. Not an apology, no, I did not want that. I wanted you to acknowledge the pain I had suffered because I loved you.

I would not hesitate, I told myself again as I saw you instead of Freyja, showing even more passion and roughness in our exchange.

Freyja was pleased that night.

9

Another week passed before we received news from my Wolves. One week, with each minute testing my patience to its limits. Ulf said that I did not used to be so restless when I was the Drake. He was right. As a leader of our kind, I had been more restrained than most Einherjar; I was more thoughtful, too. Three years in chains changes a man, I had replied, though it was only partially the reason.

Einherjar do not change much, or do so slowly. Odin, when he created the Einherjar, made sure that we kept the essence of the person we had been upon our death. This was why a man who died old remained old and grumpy, while a young one would be foolish and reckless for the hundreds of years of his afterlife. If we changed, it was a slow, discreet process. We could get fatter, stronger, wiser, and all, but it required more effort than needed from a regular human being.

I was no longer an Einheri, though. I inhabited a Jötunn body, and maybe this angry, impatient personality I was changing into was just the real me, as I would have become if given time.

It served me well, though. I enjoyed this rage. Even those who had acknowledged my identity tended to walk away from my path. Anger was a mask I wore to cover Loki's features. But it consumed me as much as I let it, gnawing at my reason every second I waited helplessly. I played with Loki's power whenever I could find some quiet corner of Sessrúmnir and tried to control its flow within my body. The heat was easy to find. It fed on my emotions, and those were aplenty. But I could not control its direction. Maybe I needed to face some danger to use it on purpose, or maybe it reacted to threats. Practicing to no avail left me frustrated, and my frustration thickened when, finally, some of my men made it to Sessrúmnir. I would have chosen anyone but those three, and their presence was far from a gift.

"I say we snatch the bloody bastard in his sleep, slit his throat, and piss on his corpse," Karl said, voicing his direct approach for the tenth time that evening.

"How many times does he need to tell you that we can't just kill him," Einar replied, though the sounds were hard to make through the lump of bread stuffing his mouth.

"Why not?" Karl asked.

I had already explained the situation and would not waste any more words. Ulf, head lost in his palms, looked as defeated as I was.

"Because he wants his body back," Snekke said. His focus, like those of the two others, was hard at work, for Freyja's hall was full of distractions.

The goddess herself was not attending our improvised *thing,* which proved smart of her. We had already lost so much time just explaining the situation, and this was going nowhere. I had not even breached the plan I was slowly cooking.

"Fuck his body," Karl barked as if I wasn't there. "That's

an improvement right there. Didn't you say that you punched a Jötunn on his ass?"

"I did," I replied, recognizing Karl's practicality.

"And you probably won't be able to if you go back to your body, right?"

"We don't know," I said, though I feared as much.

"Don't you want to have this one when Ragnarök happens?" the old man asked.

This, at least, got the small group quiet. It was a fair point. Loki's body was a weapon we could use, but I could not admit that Ragnarök, the end of the world, wasn't my priority. I took a long sip of Freyja's fruity mead and was thankfully saved by Einar.

"Screw Ragnarök," he said, splattering the table with wet bread crumbs. I had missed this old man's shrill voice and simplicity. "Everything must feel weird. Can you imagine wiping your ass, but it doesn't feel like your ass? Can you imagine, Karl?"

Fine, I hadn't missed him that much.

Yes, I told myself, as Ulf removed a face long like a Drakkar from his hands, those were the worst of the lot.

Huginn had not left his room in the past ten days, and when I knocked on his door, all I got was a request to be left in peace. He was making himself ready, or so he said. I had no idea what it meant for Odin's raven, so I let him, assured by Freyja that it was the best thing to do.

I would have given anything for Bjorn, Cross-Eyes, or Titus, but fate had offered those three, and this was all I would get. According to Karl, whom the foreigner had chosen as his messenger, Loki-Drake was keeping them even busier than usual. I dared not think that Titus had been made and just took it as another swing from the three old crones spinning our destinies.

"And think about sex, Karl," Snekke said, his eyes never leaving the door, from where a Valkyrie would sometimes pop with a pitcher or a plate. "Wouldn't you want to use your own tools? I mean, did you have the chance to try?" The question was for me this time.

"Oh, he did," Ulf replied for me, a tone barely masking his jealousy.

"How is it then? I mean, with a Jötunn's body?" Snekke asked, finally finding a source of interest in this conversation.

"None of your concern," I replied. "Listen," I said to all of them, standing from my chair, "we need to get Loki, and we need to get him in front of everyone. It's not enough to kill the bastard, as Karl suggests. He needs to acknowledge what he has done, give me my body back, then we kill him."

"Why?" Karl asked after an insulting scoff.

"Because," I said, leaning on my fists, "he has put Asgard to sleep. We need to wake everyone up with a bucket of cold water and get them moving. War is nearly upon us, and we are not ready."

"I see," Einar said, chin stuck between his thumb and first finger in a very thoughtful pose. "But how do we get a giant bucket of cold water?"

I slumped back into my chair as Karl and Ulf sighed.

"It was a metaphor, your brain-dead swine," Snekke said.

"So was my question, you tree-humping pheasant," Einar barked back.

"As if you know what a metaphor is," Ulf said in a tired voice.

"My foot up your ass is one," Einar replied, pointing a mean finger at the archer's face.

"No, that would not be one," Ulf said. Snekke and Karl

then joined the insult contest. I tilted my head when the archer looked at me, and he acknowledged how little help he was offering with a nod and a pout.

I slammed the table, using just enough of my Jötunn strength to shake it and topple a few cups. I had not meant to break anything, but a bump formed under my hand. Freyja would have a word with me for that. At least they stopped bickering. I pretended it did not hurt and gently refilled my cup.

"I'm not asking for any opinion here," I said, using my most Drake-like tone. "I am telling you what we need to do, and you will listen." I drank and let a few seconds go, just to make sure I had their attention. "We need to put Loki into a corner, in front of everyone: Æsir, Vanir, and men, especially Odin, and make him reveal what he has done. With the gods' help, we can force him to give me my body back because, yes, I would like to wipe my own ass and enjoy a woman with my own *tools*." They giggled at that, and finally, I felt like I was going somewhere.

"How do we perform this miracle?" Snekke asked.

"This is where I need your opinions. I have been out for too long, so you have to think of something. And we need to act fast; our enemies are already on the move."

The next thirty minutes passed in a hubbub of nonsense.

My men had vivid imaginations, just not realistic ones. From waiting for the next brawl, which would magically be won by one of them, to burning Valhöll, every possible idea was thrown onto the pitch. And again, the room filled with voices of men bickering over nonsensical details.

And then, when I least expected it, the Norns finally showed some generosity. They had been cheap that day, but they made up for it just as I thought to smash my cup on the corner of Karl's ugly face.

"Frigg is right," a sharp little voice said from the entrance of the room, "men truly are stupid."

We all looked at the woman standing there, though a woman she barely was. My memory was never great with faces, but I thought I had seen all the Valkyries living inside the hall, yet I did not recognize this one. She stood like a queen, a long dress of green silk gracefully shaping a body on the cusp of adulthood. Her dark brown hair, tied into a loose bun, reminded me of a pine cone, while her eyes, regal and gleaming, belonged more to a Vanir than a Valkyrie.

She was stunningly beautiful, and if Valkyries aged like human girls, she would become a splendid woman within a couple of years. She also looked familiar. The way she crossed her arms over her chest and tilted her head in a discreet shake sent me three years in the past. My mind understood who she was before my brain did, and a knot formed halfway down my throat as her name passed it.

"Lif," I said, standing up like a moron.

Lif, the girl who had crossed the Bifröst with us three years ago. A child of fate, as Odin had called her, for she was Ulf's granddaughter, and Einherjar were not able to father children. She was born with the blood of the heroes in her veins and gained access to our realm when Ulf gave up Odin's nail so she could survive the destruction of her village. And here she was, older and even more magnificent than I had left her.

"How?" I asked, opening my arms to receive her. She smiled like a child as she stepped into my embrace. Her frail arms wrapping around my waist gave me a warm feeling I was not used to. "You age," I said, though it sounded like a question.

"Even the gods don't know why," she replied, looking up at me. "Something to do with fate or with my blood." I kissed the top of her head and hugged her more tightly. "We need to do something about your body," she said. She had not even flinched when she saw this new me; she knew everything already. "I much prefer the other one."

"Me too, lass, me too."

It is strange how some people were born to be part of your life. I had met Lif less than a week before finding myself in Loki's cave, and yet, I had missed her and now felt as if reunited with a long-lost relative.

I took Lif by the shoulders and guided her toward Ulf, whose eyes would not be able to contain his tears much longer. He looked very much like Huginn when he received an apple from Freyja: pitiful, about to break, and genuine.

"Lif," he called, voice shaking like that of an old man. When he swallowed, the ball in his throat bobbed up and down as if his heart was regaining its rightful place.

"Grandfather," she said. The candles of the dining room shined in her eyes, so watery they were.

I thought Ulf was going to crush her, so strong and sudden was his embrace. He could not decide between keeping her in his arms or looking at her face, so he did both, and all the while, tears flowed down in streams. Never had I seen a warrior unmanning himself so much. Never had an Einheri been so beautiful.

If the last three years had been Hel to me, they had been a constant struggle of a different kind for Ulf. I had been chained to a rock; he had journeyed through the great winter in search of an arrow, accompanied by a lunatic Æsir, then through Ironwood, running away from monstrous beasts. And though he acted with extreme loyalty to our friendship, his goal had always been to reunite with his granddaughter. And finally, he had reached it, he had found her, and she was a sight for sore eyes.

Snekke's voice came in a sharp gasp, and when I looked at him, he was holding his ribs, wincing, and staring apologetically at Karl, who frowned him down. The veteran then pretended nothing had happened, and whatever Snekke had meant to say remained a mystery.

"How are you here?" I asked when their tears flowed no longer. Lif took Einar's chair next to Ulf, her hand never leaving his. "And how do you know about us?" She had not reacted to my body nor to her grandfather's presence.

"A little mouse told me everything," she said with a wink.

"A little mouse?" Karl asked, and it might have been my imagination, but I saw the corner of his eyes gleaming. It took me three hundred years to discover that Karl had a soft spot for children.

"You have a spy in Freyja's court?" I asked. This was impressive.

"I have a friend in Freyja's court," she corrected me. She had not just grown physically; Lif even played the gods' game now, and very well at that. "Don't worry though, she won't tell anyone."

For some reason, I thought of Freyja's maiden, the one who was so light on her feet and who brought her anything the goddess desired just as she desired it. It was probably because Lif and her looked about the same age. I later found out that I had been right, though I assumed Freyja knew about it, for even when she learned about Lif joining us, she did not react.

"So," I said, "if you called us stupid, it means you have an idea. Am I wrong?"

"Correct," she replied, "though it's not an idea, just an opportunity."

"All right," I said, grateful for having someone at the table with a good head on her shoulders, "tell us."

"There's going to be a *thing*," Lif told us.

Two days from now, the Æsir, the Einherjar, Loki, and Odin would be gathering for a great judicial assembly, the likes of which had not happened in more than a year. Everyone would be invited to attend, and a plan popped into my mind at the news.

The announcement for the *thing* was to be shared the next evening, and we would not have managed to prepare anything without Lif's information. She had given me time to organize our plan.

The fire in my chest rekindled with impatience. Two days. Two days, and I would face the trickster. It was there. I could almost touch it, my vengeance. I told them how everyone needed to act on that fateful assembly, for all of them had a role to play, and Snekke was the central piece of this scheme.

I did not envy him.

10

Leaving Freyja's domain proved harder than expected. Nothing would ever be the same after that day. I would never share Freyja's bed again, even though she had offered. I would either be back to being Drake or would die trying, and this was, no matter what, my last sunrise in the trickster's body. Passing the gates separating the estate from the fields of wildflowers, I took a last breath in and made myself strong. This would be a Hel of a day.

Freyja was leading sixteen people to the assembly. Gunhild and two Valkyries closed the march. Iona was one of them. If I had known how talented an archer and a warrior she was, I would have thought twice before attacking her in the bathroom. Astrid, Titus's lover, was also among the group, and her presence was as crucial as Snekke's.

Nine of Freyja's male guards stood among us, as well as Huginn, Ulf, and myself. The three of us were disguised as members of the guard, though the ruse was fragile. Those men all looked like prow men: bulging muscles gleaming under the sun and not one chest hair among them. The raven, the wolf, and I paled in comparison.

Ulf, though stronger than he looked, was lean and less than tall. Huginn was now a young-looking man again, with a nimble and delicate-looking frame. He had left his isolation the day before, not completely ready, he said, but ready enough. By his own words, he could mask his presence for half a day at most, which was all we needed. And I was Loki, a Jötunn known more for his brain than his biceps.

I left Crimson in Sessrúmnir because Freyja's men all carried the same type of sturdy spears and a long knife too pretty to be of real use. Those guards, though, the real ones, were chiseled. Fat had been drained out of them through a tough and long diet while their muscles shone like well-tanned leather. Today, however, to make our masquerade more believable, they and we wore long red cloaks and carried oblong shields, which we were to keep in front of us at all times. It was far from perfect, and many would notice this change, but this was the best we could do to avoid being recognized.

Then, behind us, wrists bound by a heavy chain pulled by one of the guards, walked Snekke. A face like misery, dirty hair hanging pitifully over his shoulders, and a bruise the size of Gunhild's fist under his left eye, Snekke looked less than formidable.

I did not envy him, but I preferred to remember all the times he had been a pain in my ass over the years. After this day, I told him we would be even. In truth, I would owe him, but that I would never admit. Still, I had to suppress a laugh when I saw him trying the pain on his face.

"Can't you do it?" he had asked me as Gunhild cracked the knuckles of her right fist.

"Believe me, you don't want me to," I had replied.

The bruise needed to be convincing. Or, more accurately, it needed to look like it was made by Titus. So, Gunhild, without needing much convincing, knocked Snekke on his ass. He was not faking his wobbly legs as we journeyed to the citadel, and I suspect his head was ringing as if Heimdallr had blown *Gjallarhorn* in his ears.

"You're smiling," Ulf said from a voice muffled by the helmet he wore, a fine piece of golden metal with long cheekpieces.

"I'm sorry that I'm not more sorry," I replied. He was smiling, too.

We circled the mountain, following the path of marble leading to the citadel, and soon would be in sight of the first buildings. This was probably the last time I could speak with Freyja in peace, so I stepped up to her level. I passed by Huginn, who was mumbling to himself. Not knowing his state of mind, I would have preferred to leave him in Sessrúmnir. He had not been taken by any folly since our return, but this would be a stressful situation. My faith in his stability was not at its highest. We needed him, though, and not just his Æsir strength but his face as well. Seeing him would convince his people about my claims.

Gunhild clicked her tongue when I walked past her, and her eyes lingered on my back for a long time after that.

"What is it?" Freyja asked. She spoke coldly, but I knew how much she beamed inside. It was all a game for her. Our scheme would be a challenge worthy of the best *skalds*. She would trick the trickster and reveled in the idea.

"I wanted to thank you," I said, looking straight ahead, where the tips of roofs emerged above the next hill.

"Do not thank me yet," she said. "Keep it for when Loki is drowning in his own blood." The idea had something quite unappealing, for *his own blood* was the one flowing through my body. If this was an omen, it was a terrible one.

"In that case, I wanted to apologize," I said, something long overdue.

"Apologize?" she asked. "What for?"

"For how I thought of you until I stumbled into your hall." For decades, centuries even, I had thought Freyja to be a pesky, self-centered, and arrogant goddess, while she had been more helpful in one week than any god had been in nearly three hundred years.

"My dear Drake," she said, making my name sound like the softer word in our language, "I am everything you thought I was. You just lowered the bar on the others, that is all."

Again, she was right.

"You have shown more honesty than any Vanir or Æsir I know, and you are true to yourself. I will never forget your friendship," I said. I was never one for sentimental speeches, and there were many more things I wanted to tell Freyja.

"Friendship?" she asked, almost blurting out the word with scorn. "Yes, this is what we are, I suppose, but it might surprise you to know I don't treat all my friends as I have you. Now, stop speaking with so much gloom. Things do not end today. Asgard will need you and your men more than ever. And as you owe me, you can be sure I will be collecting my debt soon."

I trusted her on that as well. Freyja, despite my new respect for her, was the leader of the Vanir, and as a good representative of her kind, generosity was never a selfless act.

"Now go back to your spot; my guards never speak to me in public."

A hammer pounded an anvil in one of the many

smithies littering the citadel, greeting us with a sound I had dearly missed. The smell of old wool and sweat found me next and, finally, the hubbub of hundreds—thousands of people swarming the paths and streets of the citadel.

Somewhere nearby would be Bjorn, Sven, Eigil, and the others, along with Loki and Magnus. Lif, Frigg, Odin, and Thor would be close, too. You, too, I dreaded as much as I desired, would be nearby.

I was home and Asgard would know it soon.

And life would never be the same.

ᚱ

The site for the *thing* was overcrowded. The hill itself stood outside the gigantic wall protecting the citadel, which made it a dangerous place; we could die there. It did not stop hundreds, if not more, of Einherjar, Æsir, and Vanir from gathering on the gentle, arch-shaped slope. Decades after decades of asses sitting on the ground had smoothened it into rows. Titus once told me people sat as such in his country to watch other men act. It sounded unmanly, but he claimed that everyone, powerful or poor, enjoyed those shows. Today, *we* would perform the greatest show of our lives, and our audience was excited.

Men were babbling like children as the sixteen of us climbed down the slope, most of them caring only about Freyja, following her curvy silhouette until they spotted Snekke, who had upped his game and now looked utterly miserable. The first onions and stones soon started raining on him. Warriors, so willing to show him respect when he stood among the pack, now spat at him and held their crotch in his direction.

Just as the slope flattened, I spotted Karl. He nodded at

Snekke, but it was meant for me. He had done his part. Titus would be ready.

The press of men tightened at the bottom. Most were drunk, but if things went according to plan, they would sober up fast.

One of them bumped my elbow and turned to curse me. I was about to react, but his eyes stopped the words in my throat. They were strong and full of authority, dark and blue, set in a hard face that had seen too many battles. I was looking at me. The helmet I wore left my face in a shadow, and our exchange lasted less than a heartbeat, but my bowels twisted on themselves. Time stopped its course, and nothing else in the world existed but this instant. He frowned, then received a slap on the back from the big bastard who was now the champion of the Wolves, Magnus Stone-Fists. Loki went back to his conversation with his men, and I forced myself to look straight ahead again.

"Fuck," Ulf said in a whisper.

"As you say, brother," I whispered back. My heart had yet to quiet down.

The fifty-steps-wide empty space separating the crowd from the raised stage on which two dozen gods sat was quiet and peaceful. A no-man's-land covered in green, lush grass agitated only by gentle blades of wind. A phallic-shaped, waist-high, white stone stood at its center. Many of my kind had lost a hand on it, or their lives, if the severity of their crimes went beyond thievery. The chunk of stone itself had been stripped from the cliff and carried to this spot by the first Einherjar to be punished on Asgard. His name was Gunnar, and he happened to become the first Drake a few decades later. I knew little about him, but we called this chunk of rock Gunnar's Stone in his memory. A ring of solid iron sprouted from the stone's top, but otherwise, it looked rather unremarkable.

We walked around the no-man's-land and climbed the wooden stairs leading to the stage, our destination. The structure was arranged to meet with the land rising behind so that the gods sat at the front, ten feet above the ground, with all their servants and guards at their back. None brought as many as Freyja, but by the time we stood in good order behind the goddess of war, the stage was creaking under the weight of a good hundred people. If I had thought my brethren were noisy, the gods' stage was deafening. They sat just as drunk as my brothers, Thor being chief of them in that regard.

The god of thunder sprang from his chair when he spotted Freyja, shoving his wife's hand from his arm in the process. He had not changed one bit, albeit he looked more tired than before. He embraced her while his wife, Sif, could do nothing but look the other way. I recognized Bragi, Idun, three or four sons and daughters of Odin, none of them being Frigg's. Heimdallr was there, too. In my time, the guardian god rarely left Bifröst. Snekke, standing as an accused, might have pulled him from his hall, for Heimdallr was nothing if not a friend of the Wolves.

Tyr, while being the god of justice, would not be here. We had heard conflicting information about him. Some claimed he was on Asgard, while others stated he hadn't been seen in months. His absence was our opportunity, for Odin was to replace him.

Frigg, queen of the Æsir, sat quietly by her husband's empty chair, and next to her stood Lif, hands clasped around a pitcher. The girl looked our way, and my heart sank. She shook her head slowly. Something was wrong. Frigg curled a finger for Lif's attention, and the girl poured some of the beverage for her surrogate mother, who looked bored beyond reason. She alone looked as such; everyone else seemed to chirp with anticipation. Entertainments were scarce in Asgard, after all, and this one promised blood.

The judicial assembly took place twice a year, on good years. Tyr presided over them if he could; otherwise, it became Odin's responsibility. One morning to solve every feud, punish every crime, and settle every score born within the citadel for the past six moons was never enough, and the trials could stretch well past noon. Punishments went from a hand to a head or some form of banishment, either from Valhöll or from the citadel, which was another form of death sentence in itself.

Once in a while, no verdict could be reached, and the two parties were then given the right to fight to the death. A real death. Those *holmgang* were the reason we came out of the citadel to attend the assembly. It might sound sordid, and most of us came for the blood, but I also thought it healthy to remind ourselves death could be final, too.

Valhöll having turned into Loki's wild realm, legal claims had flourished, and the assembly had been called two months early. Besides its length, this day's list of cases was rather dull and uninspiring, with one exception. A last-minute claim brought forth by Freyja herself and bumped to the fourth item on the program. A juicy scandal involving a Valkyrie, a Wolf, and Snekke. In all my years, I had rarely seen the justice *thing* attracting so many.

Daring a few looks between the shoulders of the guards and servants in front of me, I spotted Loki again, pouring ale into my body as if it were a barrel. Sven Cross-Eyes, Eigil, and Bjorn stood there too, the latter having, indeed, grown fatter, though not as much as I had pictured. Rune sat a bit farther and was sharing words with an even younger man. I recognized him and even remembered his name. Thrasir, a brave and kind young man I had slain during one of my last missions. The teenager beamed and laughed, then slapped Rune's back to shake his pout away. It did not work.

Of the gods, from where I stood, I could see very little.

"Freyja's men do not fiddle as such," Iona, who was walking up our line to serve her goddess, said.

"Sorry," I replied, resuming a perfectly still position.

"There will be three cases before ours," she said. "But they should not be long."

"Lif seemed worried," I whispered. Ulf tensed at my words.

"So far, everything is going according to—" The call of a horn interrupted her.

The sound of thousands of people sitting down drowned their chatter.

"So, that's what's wrong," Ulf whispered.

In one note of the horn, our plan tumbled like a Drakkar in a storm. Odin, it seemed, would not show up.

Thor left Freyja's side and walked to the center of the dais like a king, his steps resonating like the cracks of thunder on the stage. Freyja looked over her shoulder and shook her head discreetly. Ulf swallowed hard, and Huginn's tongue clicked in his mouth. We would manage, I thought, or prayed, maybe. Sticking to the plan was all we could do at this point.

"Iona," I called just as she was about to rejoin her mistress. "Have you seen Muninn?" The name sounded loud in my ear, even if I had been the one saying it. Huginn, who was right in front of me, stiffened. He had not spoken much, even after he left his room in Sessrúmnir, but had assured me that he had regained enough power to remain invisible to Odin or his sister if he chose to.

"Muninn?" Iona asked, "I don't think so."

Huginn shuffled his spear to his left arm and put his hand behind his back. Then he pointed a finger toward the left. You were in that direction. It took all I had for me not to look. I was a beardless boy dreading and praying for the presence of his dream girl at a feast. I shook the feeling with a headshake and remembered why I stood where I stood.

The first two cases went by fast, the first being a simple issue over the possession of a *brynja shirt* and the second deciding the fate of a bakery belonging to a certain Knut. The third one, however, took far longer than it deserved. Something about a warrior having won a twelfth-square brawl by cheating. No one can really cheat during a brawl, as there are almost no rules, but this man was accused of having drugged his opponents before the fight. As this was something impossible to verify and as the audience's patience was thinning fast, Thor came to a decision that sounded exactly like him. A *seidr* square was traced; both accused and accuser were given two shields and one sword and faced each other once more. Besides entertaining the crowd, the *holmgang* would prove if the accused needed drugs to beat his opponent.

He did not. A back step followed by a wide swing, and the accuser toppled against the stone, drenching it in a gush of red spurting from his half-severed neck. The duel had lasted less time than it takes to say *Svartalfheim*. The accuser died under the booing of the crowd, and the accused regained his reputation and some more.

Then it was our turn.

Everything in my chest, from stomach to heart, behaved as it did before a great battle. One of Freyja's guards pulled Snekke by the chain stretching from the metallic collar around his neck and wrists, and both vanished from my sight to reappear near the stone. I was breathless, counting the heartbeats as a man tallied his plundering chest.

A wave of murmurs spread through the crowd. This was the moment they'd been waiting for. They booed Snekke and called him names he did not deserve at the moment. The guard leashed Snekke to the iron ring and walked back to the stage. Snekke rocked his head to pull his hair from his face, revealing the greening bruise. Even in this situation, he loved to stand at the center of attention. Thousands of Einherjar shouted at his back, and some Æsir soon joined in.

It took Thor standing from his father's chair for the crowd to quiet down again. He raised his hands and opened his mouth as if about to speak but then tilted his head toward Bragi, on his right, who whispered something to him.

"Orm Hildasson," Thor called, pointing a finger at Snekke. I had completely forgotten Snekke's real name and wondered why we had changed it. Orm, the wyrm, suited him just as well. "You stand accused of intruding into a god's private hall, betraying a brother, and forcing yourself on a woman."

"Lies!" Snekke shouted.

"Silence!" Thor boomed. "Your chance to speak will come."

Snekke spat, his eyes shooting bolts of anger at the god of thunder. His acting was perfect.

"You were found in Sessrúmnir, caught by Freyja's guards while in bed with the Valkyrie known as—" Again, Thor stopped for Bragi to whisper something to him. Thor, it seemed, was as bad with names as I was. "—Astrid."

Astrid stepped forward at the mention of her name,

finding a spot next to her mistress. She kept her head low and would not look at Snekke or Thor.

"Astrid," Thor went on, "swears that you tried to force her, and—"

"The bitch lies!" Snekke said, spitting in her direction this time. "She was willing. She even got me into Sessrúmnir."

"One more word out of turn, little man, and we won't need a *thing*, am I clear?" Thor said. Snekke opened his hands and bowed to show he'd understood.

"This Valkyrie was known to have a long-lasting relationship with one of your brothers, the foreign Wolf Titus." On cue, Titus, waiting among the first line of Einherjar, lips twitching with faked anger, took a couple of steps forward, working his shoulders like a man about to do some wood chopping. "You knew of this relationship, didn't you?"

"Everyone did," Snekke replied.

"Today, Orm, you are thus being judged for betraying a brother by taking his woman, sneaking into Sessrúmnir uninvited, and attempting to rape the Valkyrie Astrid."

The crowd's issuing hoot was loud and long, though I spotted many grins in the assembly. This was a show they would not have missed. Thor waited for them to subdue.

"What do you say, Orm Hildasson? Are you guilty or innocent?"

"I'm innocent, Thor Odinson, of all three accusations," Snekke claimed, waving his head as he spoke so that everyone heard. "I was invited into Sessrúmnir by Astrid herself, who was not only willing to share her bed with me but asked for my presence in it."

The crowd laughed immediately, for no one could believe a woman would choose Snekke over Titus. Though foreign, Titus was a magnificent warrior, while Snekke's talents were more related to his tongue. On Midgard, Snekke had conquered the beds of many women with this skill, especially widows, but those men here could not comprehend it.

"She did!" he barked.

"Even if it is true, and we will know soon, you still knew of her relationship with your brother and chose to ignore it. A good man would have told his brother instead of betraying him for a pair of legs. How are you innocent of this accusation?" Thor asked.

"First, I am more a man for tits than legs," Snekke replied, which got him another wave of guffaw. "And second, this man," he said, pointing at Titus as best he could with his chained wrists, "is no brother of mine."

Titus spat toward Snekke, something he rarely did.

"All Einherjar are brothers," Thor said, "that is the law."

"And my brother he was," Snekke said. "But where was he when I was kicked out from the Wolves, huh? What did this brother of mine do to help me?"

"That's why you did it?" Titus barked, perfectly timing his intervention.

The foreigner, under the crowd's gasps, stormed the no-man's-land, stomping like a furious bear. Einar and Karl, following our plan, ran after him and put themselves between the two men right before Titus could hit Snekke, who then cowered behind the stone.

The ruckus grew on the dais, too. Titus had breached the protocol by stepping in, but he was an accuser and, as such, was allowed to speak. However, he was not supposed to do so before being invited. Acting, I had to admit, was a lot manlier than I had thought.

"Titus!" Thor shouted, stomping his foot three times. "Do not touch this man before I render my judgment."

Titus lowered his head but remained on his spot, a couple of steps from Snekke, now protected by Einar and Karl. My pieces were in place.

"Lord," Titus called, "this man has tried to bed my woman in revenge for something I am not guilty of."

"Your bitch wanted me," Snekke said, which prompted Titus to raise his fist once more. "Is this how you behave in your country? You believe women over men?"

"In my country, I would have a lion eat you in front of the crowd for what you did, *culus!*" Titus replied. The crowd seemed to like the idea. "As for your spot within our pack, I have defended you. I have asked Drake to keep you."

This was the culmination of our plan, the moment our trap would prove its worth or its failure, but Thor, it seemed, was not going to take the bait. I felt a cold line of sweat running down my back, for we needed him to call Titus out on his claim. Odin would have.

"He lies," Snekke said, trying to push Thor in the direction we wanted. But the god of thunder's interest in this story had reached its end. He would not push the point further. I could guess his thoughts. He would command the two men to fight for their honor and thus decide the whole matter in the most entertaining way. The men in the crowd probably counted on it, but we didn't.

"Do you have proof of it?" Frigg asked, the only being Thor would not order to remain silent. That the queen had spoken at all was a miracle, for she cared very little about stories involving the Einherjar. Lif had to be involved. "Do you have proof that you defended this man against his exclusion?"

Thor seemed confused by his mother's intervention. With any other god, he would have shouted for silence. Not an option with Queen Frigg. Not even for Thor. He allowed Titus to answer with a nod.

"If you allow me, I would like to ask for Drake to be my witness," Titus said. Thor waved his hand laconically, and Titus called Loki.

The trickster gave his tankard to Magnus, wiped his mouth with the back of his hand, and nonchalantly walked toward my men. The trap was closing on him, and my palms were moist around the spear I carried.

Things were about to move; chaos was about to take the *thing*. But before that, Huginn lost it.

I saw him fidgeting, rocking his shoulders, passing his spear from his right hand to his left. Impatience was gaining him. I remembered Jötunheimr and how suddenly bouts of madness conquered him. Before I could react, he slithered out of our line and disappeared into the crowd of servants, only giving me time to curse his name. I was about to follow him, for the last thing we needed was a mad Æsir ruining our plan so close to its completion, but Ulf caught my wrist.

"Too late," he said.

Thank the gods the attention of every living soul was on the scene happening by the rock, for our behavior was less than worthy of Freyja's famed guard.

"Drake," Thor called, "did this one defend that one when you decided to remove him from your group?"

"He did," Loki answered, thumbs tucked in his belt. It was most likely a lie, of course. Titus would not care much about Snekke's presence within the Wolves, and neither did Snekke since the Wolves were not traveling to Midgard anymore.

"You lying bastards," Snekke spewed, testing his chain's limits as he stepped closer to Titus and Loki. "You're no brother of mine, and your bitch said I plowed her better than you ever did."

I don't care which country or people one came from; no man could resist this insult. Titus, as he was supposed to, hammered a fist full of pretended rage into Snekke's face and pursued him to the ground, ready to release another punch. Einar dove between them while Karl and Loki grabbed Titus's arms to keep him from killing Snekke.

My heart threatened to free itself from my chest. This was the moment we had been wanting. Fuck Huginn, I thought, and fuck Odin for not being here, this was as good as it would get.

Karl nodded to Titus, and they moved as one. Titus spun on himself and twisted Loki's left arm and shoulder, while Karl did the same with the right. They shoved the trickster against the blood-spattered stone and Snekke wrapped his chains around Loki's neck while Einar pulled the knife and sword from his belt. Impeccable.

"What's the meaning of this?" Thor barked, fury taking him as fast as chaos spread within the crowd.

Magnus and his minions looked at each other with stupor, not knowing what was to be done. We had to act before they reached a decision.

Thankfully, Freyja moved first.

She walked faster than I ever saw her do and was climbing down the stairs before I could react. Ulf and I ran after her and guarded her back again by the time she stepped onto the no-man's-land.

She kept the crowd on their spot with a simple gesture of her hand. Like good hounds, they obeyed. Their dumbfounded faces as we walked toward Gunnar's Stone were worth my weight in silver.

"Freyja, what are you doing?" Thor asked, his voice barely containing his ire.

"Get the fuck away from me," Loki was shouting when we reached him. He could not see us yet, but his muscles were tensing as he tried to free himself. I hoped they did not hurt him too much. This was my body, after all.

"Silence!" Freyja shouted. Her voice echoed a few times in the sudden quiet. Even Frigg, standing with her first tightly shut, did not speak.

"This," Freyja said, a finger pointed at Loki, "he's not Odin's Drake. You have all been fooled. *We* have all been fooled."

Titus, Karl, and Snekke forced Loki up. His face was blue from the effort. I had worried that Loki could tap into his Jötunn strength just as I had, but it seemed that he could not. Just as I had gotten stronger with his powers, being trapped in an Einheri body must have made him weaker. Unless he was keeping his act up.

"*This* is Loki."

Freyja's words summoned a chorus of gasps and curses. Loki remained silent, mouth open like a dumb ox, a look I did not appreciate on my face. The only other man who kept his words to himself, as far as I could see, was Heimdallr. The guardian god stood silently next to Thor, but his frown was dark and menacing as his golden eyes peered through me. I had missed the shiny bastard and hoped his famed sight would see the truth of the matter.

"What on Midgard are you saying, Freyja?" Thor asked through the hubbub. "Loki is chained in his cave. You were there; you saw it."

"He's been among us, in Asgard, for the past three years after he stole Drake's body. Isn't it right, trickster?"

"Help me, Lord," Loki pitifully asked, turning his face to Thor. "This is ridiculous."

"I agree," Thor said. "We would have known if Loki had been here for so long."

"Remember who we are talking about," Freyja said. Thor's frown deepened.

I could not resist, and I stepped behind Loki, covering him with my shadow.

"Do you have proof?" Frigg asked. The same question she had asked earlier on.

"I have three." She squinted when she realized that Huginn was nowhere to be seen, but it was too late at this point. "This is the first."

Ulf removed his helmet, letting his long brown hair fall behind his head. Loki saw him but could not make sense of who he was looking at. I stood between them and prayed for his attention to fall on me.

"Hello, old friend," I whispered. His eyes, growing white and round as his real voice greeted him, will remain with me as one of my most precious memories. "Can't hear my thoughts anymore, can you?"

His mouth formed a "no," though no sound came out.

"This is the second," Freyja said. Her hand opened toward me.

I kept my eyes on Loki as slowly, very slowly, I removed my helmet too.

Never before had I heard the gods gasping in unison. They were looking at their worst nightmare. Loki was back on Asgard; he had escaped his prison, and Ragnarök was staring at them. Neither chains nor walls had stopped him. No god had seen him. The trickster was back.

I looked up, wanting to register the fear on their faces before I kneeled and let them see I was no threat to them.

And this is where our plan went belly up.

Odin was to preside over the *thing*. A god with a good head on his shoulders and the wisdom gained from thousands of years of existence. Instead, Thor was in charge.

His eyes turned red with rage. His roar was like the crack of thunder at the height of summer, and Mjölnir, his famed hammer, seemed huge as Thor bolted from the stage. In one leap, he breached the distance. Thor did not care for tricks, *seidr,* or illusion. Thor cared about what he saw, and what he saw was me, his enemy in the flesh. And what I saw was the end of my life. In less time than it takes to say *Tanngrisnir,* Thor's hammer would crush my skull, and there was nothing I could do about it.

11

Mjölnir was as big as a house at the center of my focus. I had seen Thor swing it against countless enemies in the past. I had witnessed the carnage its head could spread on the battlefield. And now it was my brains that would splatter the ground. Time seemed to stop. I tasted regret in the back of my throat. I would die before Loki. He would die, too, Freyja would make sure of it, but I wouldn't witness it.

My eyes closed as the god of thunder, the mightiest of his kind, arced in the sky, mouth spitting with rage, eyes marred with red veins, his hammer flicking with sparks of thunder. He was aiming for the head. Loki had killed his brother, Baldr, and was prophesied to bring death to the Æsir. Of course, he would aim for the head.

But no pain came.

When I opened my eyes, Thor was stuck mid-air, less than an arm's length from me, grunting and wriggling at the end of Freyja's grip. She had grabbed him by the throat and barely looked to be struggling.

I knew then that on our first night together, she had played weak.

"Let me go," Thor grunted through his teeth.

She tossed him back the way he came. The god of thunder crashed into the dais, breaking one of its poles. The structure almost gave way, and a few of its occupants jumped from it. I remembered to breathe then.

"Drake," she called, "would you mind?"

"I am not Loki!" I turned around and repeated myself. By Odin's beard, I was tired of those words and how few people trusted them.

"You look like him, and you sound like him," Thor said as he stood back up. His rage had not been subdued, but the threat of Freyja's power kept him on his spot.

"He even smells like him," said a Vanir I did not recognize.

"This is his body," I said, "so, yes, I do look, sound, and smell like him. But I am Odin's Drake. It took me three years to come back here, but I am still Drake."

"Three years?" Heimdallr asked, louder than the others. One of his eyes was half-closed.

"Yes, my friend," I answered. "Right after I won the brawl and went back to Midgard with Muninn. Right after Lif crossed the Bifröst."

I wished Huginn was there. His presence would give weight to my words. I could not fault the gods for their doubts at hearing anything from this mouth, but Huginn was one of them; they would trust him. He was nowhere to be seen, though.

"You must have felt things changing over the last three years. Things started getting quiet. Drills lost their edge and their frequency. Odin cared even less. Maybe you even sensed that life got more relaxed," I said, turning around to address my brothers as well. "That was the trickster at work. He was putting you to sleep while the armies of Jötunheimr,

Hel, and Múspellsheimr were readying themselves. And he did a great job of it. Look at you, trembling like mice caught in the pantry! Loki played with you. Wake up!"

The whispers changed in nature. They were not just accusing anymore; they started doubting.

"Don't listen to him," Loki, still locked down by Karl and Titus, said. "He's tricking you. Loki always puts doubts in people's minds. Don't let him deceive you."

"He is right, though," Heimdallr said as he jumped down from the dais to side with Thor. The two of them remained close to the stage. "Things have changed dramatically, though not suddenly, over the last three years." Thank fate Odin was a lecherous old goat, for at least one of his quests for flesh had produced a worthy son.

"Of course he's right," Loki replied, loud and clear. "He is Loki. He knows things. Hel, he might even have been the reason those changes happened. Shut his mouth now before he tricks you as he has Freyja. Don't let him speak; he'll put a spell on you!"

Loki was a clever bastard, all right. We had taken him by surprise, but he was already shifting the story, sowing doubts where I had just planted a few seeds. If we let him speak, I thought, Loki would win this fight. This was his battlefield, his weapons.

"Kill both!" a voice boomed from the dais. Bragi, I think.

Many agreed with him, even among the Einherjar. Not good, I thought, not good. Thor picked up his hammer; he liked the idea.

"To the one of you who is Drake, know that I am sorry," he said as he calmly cracked his neck. "Know that you sacrifice yourself for the death of the trickster, and we will honor you."

"Fuck," Ulf whispered.

Screw your honor, I thought as, by reflex, I assumed a fighting stance.

"You will do no such thing," Freyja barked, just as Heimdallr put his hand flat on Thors' chest.

"Why not?" Thor asked, the veins on his forehead threatening to burst. "Don't you want to end Loki for good?"

"I do," she replied. "But Drake deserves his revenge first, and he has promised Loki's death to me, not you."

"And how do we know you haven't been fooled?" Thor asked, pointing his hammer at the goddess of love.

"What of your third proof?" Frigg called from her spot on the dais.

"It seemed he has vanished, Queen Frigg," Freyja replied, using Frigg's self-given title to address her for the first time that I could recall.

Loki snorted, and Frigg raised her head with contempt. Damn Huginn, I thought, a second before he chose to show himself.

"I'm here."

Huginn walked around the stage, and he wasn't alone. Thought had captured Memory, and now Muninn, the lost love of my life, was our prisoner. Your beauty, barely wasted by the red trickling from your lips, took my breath away. You would not meet my gaze or anyone else's, and I can't fault you for it. Not spitting in your face took all my will.

"Huginn," a few voices called and whispered from the gods' side.

I nodded to the old raven, apologizing in my heart for doubting him. He nodded back. We had won. His presence would dispel the doubts, and his words would clear things.

Loki also realized his defeat.

My heart compressed on itself a second before a burst of *seidr* exploded. A white wave of power shoved Titus against me while Karl flew into Snekke. Even Freyja was sent off her feet, though her landing was more gracious than ours. As I pushed Titus aside, I saw Loki grabbing his sword from Einar's hands and slashing the old man's belly in a wide arc of red. Someone yelled behind us. It had to be Eigil, his son.

"I will not go down without a fight," Loki said, a Dwarven sword in his right hand and my precious long knife, Wedge, in his left. What he hoped to achieve against dozens of Æsir, I did not know, but his death did not suit me.

"Wait," I said as Thor and Heimdallr readied themselves. "He's mine!"

I don't know why they listened to me, but they did. The two of them stopped in their tracks, and I can only assume what would have happened if this formidable duo had not been interrupted.

The crowd gathered like flies to dung. Hundreds of Einherjar were now packed behind me, intent on watching the show from up close. They formed an improvised square around us, and the pressure grew suddenly as my brothers came to witness the end of the trickster or me.

"Heimdallr," I called, opening my hand toward my old friend. I would not fight with a spear against Loki and two Dwarven blades. The Æsir tossed his magnificent golden sword without hesitation. It was slightly heavier than our regular blades, but not as much as I had feared.

"You had to ruin everything," Loki said, pacing through our dueling square like a beast in a cage. He was not smiling anymore. He was in a rage, snarling and frothing from the mouth. This look suited my face much better.

I tested the balance of the sword with a couple of wide slashes, found it to my taste, and then tightened my grip on the oval shield I had borrowed from one of Freyja's guards.

"Give me my body back," I told him, "and I'll make it quick."

"I think I will take it with me," he replied. Then he attacked.

It came as a slash from above, fast and strong, ending in a loud clunk against my shield. The next one came just as fast from below. I parried it with the sword this time, taking a step back. This was but a salutation, and he broke away as fast as he came. Already, my breathing and heartbeat were hard at work.

Folks often forgot that Loki was a formidable fighter, and he was reminding us of it.

I closed the space between us and punched the shield toward his face. Loki rocked his head backward and kicked my leg at the same time. I had not seen it coming and found myself on my knee. He meant to stab me before I could recover, but I rolled on my shoulder and was behind him before he could hit. The cheers rang loud; this was a good show for the crowd. Not for me, though.

I had yet to feel the fire in my veins.

"That's all?" he asked, turning slowly. "All of this for that?"

"Give me my body, and I'll make it worth your while." This was the heart of the matter. I could not fight seriously, knowing that I would lose one of the things I wanted the most.

Loki spat his answer.

My heart told me that he would use his *seidr* next, and I jumped sideways in the blink of an eye before the thrust wave hit me. The men behind me were not as fortunate, and I heard curses as men crashed into their friends. I charged Loki, shield first, and was gratified by a curse as we connected. I pushed, but Loki was just too strong.

His fingers appeared on top of the shield. He meant to pull it down and stab again, as so many had tried before. Usually, I would slash those fingers. Not an option this time. I let go of the shield and jumped back just before the stab came.

"Oh? You don't want anything happening to those precious fingers, don't you?" Loki asked, curling his fingers one after the other. He brought the long knife to his palm and drew a red line.

"You bastard." He knew of his advantage.

"How do you hope to win if you can't even damage this vessel?" he asked, this time dropping the blade to his thigh, marking it with another line of blood.

"Wait!" I said urgently, this time looking over his shoulder toward Thor.

Loki turned his gaze in Thor's direction. He realized he'd been tricked when I pummeled his nose with my fist. The sound of my own bone being crushed did not please me, but it would mend. I had tricked the trickster with one of the cheapest tricks, and the crowd cheered for it.

Loki tried to reply in kind, but I had the momentum. I prayed for my aim to be true as I slashed at Loki's right arm, forcing him to drop his sword. Then I kicked his knee right after avoiding a lunge. The fire was finally in my body, fueled by rage, making my hand faster and my arms stronger.

Loki was trying to fend me off with Wedge, but he was failing. Each stroke brought a new cheer from the crowd and me closer to losing my real body for good. He was stronger than I had been as an Einheri, but those years away from his Jötunn self had weakened him, while I had gotten stronger since his cave. His powers had abandoned him, and maybe it was due to me using them now. Even his thought-hearing was gone, it seemed. Jötunheimr had made me ready for this fight.

I looked at myself, bloodied and panting. I had to trick Loki again if I wanted to keep it. He would not willingly give what belonged to me. I had ruined his plan, whatever it was, and he was hopeless. I had to give him something.

"Now, *I* am disappointed," I said.

Loki spat a gob rich in blood before he spoke. "I could snap you like a twig."

"Not with an Einheri body, you won't."

"I am dead anyway," he said. "My last trick will be to keep this vessel from you."

"Still a cunning old bastard," I said. "I thought you would prefer revenge as your last act."

"I will never satisfy *this* thirst," he replied.

"Not revenge for you," I said, "for Sigyn."

Why the idea only came then, I did not know, but Sigyn would save me again. Only I knew of Loki's true love for her. She had cared for him for many years while he helplessly waited for the end of the world in his cave. She had sacrificed her sanity for him, even after the loss of their son. Loki could only love her. This realization had been the key to my escape from the cave, at the cost of Sigyn's life. Yes, Loki loved Sigyn, and the way he looked at me confirmed my theory.

"What have you done to her?" he asked, wrinkles of fury marring his brow.

"What you never could," I replied. "She did not even call your name when I killed her. Or rather when the snake killed her." In my chest, I felt Loki's *seidr* once more. It was burning with rage this time; I could sense it coiling around my heart. "I hit her right there," I said, pointing at my forehead, "and the snake took its chance. It bit her in the throat and curled around her neck until she could breathe no more. But don't worry, she still managed to tear the snake apart; I owe her that."

"Shut up!" Loki called as his magic tensed, shaping itself like a second skin, dark and blue.

"The poison killed her. She died, foam spewing out of her toothless mouth, struggling for air. She died pissing and shitting herself while you were enjoying Asgard. And once free, I tossed her rotting carcass over the mountain, and I doubt even wild beasts found something edible from it. If they did, she's now nothing but frozen feces and broken bones. Her marrow fed the beasts of Jötunheimr, and they're using the rest to sharpen their fangs."

"I will crush you," he grunted, "like an ant."

Loki's power was a furnace, and I was the bellow. I had woken up the god of mischief and had blinded him with boiling anger. All he needed now was his vessel. "You want your body?" he asked, reversing his grip on Wedge. "Take it."

He stabbed himself in the abdomen, exactly where I had been stabbed the first time. His *seidr* flew from the wound in a liquid-looking fume. "Come!" he said, opening his arms.

"Drake!" a voice called, though I could not recognize it. Lif, Freyja, or Iona, maybe.

It did not matter; I was in the maelstrom of Loki's magic. It twisted everything around me: sounds, colors, feelings. I walked to him as much as I was sucked in. I could not resist and did not want to. My hand curled around Wedge's hilt.

"You will die in your own body," he spat.

"Try me," I replied.

The fire was sucked from my chest to my arm, then to the blade, and then back into the wound. My wound, my pain. Everything turned dark, and everything hurt. I yelled, and as I did, my voice shifted. Loki's clear, like water, voice morphed into my very own low and rocky shriek of pain. I felt my wound, my throat, my hand, my thigh, my nose, every little pain inflicted during the *holmgang*. Then I felt my fingers, my beard against my throat, my toes in my boots, and the familiar weight of silver rings on my arms. It was like kissing a lover after months at sea.

There was a flash, a push, and both Loki and I fell on our backs. *Our* backs.

"Drake!" Lif called. This time, I was sure it was her.

"I'm here," I said through the pain.

"Don't listen to him," Loki said, sitting faster than I could. "He did nothing; this is still Loki."

Fuck, I had not seen that one coming. In the blurred crowd of men looking at me, I spotted Bjorn, his stupid face struggling with what was happening. They all bore the same expression.

"Don't look at me like that," I said as I painfully leaned on my elbow. "It's me, you dumb ox. How many times do I need to save your arse before you recognize your real Drake, huh?"

"Thor," Loki said, "kill him before he recovers." He was wobbling to his feet, using Heimdallr's sword for support.

"Screw it, I kill both," I heard Thor say as I plucked Wedge from my belly. His shadow fell on me while my blood oozed from the wound. He looked as big as a mountain as he raised his hammer, ready to strike me down for the second time that day.

"Don't!" Heimdallr said as he put himself between his brother and me.

Heimdallr was a believer of fate. Ragnarök, he thought, was the best-case scenario, no matter how awful the prophecy sounded. Loki, he used to say, was a necessity and could only die during Ragnarök, as the two of them killed each other. This was his destiny, and he would not let it be stolen by someone else, not even Thor.

"This is Drake," he then said. Heimdallr stooped and offered me his hand as well as his golden teeth in the warmest of smiles.

"I see you, my friend," he said. "Welcome back."

I grabbed his massive hand, and for one second, the pain was subdued.

The sword appeared through his chest before I could register the shriek coming from Lif. Blood came out of Heimdallr's mouth, spotting his perfect garment of gold and white with red. The confusion in his eyes hurt before the tears came in mine.

The world stopped. I could not move or breathe as Heimdallr, the greatest of his kind, was killed by his own blade. The sword swooshed out of him, and he stood as if nothing had happened. Then he turned to Loki, who stared viciously, bloody sword in hand.

"So much for Ragnarök," Loki said before thrusting the blade back into Heimdallr from the front this time. A gasp spread through the crowd as the sword pierced its master once more. Not even Thor reacted, petrified as he was at the sight of Heimdallr's last moment.

The guardian god took one more step. A breath away from his killer, he grabbed the trickster by the throat and lifted him as he would a chicken. Loki's face turned red faster than Heimdallr's shirt. He fought for air, punching Heimdallr's arms pitifully. It reminded me of Sigyn's battle with the snake. Then, Heimdallr used the last of his great strength, and all those present that day heard Loki's throat crush under the golden Æsir's fingers.

His whole body dangled lifelessly from Heimdallr's arm, then dropped on the ground like a bag of wheat. Loki had met his fate. So had Heimdallr. My friend got on his knees, then on his back.

I crawled to him, unable to speak. For once, I did not even try to prevent the tears. I took his hands in mine again. They were turning cold already. Heimdallr, struggling for air, looked at the sky, and I can only imagine the things those eyes could see in the clouds.

I felt more than I saw people surrounding us, their presence casting long, fingers-like shadows over Heimdallr as if fate itself were coming to take its champion.

His left hand trembled as he shuffled with the bottom of his shirt. I knew what he was looking for, even if he could not ask for it. I bent over him and freed his horn from his belt, then brought it to his lips. He nodded in gratitude.

Heimdallr gasped for air a few times, making *Gjallarhorn* breathe some pitiful sounds. Then his chest rose like a barrel, and he emptied his lungs into the horn.

It was the most feeble call that ever boomed from Gjallarhorn, but we understood.

In his last breath, Heimdallr had called for us to gather.

Ragnarök had just begun.

And Odin was nowhere.

"First, you miss the big things, like your wife's cooking or the sight of the sun going down from your doorstep. Then you miss the little things. Market day, the fresh barrel of ale from your neighbor, grooming before a thing. Finally, you miss the annoying stuff, like plowing your field, reaping under the rain, stitching fish nets. And then you slowly forget all of this, and you're an Einheri at last."

Gunnar, son of Hrolfr.

12

"How could I miss it?" Bjorn asked for what seemed the hundredth time that morning. His breathing was loud as we walked toward the mountain, and he struggled to keep up the pace.

I had found my champion changed. Laziness had taken its toll on him, making his belly larger than his chest and his lungs weaker. I still gave him his spot back, for Bjorn was nothing if not the greatest of our kind. But that he had been tricked by Loki did not sit well with him. If anyone could have seen through his act, he thought, it should have been him.

It was easy to see it this way afterward, but Loki had worked patiently, slowly boiling the water in which my friends bathed in my absence. That's what I had replied the first time. Now I just left him to his sighs.

"Loki tricked everyone, not just you," Tyr replied, gracefully patting Bjorn's back.

Tyr, as it turned out, had been on the other side of Asgard, closing all existing gates connecting our realm to the others per his father's request. He had almost finished his task when he felt the loss of his brother and rushed to the citadel, only to find Heimdallr's body in my arms and the members of his clan crying for their loss.

We sent Heimdallr away with honor. His body was wrapped in his golden armor, itself wrapped in golden silk. We put his sword on his chest, his fingers around it. Some had argued that since the sword had betrayed him, we should break it first. I told them Heimdallr would see it as fate, not betrayal, and they relented.

We filled a ship with nine barrels of his mead, a waterskin of water from the Bifröst, and hacked silver in a hundred pieces. We kept Gjallarhorn, for it was the key to Asgard and contained too much magic. No one but he and Odin could use it, so as it was, locked into Thor's hall, the horn was as useful as nipples on a dog's arse.

One of Odin's sons shot the arrow that set the ship on fire, and we watched my friend as he vanished under the water. I hope he found his way to his grandmother's realm at the bottom of the sea.

Three days later, Asgard had yet to recover from his death and from all that had transpired on that wretched day. I kept myself busy with whatever I could get my hands on to avoid the one thing I needed to do the most and was now on my way to take care of.

I reorganized the Wolves first. Magnus Stone-fists and his dogs were kicked out. That I could not prove they knew of Loki's identity saved their lives, and something in the way Magnus bleated for us to trust him led me to believe him. Snekke and Karl rejoined the ranks, and we welcomed a new member. Gunhild did not thank me for it, but at least I had fulfilled a promise to Freyja. The other, which had been a slow death for Loki, I had broken. The goddess did not seem to hold it against me, but our new friendship had taken a hit. Welcoming Gunhild was a small gesture but a much-deserved one. And since there were two empty spots, I might as well have accepted a strong and reliable warrior like Gunhild. Einar survived his wound, but his fighting days, as he declared, would wait.

And, finally, after all he had done, I freed Ulf from the pack. He wished to remain with his granddaughter and make up for all the lost time, and nothing I could have offered for his presence would have changed his mind. The Wolves were not needed anywhere, so I just gave his spot back to Arn. We had joined the pack at the same time and, for a while, competed for the title of Drake. He was a dependable fighter with a calm nature, quick wits, and a unique sense of humor. We had shared much over the years, but, being loyal to the previous Drake, Arn had chosen to leave the pack and was taking care of the man whose mind had never recovered from his last mission. But now I needed him more than our old Drake did, so I forced his ass back in line, and I believe he was grateful for it.

I put Titus in charge of reorganizing our thousands and thousands of brothers into a proper army. Fat had to be drained, habits had to be recovered, and Valhöll had to be cleansed of Loki's presence. This was why, with Thor's approval, we emptied the hall for the first time in its history and kept the men out in the open, where Titus would make them run through Hel.

"Will you talk to Rune?" Bjorn asked, puffing and sweating.

"Why to Rune?"

"You know why," he replied obviously.

"I don't. So why don't you make yourself clear?" I asked. I was in no mood for politeness.

Bjorn, accompanied by Tyr, had forced me out of some

non-urgent task. My champion did not know I had learned some unfortunate truth about Tyr and currently despised him. As for Rune, I assumed Bjorn meant that I had been less than warm with the young Wolf since I had recovered my body. I did not completely trust him, though, according to the others, he was the first who had voiced his concerns about the Drake of the last three years. The jolly young warrior I had left in Asgard had become a sullen man whose first smile had been for my presence when I had gathered the crew. By now, I was fairly certain he had nothing to do with Loki and Muninn, but my instinct still warned me that something was off with him.

"You might be Asgard's hero and all," Bjorn said, using his axe for support, "but I can still kick your ass like you were a bairn. So mind your tone, or I'll show you why you made me your champion in the first place."

"You'd have to catch me first," I replied as I took a bold step inside his reach. Now that I was an Einheri again, I doubted my chances against Bjorn, but I also doubted his will to test me.

"Enough," Tyr commanded, getting my darkest stare in response. "Save your words; you'll need them."

He was right, but I wanted to play petty.

"I can get there by myself, you know."

"I also want to speak with her," Tyr replied.

"I don't know if you'll be able to," I said.

"Drake," Tyr said, dropping his hand on my shoulder. "You will not harm Muninn; we need her."

We had burned Loki's body on the very spot where he died, naked and unwashed. I felt a certain kind of unease as the flames crept over a body I had inhabited for more than three years. It might have been the heat, but as his face melted, the corner of his lips rose to a vicious, ominous smile.

Later that afternoon, we found out about Loki's very last trick for us.

Odin had vanished the day before the *thing*, just after a meeting with Loki. Frigg, who recovered her grandeur faster than Thor or I did, told us how much Odin had come to trust Drake-Loki over the past few years. Some members of the All-Father's guard had seen him leaving his hall, clad in armor, a sword in hand, Gungnir, his legendary spear, in the other, hiding under his old hat and inside a gray cloak. Odin was wandering again, just as Ragnarök loomed on us. No one knew where the All-Father had gone, but it had to be Loki's doing. Now that he was dead, only one person would know Odin's whereabouts, and she had remained silent so far.

The queen had tried, Thor had tried, and Huginn was still trying, but no one, it seemed, could get a word out of you. No one more than I wanted to speak with you, yet no one more than I wanted to avoid it. I was afraid to face you, for you had been my weakness and might still be. But Tyr, who knew of my past affection for you, had insisted. I was to make you talk.

The path to the mountain was sinuous and unsteady, but the entrance of the prison stood large and threatening, like some beast's maw jagged with sharp fangs of stone.

"Remember—"

"I know," I interrupted him, "we need to know where Odin is, what was Loki's plan forward, and what secrets have died with him. Hel, we know so little that I could ask her the color of Surtr's undergarment and that would still be a gain."

"I don't think Sutr wears clothes," Bjorn said as if it was the point of the conversation.

"We know Ragnarök has started, and we know that our enemy is ready while we are not," Tyr said. "We know so much more thanks to you, my friend. We are all grateful to you, and you have recovered your body. So why do you look at me as if bugs were crawling under your eyes?"

Why? I asked myself the same question. Why was I still filled with so much rage? I was back. I had brought Loki's death upon him and had protected my people from a humiliating defeat. But the ire was still flowing in my chest. I was hungry for more. And you, Muninn, were all I had left.

I was angry at Tyr for his betrayal of Fenrir, knowing how close they had been. But Tyr had done nothing to *me*.

I was angry at Bjorn and the others for having been fooled.

I was angry at Gunhild for not showing more gratitude, at Thor for acting so meekly since his brother's death, at Loki for having died so fast. I was even angry at the trickster for having left my house to rot and mold while he enjoyed every shiny hall in Asgard.

"Don't worry about me," I told him as I removed his hand from my arm and entered the prison, leaving the two of them outside.

13

Asgard's prison, now

"There, you know everything."

Muninn had not made a sound since the retelling of Heimdallr's death. Unless it was Loki's who kept her quiet. The torch had died down a little before that, so we were now bathed in the darkness of her cell. I should not have told her why I came here, but she probably knew already.

"I was the one who screamed," she said, "when Loki stabbed Heimdallr. It was me."

"Why?"

She scoffed. "It might surprise you, but when a sword bursts from a friend's chest, I react."

"A friend," I said through a chuckle. How dare she call him such?

"Yes, a friend," she replied. "I liked Heimdallr and cried for his death. He was kind, almost human. If he alone among us Æsir could survive Ragnarök, this would have been a good thing. But Heimdallr's fate said otherwise. He was always going to die, Drake. That it happened so suddenly was unfortunate, but it was always going to go this way."

"Isn't that convenient?" I asked in a voice dripping with sarcasm. "Fate made you act the way you did, it's not your fault?"

"I own my actions," she replied. "I did what I did willingly. I will not lie, or protest, or beg. I betrayed everyone, and nothing I say will change that. And, yes, my actions were always going to happen the way they did, as fate would have it."

"But why?"

My questions echoed in a long sigh.

"Because you are not Heimdallr, Drake," she answered when my voice stopped bouncing between the walls. Her chains shuffled; she was dragging herself closer. "You are not Thor or Odin or Freyr. You are a nameless Einheri and could be saved. Your fate was not written; I could save you."

"By keeping me chained in that cave?"

"Do you think I enjoyed it?" she asked, voice trembling. "I stabbed you and left you behind, believing I would never see you again. This was Loki's plan, and I hated it, but you would have survived the end of the world, and it was worth it in my heart," she replied. "I didn't even care that you hated me as long as you survived."

"Why didn't you tell me?" I asked. "The moment Loki reached you in your dreams, why didn't you tell me?"

"You would never have let me try. I could never have convinced you to abandon your brothers or my father. The moment I told you about Loki's plan, you would have run to the All-Father to let him know about Loki, and my only chance to keep you safe would have vanished." She was right. "Loki insisted that I did not tell you."

"And you listened to him?" My voice bounced against the wall of her cell again, distorted to an even higher tone.

"He offered to save the only person I ever loved," she replied, dragging herself a little closer still.

"How about your brother? How about your father? You never cared for them? Is that why you erased his memory of sending Huginn to Midgard?" I asked, forcing myself to sit straighter.

"Erasing his memory wasn't my decision," she replied. "He asked me to."

"What did you just say?"

"Odin asked me to remove his memory. He called for me right after Huginn left and asked me to remove anything that had happened on that day, all of it. Until Huginn told me a few minutes ago, I had no idea what Father had ordered him to do on Midgard."

Huginn had voiced this possibility before, but I could not completely believe it until now. Odin had asked his memory to be cleansed. Everything that had happened to me, to the twins, to himself, and even to Heimdallr was part of his vision. And this vision was the best-case scenario. The All-Father knew that his foretelling of those events would test his limits, and he would have done something to prevent them, especially his son's death. He sent his raven-son to Midgard and made sure he forgot about it. This was twisted, even for Odin.

"Odin knew what he was doing," Muninn said as I still struggled to grasp the whole meaning of her revelation. "He could never have left you in the cave or let Heimdallr die if he had kept that knowledge, so he made me take it away. Don't you see? He even knew I would act as I did, and he let me."

"That's your excuse, Muninn? Odin knew, so you should

be forgiven?" I meant the question, but when it came out of my mouth, it sounded like an accusation.

"I betrayed my kind; I do not want forgiveness," she replied. She sat so close to me now that I sensed the moment she closed her eyes to look the other way.

"But Odin would give it to you," I said. "So why don't you ask to wait for him?" She would not look at me, and I felt the world weighing on her shoulders.

"You know why," she said.

"Because he's not coming back," I answered for her.

She nodded.

Odin had gone to his death, and I had wasted three days to find out about it.

"Muninn," I said, filling my voice with all the scraps of love I yet held for her. I crawled on all fours until my hand touched her fingers. She meant to remove them, but I gently grabbed her hand and held it in both of mine. There was a time I would have burned Valhöll for this touch. "If you love me, if you want me to believe you, tell me where Odin has gone."

"I can't," she said, her lips trembling as she fought tears of frustration.

"Why?" I asked, gentle as a lover. I lifted her hand to my chest. "Because I would not make it back either?"

"You wouldn't," she confirmed, "not this time."

"Not this time?" I asked, confused.

Her hand stiffened, and she almost jerked it from my grasp. Muninn had said too much, but her attitude told me more than her words. My heart froze, and my belly twisted on itself. I knew.

Fuck, I thought. *I should have known.*

"Drake," she called, panicking. She meant to grab my wrist, but I moved before she did. I stood and took a step back to put myself out of her reach. Her chains tensed. It was so obvious and none of us had realized. My head buzzed and spun; I needed to get out of there.

"Drake, don't go there!" she yelled as I stepped through the bars. The feeble light of the torches were blinding after so long in the dark. I used the wall for support and peered through the bars once more.

"You let your father go to Fenrir!" I barked. "You let him go to the one being whose fate is to kill him, and you want me to trust you? Pray that I bring Odin back, Muninn. Only he can save you now."

"Drake, I did it for you!" she shouted as I stormed back to the open air. Her voice woke the creatures in the other cells, who then screamed and roared and whimpered. I could no longer hear her plea through the ruckus, but her sorrow was like a dagger in my belly. I would have given anything to believe her and then some more to defend her at her trial so that we could spend the last few days before the end together.

Instead, I was going back to Jötunheimr and Fenrir.

I was going to save Odin or die by his side.

ᚱ

Valaskjálf, Odin's silver hall, was meant for brief, private meetings with the All-Father, not for the greatest gods gathering of our time. Its walls had been erected to make Odin's voice boom and echo with more strength. The slabs of silver had been forged to reflect the light in all directions but toward the throne, making the guests lose their focus before our lord did. The way the ceiling curved inward gave an impression of being slowly crushed by a cloudy sky. Odin did not want his guests to stay, and he did not want them to come in numbers.

On that day, Valaskjálf was making things worse.

Hundreds of deities crammed the main room, and still more waited in the antechamber. Their voices rang as each of them tried to be heard above his neighbor, creating a beehive mess of a noise. The light bounced on jewelry and polished armor, turning green, red, or golden accordingly. If not for the atmosphere, one would have thought Valaskjálf was welcoming a grand feast. But no matter the company, the beams of colors, and the shiny hall, the atmosphere was somber.

I stood right in front of the throne, the only one of my kind in Valaskjálf. Tyr stood on my left, Huginn on my right, both of them trying hard to keep their faces of stone as the hubbub refused to subdue.

Thor, on his father's throne, looked as if he was growing the mother of all migraines, while Bragi, by his side, repeatedly butted the floor with his cane for silence, louder and louder with each strike. Frigg, standing on Thor's left, shook her head with disbelief at what she was witnessing.

"We need to go," someone said, not too far from me.

"Yes, after Father," said another.

"No, from Asgard," replied the first.

"Coward," said a woman, "we should get ready for war."

Their voices got lost in the maelstrom of Æsir and Vanir insulting each other. Thor, eyes shut as if it could keep the sound out, was crushing the throne's armrest. And then he could take it no more.

"Shut up!" he barked, springing to his feet. He never was a patient one, our god of thunder. It did the trick, though, and a heavy silence fell in Valaskjálf.

This situation was partly his fault, though.

I brought him the news of Odin's destination as soon as I left the prison. And since the gods never tarried far from the throne room since Heimdallr's death, my news had interrupted some useless talk and thrown the hall into chaos. This current situation was my doing, but Thor, by hesitating, had let it slip into the madness we currently bathed in. Thor had changed since Heimdallr's death, and not for the better, though Heimdallr's death mattered less to him than what it announced; Ragnarök and his own demise. When Gjallarhorn blew, the gods remembered their mortality and realized its imminence. They have behaved more like children than deities since.

"We stay and get ready for war," Thor finally said, raising a wall of complaints.

"You mean we just wait behind our wall," Freyja spat after Thor threatened the hall with Mjölnir.

"And what would you have us do, goddess of love?" Frigg asked with contempt.

"I would have us ready to win the war, not just wait with our belly exposed like beaten dogs, as your son suggests," Freyja replied, and that she said those things without getting much reaction from Thor showed how far he had slipped. "A great number of my people live in Vanaheimr; some Dwarves would fight as well, and—"

"Your people in Vanaheimr never recognized the truce," interrupted Frigg. "And not all of us have as great a relationship with the Dwarves as you do, Freyja." Once again, mocking laughter rose in the hall, for Freyja's *great relationship* with the Dwarves had been one of those bawdy stories told over and over again for the past centuries.

"Insult me once more, Frigg, and you'll have no Vanir to fight by your side at all," Freyja replied, a threatening finger pointed at the queen. Frigg's lips shut even tighter than usual, and it took Thor to gently grab her hand for the queen to relax a little. "Let's at least call for my brother," Freyja offered, using her small victory to express her one true desire.

Freyr was Freyja's twin and the only rival for Thor's might, or so they said. Self-exiled to his own realm, the Vanir had not been seen in Asgard for hundreds of years, shame keeping him away from judging eyes. I had briefly known him and even went to his realm with the Wolves once, ages ago. The Vanir prince and god of fertility was handsome beyond words and wielded a magnificent, *seidr*-filled sword. He lost the blade, and while I did not know all the details of this story, Freyr's shame weighed too heavy on his shoulders, and he left. A rival to Thor in our army would not only be a welcome addition, but it would also boost morale, something we direly needed.

"Would he come?" Bragi asked after using his staff to reclaim silence.

"With a bit of a push," Freyja answered. I knew her enough by now to hear doubt in her voice.

"I would not have any of us leave for a maybe," Thor said laconically. "Not when Ragnarök and the armies of Surtr could reach Asgard any day now."

Freyja slapped her thigh in frustration and looked the other way. I understood her. This was not the Thor we knew. For all his faults, we could have used the god of thunder right now but instead had to deal with his hesitating, trembling shell.

Thor had always been extravagant and uncaring. His strength had turned to arrogance, which in turn had made him a strong disbeliever of the prophecy. Thor could not imagine for one second that the great serpent could really kill him. He would be the victor of his fateful duel, and even if he were the last to stand, he would defeat Surtr, the Jötnar, and Hel's soldiers. There had been no doubt in his heart of hearts until Heimdallr's death.

For the first time in his life, Thor had to acknowledge the prophecy and recognize his mortality. *The bigger they are*, I could hear Cross-Eyes say in my mind.

"Let me go after Odin," I said over the din. "You won't lose an Æsir if I go."

Frigg meant to say something, but no words passed her lips. She would agree to send me after her husband, but the decision had to be Thor's. Answering for him now would wound his authority.

"Why?" Thor asked from the depth of this father's throne.

"I know the place. I've met Fenrir. If we need to go all the way to the Wolf King, he would be more welcoming to me than to anyone else here."

Tyr had the decency to look away as I spoke.

"Even after you had his father killed?" someone asked.

"Especially after I had his father killed," I replied.

"I meant, why would you go after Father by yourself?" Thor asked. For the first time in ages, I missed the real Thor.

"We need him," I replied. If Thor recognized the implied insult, he did not show it.

I had enough of those gods who behaved so genially when things went well but turned to children as soon as a threat knocked on their doors. No wonder Odin put his trust in Einherjar. At least you could find warriors with balls in our ranks. Of course, I could not tell them why *I* needed Odin.

He alone could save Muninn. She had planted seeds of doubt in my mind, and the vines sprouting from them were coiling around my heart. An echo of the life I dreamed with her passed behind my eyes, and though it would be short-lived, maybe she and I deserved it. I hated my weakness for her and could not think about Muninn with a clear, unbiased mind. I needed the All-Father to see the truth in her claims and deal with her.

"Odin left to face Fenrir," Thor said. "Fenrir is the beast fated to kill him. You know what it means."

"No, I don't. And neither do you." I replied. "I piss on the prophecy! It made you weak, all of you!" I was losing supporters here.

"What are you doing?" Huginn whispered.

"Be careful how you talk to me, boy," Thor said, grabbing the edge of the throne as if about to launch himself at me.

"Look at you, Thor Odinson," I said, pointing a finger at him with all the disgust he was inspiring me, "shaking like a maiden at the sound of boots on her doorstep. The Thor I knew would have been the first to go after his father. You would have grabbed him by his belt and dragged his ass back on the throne. You would have laughed at Ragnarök and put ease in our minds instead of sowing fear. Let me save your father, for clearly, you can't."

"And you can?" he asked, snorting with derision.

"He's proven capable," Freyja said.

Thor's tongue clicked in his mouth, and his eyes dropped. He was tempted. Frigg's hand fell on his shoulder, and the queen nodded to her son.

"What do you need?" she asked with the gentlest tone I ever heard coming from her mouth.

"My men," I replied instinctively, "as well as some volunteers. If anyone knows the path Odin took, this information would help as well. And, Queen Frigg, I would ask for a favor."

"Bring my husband back, and I will give you this very hall."

Frigg and Odin had bickered like an old couple for as long as I had known them, but their love shone like the Bifröst when faced with adversity.

"Keep Muninn alive," I said. A new raucous wave shook the hall, only finding an end when Frigg waved it down.

"You, more than anyone, should welcome her death," she said.

"My instinct tells me she might yet prove useful," I said.

Frigg watched me as if she could read my mind, but I kept a face of steel, determined to show nothing of my weakness. I was certain she knew; women sense those things, but she agreed nonetheless.

"Very well, you have my word."

Huginn sighed with relief.

"Drake," Thor said, speaking in his most commanding voice, "I hereby command you to go after my father and bring him back to Asgard. You may leave with my blessing."

Ass, I thought as I bowed. No one was fooled, but Thor needed a win. I would let him have it. That was probably the last time I would ever see him, after all.

I went immediately, slithering through the pack of gods and receiving a fair share of pats on the back. I left them to resume their endless discussion, knowing that when I came back—if I came back—nothing would have changed.

"Drake," Huginn called as we emerged from the back of the crowd and into the open. "I'm coming with you."

"You would go back to Jötunheimr?" I asked, surprised by his courage.

"You saved my sister and are putting your life on the line to rescue my father. Of course, I will go. Plus, if I had been strong enough, I could have simply flown back to Jötunheimr, and we wouldn't be in this mess."

I did not know what to expect of him once back in Jötunheimr, but there was no doubt he would be useful, if only by sensing his father.

"I will come too," Tyr said as he, too, cut his way out of the hall.

"I can't let you," I said. I did not want Tyr anywhere near Fenrir. Nothing good could come out of it. And if Ragnarök's shadow was really falling over Asgard, Tyr would be needed here.

"A one-arm Æsir won't change anything here," he replied when I told him so.

"I've seen you fight," I replied. "You can do more with one arm than most Æsir if they had three."

"Which is why you might need me," he said.

Fine, I thought. If he wanted to face his former lover and risk his ire, it was his choice. I had pampered enough gods for the day.

"And I know which path Odin used," he said, which is what he should have led with.

"Drake," someone called from the hall.

Can't a man simply walk toward his death in peace?

"Meet me by my hall when you're ready," Tyr said when Freyja climbed the few steps down to us. Then he and Huginn left me with the goddess of love.

"Freyja," I said, bowing my head. Loki had been taller than me, so looking at her from a lower height was like seeing another person.

"Iona will accompany you," she said.

"As I told Frigg, I will only take volunteers."

"Oh, she volunteers, don't worry. You've made an impact on more than just this goddess here," Freyja said with her most malicious smile. "Besides, you will do what I ask; you owe me as much."

"I owe you a thousand times over," I said. "But I doubt we will come back. You'd lose a precious Valkyrie."

"You will come back," she said. "I believe."

I wish I could have shared her faith. Part of me trusted the Norns to have more in store for me. The three crones had found an entertaining pawn and would use it until it broke, or so *I* believed. Yet even the gods' threads could be snapped, and my arrogance might be the end of me.

"When you do come back," she went on, "I will collect my debt and fulfill a promise." The last part she said with her finger on my chest, her beautiful nail tracing a line from my heart to my navel. I had not forgotten her promise, though I had expected she would. As far as I knew, Freyja had never taken any human into her bed.

"Oh," she said, surprised, "I see. You are already someone else's again. What a lucky little raven." Freyja's tone was mischievous, and I did not like that she could see so clearly into my heart when even I could not.

"When I am back, I will make sure you keep your promise," I said, trying my best to sound naughty.

"Drake," she called, serious and cold, "do not play with love."

I had not expected it, but in a split second, Freyja had gone from playing with me to frightening me. Her menacing aura vanished just as fast, and she was the playful goddess I had come to adore once more.

"But come back to me nonetheless," she whispered in my ear before kissing me on the cheek.

She left, leaving me dumbfounded.

When the goddess of love tells you this is what you feel for another, you have to believe her.

14

"I cannot reopen passages I have closed," Tyr said as more of our group gathered by the door of his hall. "Even for Father, it would be a tough job."

"So?" I asked.

"If he left the day before the *thing,* there are only a couple of bridges he could have used. I have closed the others before that. Of those few which remain open, I know only of one which might get him to Jötunheimr."

Tyr had dressed for war, wearing an attire I hadn't seen on him for ages. A mail shirt of dark iron, a helmet of the same color mounted by a horsetail of pure black, a cloak made from the pelt of a white bear, and boots of dark leather. A sword was attached to the stump of his missing arm with a custom-made harness, while in his hand Tyr held a small and sturdy shield painted black and white. Tyr was never the most impressive of his kind, but he impressed nonetheless.

"Might?" Gunhild asked.

"It is not a direct passage to Jötunheimr," Tyr replied, "those I have closed first."

"Where does this one lead?" Huginn asked.

"Nidavellir."

Bjorn, who was busy stretching his belt, immediately looked up at me and I at him, the two of us sharing the faces of children on the eve of Yule. It had been our long-shared dream to visit the Dwarves' realm. Bjorn, because those people were said to brew the best ale of the nine realms, and I because I adored their crafts and dreamt of seeing their smiths at work. Relations between Asgard and Nidavellir had halted shortly before I became an Einheri, and I had never even met a Dwarf.

"Why did you keep it for last?" Gunhild asked, not sounding too impressed by our destination.

Just then, from the corner of my eye, I saw Iona coming up the path leading to Tyr's hall, clad in a clean and unmarked set of gold and leather armor. She carried two quivers of white-feathered arrows, one on the back, the other hanging from the hip. She wore her long chestnut-colored hair in a loose plait, stretching her face to a more warrior-like appearance, which in no way impeded her beauty. She blushed when our eyes met, and I cursed fate for making me love Muninn rather than a woman such as Iona.

"Let's say I would have preferred not to close it at all," Tyr said without much confidence.

"Is it a big one or something?" Gunhild asked.

"It's not the bridge; it's its guardian," he admitted.

"Oh no," I said, understanding what he meant.

"What is it?" Bjorn asked.

"Skadi?" I asked.

"Skadi," Tyr confirmed.

"Oh no," Bjorn said.

All the major bridges and passages connecting Asgard to

other realms had designated guardians. Some gates, being rather small or remote, were put in the trust of a few Einherjar. But the big ones, those through which large creatures or groups of enemies could pass, were watched over by mighty guardians. Just as Heimdallr had been the protector of the Bifröst, so were other Æsir and friendly Jötnar put in charge of bridges. And then there was Skadi.

No one liked Skadi.

Skadi had lost her father to the wrath of the gods in a story involving Loki. As compensation, she had been allowed into Asgard and given her choice of husband among the main gods. While she had been madly in love with Baldur, she was tricked into choosing Njord, Freyja's father. The marriage did not work, and Njord fled back to his watery realm. Life had not been kind to Skadi, but according to anyone who knew the Jötunn from her young years, she had it coming.

Despite her husband's escape, Skadi remained in Asgard, forever hating Loki and lusting after Baldur, who only accepted the most beautiful creatures in his bed. No one knew what to do with Skadi. In the lucky years, she could be gone for months at a time. Otherwise, she was just a pain in everyone's backside. I had never heard her laugh unless it was at someone's expense. She was a pessimistic, bitter Jötunn, and it had not taken long for Odin to grow tired of her presence.

He put her in charge of a bridge and gave her a hall high in the mountain, where snow never melted and from which she needed a long time to come down. Then the All-Father ordered for one Einheri to always look up the path leading to her hall to warn the citadel whenever Skadi climbed down.

Bjorn's neck threatened to snap as he looked up the said path.

"I'd have kept it for last, too," he said.

But Tyr had not kept Skadi's gate for last because of the path. He'd done so because once the gate was closed, Skadi would return to the citadel, and no one, not even Skadi, would enjoy it.

As for myself, I had a score to settle with the Jötunn.

She had lost her father because of Loki, and then Loki had Baldur killed, two reasons for her to hate the now-dead god of mischief. When he had been caught, she had hunted the most vicious snake in the nine realms and had trapped it in the rock above Loki's face, from where its venom dripped. This gift of hers had made my life miserable for three years, and I could not wait to tell her what I thought of it.

We waited for the last three to join us, then took the first painful step of a journey hopefully leading us to the All-Father.

ᚱ

Heimdallr had once told me that the mountain at the center of the citadel was a root of Yggdrasil sprouting at an odd angle. As usual with the golden god, it was hard to tell if he'd been joking. Neither would have surprised me. But as I scraped my knee on the mountain's floor, it felt very much like rock to me. The loss of my Æsir friend was still fresh, though, and thinking of him brought so much sadness that I kept my curse inside.

"Getting too old for a stroll in the mountains?" Arn asked, offering his hand for me to get up.

"Getting old happens when one leaves the comfort of home," I replied as I accepted his offer.

"You stinky fart, you were old from the moment you were born. I'm sure your mother thought she gave birth to an old goat."

"Oh, is that why your mother took me to her bed when I was barely seven years old?" I asked, which made no sense, but it never really did when the two of us were together. He made one of his most ridiculous faces, as did Gunhild, who walked by us, and we laughed like I had not in ages.

Arn had a young face, despite being nearly as old as I was when he became an Einheri, with hair so blond it looked gray. He had never managed to grow a proper beard, so he kept it short. He stood an inch taller than me, something he was fond of reminding our audience. His jaw was strong, his nose straight, and he possessed deep, bracken-green eyes that could sway the hearts of women in seconds. Any weapon was deadly in his hands, even shields. But it was his optimistic spirit that I had missed the most and would need during this journey, for few of us had much to offer of that particular asset.

The last two warriors to join us also possessed a talent for foolish confidence, but such is the nature of the young, anyway.

Rune had insisted on joining the group, and Bjorn's nod got me to accept. That and the fact that we would be nine, and nine, as everyone knew, was a lucky number. I also hoped it would give me a chance to finally make sense of Rune and this unease he gave me, and me alone, apparently.

The last of us was Thrasir. The boy had not only volunteered but also been forced into the group per Frigg's order, though the directive was delivered through Lif's lips. I found it puzzling that Frigg required a specific Einheri to accompany us—we were all the same to her— but the gaze the boy and Lif exchanged explained it all.

Though he was born three or four years before Lif, she had grown while he had not, which put them in the same age range. As was bound to happen, the two teenagers had developed an attraction for each other. I wondered if Ulf knew of this and, if so, how he planned to kill Thrasir.

"Can he fight?" I asked Arn as Thrasir and Rune, the best of friends it seemed, walked by us. Thrasir did not lack courage, but of his skills, I knew little.

"He isn't a Wolf yet," my old friend said, "but he shows promise."

"We need more than potential this time," I said.

"Well, Frigg asked for him. So, it's not like we have a choice in the matter," he replied, a mocking smile on his lips.

"If you two maidens are done chatting," Bjorn said, closing the march and puffing like an old bull, "maybe we could go on with saving the nine realms." He was using the butt of his axe as a cane, and I wondered if maybe I should worry about my champion more than the young pup.

He was struggling with the path when it was just that, but when it turned to a proper climb, none of us fared much better. Tyr managed well for someone with only one arm, and Iona was light enough to ridicule us brutish warriors.

She was a warrior-Valkyrie, not a ghost one. She could shift as well, like those who chose the slain after the battles, but only for a brief moment. Her bowmanship, her beauty, and her athleticism had gained her access to Freyja's hall. But even she was red and sweaty by the time we reached Skadi's hall, where snow had given up the path at last. A sudden heat swarmed us as we entered the mountain. So much so that we had to remove our cloaks and pelts before we met the guardian.

"So many visitors recently," Skadi said without warmth.

She stood, arms crossed in front of a closed door, almost naked save for a thin dress of linen hanging from her shoulders. Skadi, like Eggther, was one of those Jötnar on the taller side, but contrary to the herder, she was not pretty. She reminded me of Gunhild. Their behavior also had a lot in common.

"So, Father passed by here?" Tyr asked.

"He did," Skadi replied. "Was in a hurry, so we didn't chat much. I hope you feel the same."

"Will you let us pass?" I asked, for I had expected some resistance.

"Why not?" Skadi replied. "Odin told me not to let anyone after him, but when have I ever listened to him? Do I know you?" she asked me.

"I'm Drake," I replied, wondering if it would be enough. It wasn't, and she shrugged. "I met your snake," I said, which finally got me some attention.

"In Loki's cave?"

"The very one. A mean old bastard you found. I even named it after you. I killed it. Well, technically, I got it killed," I said, enjoying the dozens of questions seemingly popping into her mind.

"What about Loki?" she asked.

"Him too, I got killed."

Skadi laughed, first with a short burst like a whip and then like long thunder, echoing between the corridors on each side of the entrance.

"You got to tell me everything."

"I thought you didn't feel like chatting," Huginn said, instantly killing the mood.

"Not with you, old crow, that's for sure," Skadi replied. "But you," she said, pointing a finger at me, "will tell me all on the way to the bridge. For this is why you came here as well, isn't it?"

"It is," I confirmed. "Shall we?"

Skadi did something that looked like a smile and stepped back into the corridor, where the temperature increased with each step.

I was no skald, but I had a very attentive auditor in Skadi. Surprisingly, I came to like the mean giantess. She laughed at Loki's end, seemed sorry for Sigyn, and spat on the floor when I mentioned Eggther. It was so hot by then that her saliva hissed where it landed.

We were walking down, of that I was certain, but for how long or deep I could not say. For all I know, we went below Asgard's floor. Whatever the case, we were sweating again by the time we reached the bridge, which turned out to be a pool of magma. Bubbles popped in a basin nearly as large as Bifröst had been. She seemed to enjoy the fear painting itself on most of our faces.

"Drake," Bjorn said, "are you sure?"

"As long as you avoid the edge of the pool, you're fine," Skadi replied, "and a small patch near the center. I don't know why, but it's just magma there."

Despite the heat, I felt a cold sweat running down my back.

"We don't have nails either," Rune said. "How do we come back?"

"Coming back?" Skadi replied after a snort. "Isn't he the optimistic one? You don't need a nail or anything with this bridge."

"And Huginn's feathers can do the trick as well," I said.

"They can?" Bjorn and Rune asked at the same time.

"Well, we think, but probably not for long, so don't start plucking him already."

Huginn sighed, but even he did not look extremely confident, his eyes lost in the burning pool as if he were staring at death itself. Odin had passed by here, though, and we had to do the same.

"Thank you," Tyr said dismissively, "for not making it more complicated."

"This one killed that piece of shit Loki; I owe him as much," Skadi said with a wink in my direction. "For the others, as a sign of gratitude, let's see—" She scanned our group as if judging how much silver she would ask for the passage. "I'll take this one for a night. If he comes back, of course."

She pointed at Rune, who looked mortified at what had been asked of him.

"Deal," I said before he could open his mouth. Thrasir patted his friend on the back, his lips twitching as he tried not to break into laughter.

Skadi, smiling, brought her fingers to her lips and whistled the way hunters do to call their hounds. The room shook, and the bubbles boiled at the center of the pool of magma. The bridge connecting Asgard to Nidavellir had been opened.

Tyr jumped and was sucked in as if it had been Bifröst. Huginn went next, eyes closed.

"Were you serious?" Rune asked. "I am to sleep with her?"

"Hey, you might even enjoy it," I said, though I highly doubted it, as he did, judging by his pout. He was probably the most eager to jump away from the place.

As I sometimes did with my men, I put my hand on Iona's back to put a bit of pressure before the jump and felt her tremble under her lamellar. This was, I realized, the first time she'd ever left Asgard.

"The crossing is fun," I told her, "I promise." I meant my most reassuring smile for her, but I guess I failed, for she did not reply in kind. She still jumped without much hesitation.

"Don't play the shiny protector with her," Gunhild said as she took the Valkyrie's place. "She doesn't need that, and that's not what she wants from you."

"Have you always been such a pain in the ass?" I was reaching the end of my patience with Gunhild. She looked as if she was giving it an actual thought.

"As a human, I was actually fun," she replied.

"Let's work on that when we come back, all right?"

I was last and about to follow the others when Skadi dropped her hand on my shoulder quite gently, I must say.

"No need to be a seer to know that not all of you will return," she said. She looked concerned. "If any of you even do."

"We've got to try," I replied.

Skadi grunted, though I don't know if it was in agreement or the opposite.

"Odin wasn't himself," she said. "Maybe he never will be again. So don't sacrifice any of them for the old goat, all right? As Odin was when he came here, you nine are more useful to us than the All-Father."

"I will keep it in mind."

"No, you won't. Not until it's too late. But at least I warned you."

I did not thank her; Rune would do it for me. Instead, I jumped after the group, leaving Skadi to her hall in the mountain and Asgard to its problems.

"Aye, I remember the Dwarves. They used to come often, and Valhöll was all the merrier for their presence. A bunch of champions won some Dwarven stuff when a delegation witnessed the brawl. Then they'd lose it at some stupid game, but at least we had some new asset to bargain with. I wonder how many Einherjar from that time still remain on Asgard?"

Frode Goose-feet, square thirty-eight.

15

Living on Asgard was an endless source of disappointment. Folks grow on Midgard with stories of the gods to fill their imaginations with wonders. The reality was far less legend-worthy. Gods occasionally farted; they puked when they drank too much and suffered the next day. Their halls could smell as bad as a farmer's hut, and Asgard also had its issues, like bugs and storms, only much bigger ones. When Einherjar learned the truth, the gods lost some of their brilliance; it was inevitable.

But Nidavellir was everything I expected of it and more.

I emerged from the pool as if it spat me out and landed flat on my back. The bubbles of the bridge immediately lessened. When I managed to open my eyes, they were filled with one of the greatest sights I had ever seen.

A city, just like in my dreams, dug inside the rock, with hundreds upon hundreds of small troglodytic houses mounting each other in rows. The sky was an arched vault of rock, ending at its center with a hive-like structure where hundreds of torches and mirrors reflected a warm light throughout the city. There would be no night or day in here, and Dwarves could mine and forge without interruption. Until, of course, nine people came out of their pool of magma.

Small rivulets branched from the pool to the rest of the city, carrying the lava to the workshops needing its heat. The whole cavernous city was bathed in orange and gold from the fires and metal marring it. It smelled like copper and earth. I loved Nidavellir from the moment I breathed my first breath of its air.

The guards who encircled us, I did not like as much.

"He said no one else would bother us," a burly Dwarf spat in an accent so thick I could have cut through it with a spoon. He was clad in heavy pieces of iron, but even those were decorated with intricate shapes and stones. His squared helmet looked ridiculously heavy, as did his spear and his shield.

"I guess you are talking of Odin," Tyr replied, his arm and blade up. Bjorn helped me to my feet as the circle of soldiers tightened.

"Aye, I speak of Grimnir. Who else?" the Dwarf said. Now standing, I realized that Dwarves were not nearly as short as legends made them unless their soldiers were chosen by height. Those walking toward us stood half a head shorter than me, and their shoulders were much wider. I saw some people hiding in the closest buildings, their curiosity strong enough for a head to pop through a door frame or window, but no more.

"We're after him," Tyr said.

"You're out of luck then. Grimnir's gone," the captain of the guards said.

"If you could be kind enough to take me to the bridge he used, Atvardr, we will be gone as well," Tyr said, using his most diplomatic tone. The guards were so close to us now that I could see myself in the spearhead pointed at my throat. I could barely see his eyes under his helmet, nor his lips, lost inside a shaggy red beard, but the bynamed Atvardr was not smiling, of this I was certain.

"Oh, you remember my name?" the captain said ironically. "That's so fucktasticly nice of you, my dear Ernozes."

Arn mouthed the name we had just heard, a frown marking his question. I had no reply, for I had never heard the name Ernozes before. It could have been a Dwarven sobriquet for Tyr or the Æsir, but it meant nothing to me.

"I do remember your name and your mother as well, who I saved from a wyrm when your people still lived in Austri. Surely you've heard the story, captain?"

Atvardr did not reply as fast this time. His bulbous nose wrinkled as he pondered on what to do, but we all knew where this was leading.

"Aye, well, not like I can just behead the lot of you here anyway. Let's go see lord Eitri. He'll decide your fate."

"Lord Eitri?" Tyr asked just as Atvardr was about to turn around. "Brokkr doesn't lead here?"

"Only an Ernozes would assume things don't change in five hundred years," Atvadr said as he forced a passage between his men. I received a shove in the back, and like cattle, we were driven from the square and into the streets.

I would have liked to join Tyr, who walked in front of us, but the guards were keeping us lined in twos and made it clear we were not to move in any weird way.

I knew of the two names, Eitri and Brokkr, the legendary brothers.

Eons ago, Dwarves had been at war with each other over the quality of their crafts, each clan or tribe claiming its superiority. They had sought the Æsir, then all glorious and powerful, to judge once and for all who among them had the greatest skills. The Æsir had won much during the competition. Thor had received Mjölnir, Odin the spear Gungnir, Freyr, a magic ship called Skidbladnir, and many other treasures without equal. Brokkr, king of Sudri, and his brother Eitri had been declared victors and enjoyed fame over any other smith in the nine realms.

This was before most of the said treasures turned out to malfunction. Odin, for example, had received a golden ring named Draupnir, which could multiply by nine every night. On the second day, Odin realized that while the ring did produce nine more, the nine from the previous day vanished every time, making it a near-useless piece of junk. Soon after, relations between Asgard and Nidavellir had stopped.

The noise of hammers hitting anvils rang around us again as life resumed its course in the mountain city of Surdi. Smitheries of all sizes lined both sides of the main street, outnumbered only by drinking establishments and breweries. The smell of fermenting ale, melting iron, and sweat mixed in this world of workers and craftsmen. This was a place I would have loved to linger in. Every shop displayed tools and weapons, the likes of which had become rare on Asgard.

"Look ahead," spat the Dwarf on my right. Their steps were heavy and marked our tempo with an alarming regularity. Titus would have loved to see the synchronism of those soldiers.

"Can I ask you," I said, "what's Ernozes?"

I heard the Dwarves in front and behind giggle, but the one I asked the question to simply grunted.

"That's an Ernozes," he said, pointing at Tyr. "And this one, too," he then said, moving his gloved finger to Huginn.

"Is it how you say Æsir in your language?" I asked, and

this time, even my surly new friend could not suppress a laughing snort.

"That's from *your* language," he said.

"No, it's not," I replied.

The Dwarf sighed. The one behind him said something in their language, of which I knew nothing. I guess he said something like, "Just tell him," for the Dwarf explained himself.

"They're so arrogant that we always see up *their noses*. Ernozes, get it?"

The other Dwarves boomed with laughter, and some of us did too.

"What do you call the Vanir, then?" Bjorn asked. "Erasses?"

"Hey, the big man is cleverer than he looks," the Dwarf on Bjorn's left said.

"Aye, that's what we call them because if they want anything else from us, they can shove it up—"

"We get it," I said, for Iona and Gunhild loved Freyja, and I wanted no bouts of violence before we had the chance to meet the king of the mountain.

"Don't want to know what you name us folks from Midgard," Arn said.

"We don't have a name for you," the one on my right said. "Not worth the hassle."

Dwarves, it seemed, also had their fair share of assholes.

The farther we went, the bigger the shops and houses appeared to be. And after another minute of walking, they were the size of a respectable longhouse on Midgard. The inhabitants did not change, though. Nothing marked them as richer in their attire. They looked just as strong, proud, and tired as their counterparts from the square, and I assumed it must have been the same in whatever passed for the lower town here.

"Are you sure you're not half-Dwarf yourself," the one on the left asked Bjorn, who indeed shared a lot with those men, especially now that his hips' width matched his shoulders.

"Only if one of you plowed a Jötunn," Bjorn replied. "I am three heads taller than any of you."

"No, my friend," the Dwarf replied, "you are three heads farther from the ground, and I don't envy you."

"That was a smart answer," Bjorn said, dropping his hand on the shoulder of the Dwarf. "I might be half-Dwarf after all. And I'd drink to that if I had something to drink."

His new friend knew where this was going. He removed a flask from his belt and handed it to Bjorn. My champion didn't need to be asked. He uncorked the thing and downed some of its content in a series of loud gulps, then smacked his lips even louder.

"The legends are true! Gods be blessed. Sorry, I meant, Ernozes be blessed!"

Even the bitter Dwarf on my side laughed at that, and I was left to wonder at how easily Bjorn befriended people anywhere we went. He meant to give the flask back to its owner, but the soldier invited the beverage to be shared, and I came next. It was, I must admit, the greatest ale that ever passed my lips. Ernozes be blessed indeed.

The cohesion of the soldiers slowly faded. By the time we reached the king's hall, the back of the line looked more like a group of farmers coming back from the field than a serious procession of guards and captives.

To call it a hall would be generous. Eitri lived in the last of the long series of buildings, and it was even smaller than some of the houses we passed by. It faced the same direction as the others on this side of the street. Its door, while slightly larger than any we had seen so far, was neither richly adorned nor made of a particular alloy, just a plain piece of redwood. It was a regular Dwarf's big house, and that was it.

"I like them," Bjorn said as we entered, leaving most of the guards outside.

"Me too."

After the pomp of the Æsir and their perpetual quest for grandeur, the Dwarves' simplicity and brutish pride were refreshing. This impression did not diminish when we were introduced to the king of Sudri, Eitri, the greatest smith of the nine realms.

The throne room was a large guest room, with half its walls covered in bookshelves. A wide table of rock stood in the middle, with countless cups and tankards scattered on it, some of them used to keep the corners of parchments from coiling back into tubes. And on the other side of the table, leaning over a paper with runes and sketches, stood Eitri. The interruption of a dozen of his guards and nine other people did not take him from his document. The Dwarf next to him tapped the king on the arm, and finally, Eitri noticed us.

"Tyr!" Eitri called, opening his arms as he rushed around the table.

Eitri was leaner than his soldiers. His hair and beard were gray, with some red strands resisting here and there. He was dressed simply in wool and linen, though some golden threads formed runes over his chest and shoulders. He still wore an apron over his chest, a filthy, soot-stained piece of leather worn beyond the point of washable. Tyr did not look surprised when he received the king's embrace and did his best to return the gesture.

"I knew Odin was lying," Eitri said with a wink and a

finger pointed at Tyr. "Of course, more of you would show up."

"He didn't know we would," Tyr replied.

"Huggin, my friend, it has been too long," Eitri went on, paying no attention to Tyr's words.

"It has, Eitri," Huginn said, offering one of his rare genuine smiles. And just as with Tyr, the raven was pulled into a bear hug. "Will you forgive our intrusion, Forge-King?"

"Intrusion?" Eitri asked, rocking his body back as if he'd been hit. "You are my guests and have always been! Not my fault you people can't take a joke and decided to sever ties."

"It's not the impression we received," Gunhild said with one of her signature stares for Atvardr.

"You're a woman!" Eitri said, slapping his thigh. "Would never have guessed. Don't look at me like this, lass; I meant it as a compliment. Well, you'll have to forgive Atvardr; he was born under the sky. It doesn't make well-mannered Dwarves."

"Or anything else," Atvardr replied.

"Atvardr, *zöndöö garaad bidniig alei!*" the king snapped in his language. It must have meant that the captain was to get out, for the Dwarf left us immediately, and it must have been less polite than that, for he did so with a fair share of grunts.

"Sorry about that," Eitri said. "We don't keep a great memory of our dealings with your people. But sit, sit, all of you."

The king pulled on a chair and invited Tyr to take it while we spread around the table and occupied most of the empty chairs. Three other Dwarves were already seated and far advanced in their drinking, judging by the rings of ale on the rock.

The one on my right offered me a bear paw of a hand to shake and gave me a warrior's nod when I accepted the honor. He had bushy eyebrows and a mustache to sweep the floor with. Dwarves were more recognized for their crafts than their soldiery, but this one nearly crushed my hand, and I could only imagine what an army of people like him could do on a battlefield. The one on his right was even more impressive.

I shifted Crimson as I rearranged myself on the chair, and my neighbor's eyes squinted at the sight of the blade. He could only see the handle and guard, for the rest was hidden in a scabbard of leather given to me by Freyja, but what he saw seemed to please him. He nodded once more and held his thumb up in approval.

A group of female Dwarves stormed the room, arms filled with tankards and platters of smoking meat. Once again, the legends proved wrong. Female Dwarves were far prettier than I had heard. In fact, besides their strong jaws and thick fingers, they would pass for beauties on Midgard. They dropped food and drinks on the table and kept chatting without care. I barely received a glance, but Bjorn was honored with a pat on the back from the oldest of the lot. Had he not been so enthralled by what they had brought, he would have paid more attention to those ladies.

I banged my tankard with my neighbor's, and we proceeded to a long and appreciative gulp of this sweet ale. It tasted like honey and something I did not know but loved. I later learned from Huginn that it was a root that grew only under certain soil and was said to make a man hard for hours if consumed in enough quantity. My new friend drank for longer than me, but as he did, he never left Crimson from his sight.

"Thank you for your hospitality, King Eitri," Tyr said on the other side of the table from me. Eitri waved it off.

"If you don't mind me asking, what happened to Brokkr? I thought he was the king here," Huginn asked. My friend had used his crow mouth the wrong way once again, and the mood soured in a heartbeat. The Dwarves looked at each other with an expression suggesting how unfortunate the question had been, but Huginn did not seem to notice. Eitri stared down his tankard.

"My brother's dead," he replied, his voice breaking with sorrow.

"My condolences," Tyr said, dropping his hand on the king's shoulder.

"Aye, well, it has been so for a very long time," Eitri said before lifting his tankard and swallowing its content in one long series of gulps. Tyr filled it up again. I thought the point would be abandoned, but the king himself told the story.

Brokkr was the older brother, but Eitri was the most talented. He could carve runes of power in blades and enchant them like no other smith, while Brokkr was left to man the bellow.

"Keeping the fire going," Eitri explained, "is more difficult than it looks. And the more complicated the blade, the more precise the temperature needs to be. Doesn't sound much, but Brokkr was a genius in that regard. Nevertheless, after we won that contest on Asgard, folks and kings came every day, asking for such and such weapons and items to be forged. They spent fortunes they barely had on something made by *Eitri*. Brokkr was the king, but they came for me, his little brother."

His name traveled far and wide among their people, while Brokkr was but a footnote in Eitri's fame. The kind and big brother's pride was wounded beyond healing, and Brokkr grew jealous of his talented sibling.

"I paid skalds to sing his praises. I told him many times over that without him, I could not forge as I did. But it only made it worse," Eitri said, his eyes watering as he spoke. "Oh, Brokkr tried to forge some blades, and they were magnificent, let me tell you that. They just had no magic in them. And then, one day, he had enough and left. No explanation, no nothing, he just left. I guess he wanted to do something worthy of the legends, but we never heard from him."

"I am truly sorry, my friend," Tyr said. "Brokkr was a great king."

"I waited for twelve years," Eitri went on, "but our people need a leader, so I took the throne I do not deserve."

"How do you know he's dead?" Rune asked. I had forgotten that the young Wolf, just like Huginn, had a talent for speaking out of turn.

Eitri lifted his head and noticed Rune, probably for the first time. He wiped his tears with the back of his sleeve and replied.

"It was 'bout four hundred years ago, lad, so by now, we would have heard," Eitri said without any animosity. "But enough of these sad talks; we have a friendship to renew," he continued, exorcising the mood with his jolliness.

"That would be with pleasure, Forge-King, but we cannot stay long, as you know," Tyr said.

"You shouldn't go after your father," Eitri replied. "You won't come back, not without sacrificing too much in the process. And seeing how Odin was, I don't believe any sacrifice would be worth it."

"Someone else said the same, back in Asgard," I said, thinking of Skadi. "Tell us, Forge-King, how was Odin?"

Eitri stared back at me, his gentle eyes turning sharp as he weighed me.

"Your father wasn't himself." I didn't know if he meant All-Father or if he confused me for an Æsir, but I was more intrigued by what he meant. "He sounded desperate to go after Fenrir as if the idea was the only thing making sense to him. We tried to dissuade him," Eitri went on, opening his hands toward his counselors, who nodded as a sign they had indeed tried to resonate with Odin. "But he barely listened. He kept rambling about ending Ragnarök before it happened and making things right. I understood less than half of what he said. It's like he was speaking to himself. But Odin is Odin, and I am no Dwarf to keep a man from his destiny."

"And he paid a good price," one of the counselors said.

"That he did," Eitri said.

"What did he pay?" Thrasir asked in all seriousness.

"Let me show you," the king replied, an eye half-closed mischievously. "*Khüüye, jadyg avchir!*"

One of the two guards standing behind the king's throne left the room and came back a few seconds later, accompanied by another, for two of them were needed to carry their load. I don't know what I had expected, but certainly not that.

Tyr stood up from his chair, horrified, and Huginn paled when the two guards dropped Gungnir on the table. The spear was so heavy that it knocked an empty pitcher simply by bouncing on the flat rock.

"Father went to fight Fenrir without Gungnir?" Tyr asked, his voice betraying his growing fear.

Gungnir was, by far, Odin's greatest weapon. It was famed for never missing its target, and in the All-Father's hand, it could pierce any shield or armor.

"I didn't ask for it," Eitri replied in defense.

"But you accepted it," Tyr said, accusingly.

"And what was I supposed to do, just let him pass without any form of payment? Do you know what my people would have said?" Eitri asked, his voice growing in authority as he spoke. "If Odin was stupid enough to go after the beast without Gungnir, that's his problem. Better for us to keep the spear than let it rot in Fenrir's lair."

I thought Tyr might well break any sign of diplomacy here and jump at the king's throat. Any other Æsir would have acted so.

"How about us?" Arn asked.

"What about you?" Eitri asked, struggling with his temper as well.

"What do we pay for our passage?" my friend asked, which was the only sensible question.

Eitri sat back in his chair, puffing, and I could almost hear the gears in his brain as he tried to resume his previous friendliness. Arn had been smart. Bickering would only slow our progress or even halt it.

"Odin gave a treasure of Dvalin for the right to use our bridge to Jötunheimr," Eitri said. "You don't have anything of the same value, and you are nine." He picked his chin between two fingers, assuming the look of a merchant calculating his price. There was a tense silence as the king pondered, interrupted by the mastication of the few among us still eating.

"I know," Eitri said, clapping his hands victoriously, "let's make a game of it. I've got three counselors here. Each will challenge you to something. For each victor, three of you can pass the bridge. Deal?"

"We don't have time for this kind of thing," Tyr said, his patience completely depleted by then.

"In that case, be my guest and jump back in the pool of magma," Eitri replied, waving in the direction of the bridge. Tyr had used up all the king's good grace, it seemed.

"What's your first challenge?" I asked.

Eitri opened his hand toward the first counselor on his left, inviting him to speak. The Dwarf stood, though it barely changed its height, for he was rather short. He wore a piece of round glass on his right eye, linked to a pocket on his shirt by a small golden chain, and on his wrist rested another disk, of metal this time, mounted by a thin needle of copper. He was more of an intellectual, I thought, and his challenge proved it.

"Hum, hum, a riddle. You will answer my riddle," the Dwarf said as he searched the inside of his shirt. He bore almost no accent and spoke fluidly as if our language was as natural to him as the Dwarven one. "You can only give one answer, and you will do so in less than a minute." He dropped a small item with two glass compartments, the bottom one half-filled with sand. He then removed his eyeglass, the needle ring, and three more items of the kind, which he lined up in front of him.

A riddle, I thought, was so typical of legends involving Dwarves and Elves. If we had not been on the hunt for a mad Æsir, I would have enjoyed the moment greatly, though, in truth, I have always been terrible with riddles. I wished Snekke or Karl had been here, for this was more their specialty.

"I have something here," the Dwarf said, showing the objects in front of him, "that belongs to me but that everyone else uses. What is it? You have one minute." He flipped the item with the sand over, and the grains went from the first compartment to the next.

I took a quick look at Eitri, who did a poor job of

masking his grin behind his curled-up fingers. The rest of us looked miserable, eyes focused on the five items as if we could read the answer. The object he had just used was an instrument to measure the time; this was clear, and I could not imagine everyone using it. The glass he had removed from his eye was some sort of magnifier, I assumed, and as such, was tailored for this Dwarf alone. That wasn't it.

Bjorn was making the sound of a purring cat as he forced his brain to more activity than it was used to, which only made things worse for me. I was about to curse him and his mother, but a look at the sand showed that more than half of the minute had passed.

A fat pearl of sweat ran down my neck as I tried to make sense of what I was looking at. All those things were complex, probably made by the Dwarf himself, and he had taken them out of his shirt or from his face. None of it would be used regularly by everyone.

I swallowed hard as my focus went from thinking to observing the sand vanishing from the upper compartment. I could not find the answer; of this I was certain, and our allocated time turned to a few grains.

"Your name!" a voice blurted. The last grains disappeared. "It's your name," Iona repeated, breathless as if she had fought a battle.

We all looked at the Dwarf, for as soon as it was said, it made complete sense.

He picked up the round piece of glass and put it back on his eye. His whole body then shook with a wave of silent laughter.

"The young lady is right," he said. "It was my name."

We sat back collectively, sighing heavily and going back to our tankards, for our mouths were dry. Rune dropped his hand on Iona's arm in congratulation, and for some reason, I felt a hint of jealousy.

"That wasn't your toughest," Eitr told his counselor, seemingly as happy as we were.

"It's not a challenge if it's impossible," the first counselor replied.

"My turn!" the second counselor said, standing up abruptly.

A tall one, with a chest like an oak trunk and arms thick as my thighs sprouting from a sleeveless wool shirt. He was the complete opposite of the first, and I assumed one was in charge of administration while the next led the army. His skin hinted toward a yellowish tone like some old butter, and his hair was long, black, and tied in a bun, while his beard was straight and well-oiled.

"What's your challenge?" Eitri asked, amusing himself.

"Not a riddle," the Dwarf replied, butchering our language with his accent. "Arm fight," he then said, crooking his right arm and making the bicep bulge to a most impressive size.

"He means arm wrestling," the first counselor said.

"Who do you challenge?" the king asked. Bjorn and Arn shuffled on their chairs, their interest rising fast.

"Fate decides," the warrior Dwarf replied.

"All right," Huginn said, "and how do we do that?"

"Like this," I said, standing up. Wedge was in my hand, and I dropped it flat on the table. We would spin my knife, and whoever it pointed to would answer the challenge. "Agreed?" I asked.

While it seemed fair in appearance, I did not want to let fate meddle with this one; too much was at stake. I knew Wedge as if it were a part of my arm, and I was fairly certain I could more or less spin it to land near Tyr. While being one-armed, Tyr would break the Dwarf in a second. And if I missed, it would point at his neighbor, Huginn, who, though probably weaker than Tyr, was also an Æsir and could summon incredible strength when needed.

"*Khar chuluu!*" the Dwarf said when he saw my knife. "That's good blade." He held his thumb up and gave me an appreciative smile. "Agreed."

I dropped my hand on the handle of Wedge, ready to make it spin, but the warrior Dwarf leaned over the table and caught my wrist with astonishing speed. "Not you," he said before grabbing my knife and bringing it back to his spot. Fate had not liked my idea, it seemed.

Wedge spun on itself longer than I would have made it. The tip slowed down and passed in front of Tyr, Huginn, the king, and then the three counselors. It rocked a little as it passed in front of me and almost completely halted its course in front of Arn, who sucked his breath in. And finally, just as I worried that it might continue all the way to Thrasir, the knife became still, its tip pointing at Bjorn's heart.

"All right!" my champion yelled as he slapped the table with both hands.

I would have preferred Eigil to be here. In terms of brutish strength, he was a notch above Bjorn. In fact, arm wrestling was the only form of competition where Eigil shined. Magnus Stone-fists would also make a better adversary for the Dwarf. But as it was, Bjorn was a great asset, and I wondered who Titus would have bet on. My silver was on Bjorn, for it never paid to bet against our champion.

A smaller round table was carried next to the big one, and the two challengers dragged their chairs as supporters took their spots in a crude circle. Bjorn only had eyes for the Dwarf, who rolled his shoulder a couple of times before taking his seat. I lost a bit of my confidence when I saw the sinew of his well-carved muscles working together while Bjorn's arm looked soft and meaty.

My champion dropped his elbow on the table and gripped its edge with his left hand, fire in his eyes, teeth gritted.

"This is Nidavellir; we don't do like that," the Dwarf said before extending his left arm. It got us confused. What kind of arm wrestling was that?

Then the Dwarf who had been seated on my side put a tankard, three-quarter full, in the empty hand. "This is how we do," the Dwarf said with a grin of satisfaction.

Bjorn looked at me with an expression of amusement mixed with horror, for he could imagine the difficulty of the task.

"If you drop some ale, you lose. If you bend your extended arm, you lose," the king said. "And, of course, if your right hand touches the table, you lose."

Bjorn had the advantage in size, his longer arm being a great tool in such a competition, but the Dwarf was strong and used to this particular bout. I grew worried and excited at the same time. For a second, I even forgot why we were here in the first place.

They grabbed each other's hand and locked the position like statues. A tankard was given to Bjorn, who extended his left arm as well. He gave no clue as to how he felt about it.

The king put his hands on theirs. The two competitors nodded. Then Eitri yelled, "Begin," like a whip.

The table creaked pitifully as the two wrestlers grunted like cows giving birth. They barely moved, which was a testament to their strength, but the liquid in the two tankards swayed dangerously. None was spilled, and both left arms remained locked straight.

Bjorn's face reddened. A vein turned purple and thick on his temple. The Dwarf, whose name was Horr, judging by his comrades' cheers, maintained a peaceful face. I prayed for it to be an act. Ten long, nerve-wracking seconds later, my prayer was answered, and he, too, shifted to a different color.

Horr's bicep became so round that you could bounce a piece of silver off it, and his shoulder worked so hard that it looked as if a beast had used its claws on it. But Bjorn surprised me even more, for under the layer of fat, angry muscles trembled. With a vengeance, those arms that had been put to sleep for too long bulged and thickened.

Bjorn rocked his chest and shoulder as if pumping air into the bellow. It gave him a bit of power over the Dwarf, but it also threatened the tankard's balance. He stopped acting so but had gotten the upper hand. It might have been my imagination, but I saw Horr's hand going down very slowly.

Usually, during such an event, people shout, names are called, and mothers insulted, but this time, we were silent. It was a great contest of strength, and fate could not have picked two better opponents.

The Dwarf grunted and puffed. I could count his teeth. His face turned from red to purple, his tankard was shaking, and just as I thought that it might have been an act, Horr spat a "bastard" through his teeth. Bjorn heard and knew he was winning. He moaned with one more effort, making the veins on his arm pop dangerously. Horr's jaws finally unlocked as he yelled with all his might, but nothing declared a winner more than this action.

Bjorn banged Horr's hand on the table, forcing his arm to an odd angle and making the Dwarf swear in his language. My champion stood and yelled as well, though in victory.

"Who's fat now?" he asked no one in particular.

"You're still fat," Arn said as he patted Bjorn's shoulder, "but you're gods damn strong as well."

"That was fantastic," Bjorn told Horr, his right hand now opened for the Dwarf to shake, which he did.

"Aye, you're great strong man for a folk. But I lost because I did not want to spill this," Horr said, showing us his intact tankard. They banged cups and emptied them in what could pass for another competition of who would finish first. It was a tie. Lips smacking, they fell into an infectious laughter.

Receiving their fair shares of pats and praises, the two wrestlers went back to their seats at the big table, and I smiled when I saw Bjorn massaging his wrist. He tilted his head when he saw that I saw. It had been more difficult than it looked.

"What is your third challenge?" Huginn asked.

The king wiped a tear of laughter away and invited his third counselor to speak. The Dwarf on my right was the oldest of the group, and I did not know what his role was among his people. If I had to guess, I would say he had been a minister of Eitri's father. He looked like a veteran of many wars but also like someone who had hung his axe a long time ago, trading it for food and comfort. And as with all those who survived a lifetime of battlefields, his eyes brimmed with cunningness.

"*Nadad yamar ch sorilt baikhgüim,*" he said in a voice that came from the depth of the earth. "*Bi yamar neg züil khüsch baina.*"

"*Naiz mini, chi yuu khüsch baina?*" the king asked with obvious respect.

The Dwarf made a long hum from the back of his throat and passed his fingers through his venerable beard.

"*Bi üügeer togloom khiikh bolno,*" the Dwarf said.

"What is it?" Gunhild asked.

"Master Fullangr said he wants no challenge; he wants something from you," the first counselor said.

"What does he want," Gunhild asked.

"This was the king's question as well," the Dwarf replied. "He said that he will make a game of it."

Fullangr, who had been waiting for his peer to finish, then said, "*Bi yamar neg züil asuukh bolno, ta tatgalzaj bolno.*"

"He will ask something; you can refuse."

"*Bi öör züil asuukh bolno, ta tatgalzaj bolno,*" Fullangr said before inviting his comrade to translate.

"He will ask something else, and you can refuse."

"*Gekhdee gurav dakhi udaagaa ta tatgalzaj chadakhgüi.*"

"But the third time, you cannot refuse."

"Agreed?" Fullangr asked in our language, though I could barely make out the word.

"I must warn you," the king said, "Master Fullangr is famously greedy. You have already won passage for six people; you might want to stop there."

"Let's hear what he asks first," Huginn said, though I had an idea what the old Dwarf would ask. Eitri opened his hand in an invitation for Fullangr to make his first request. If I were right, the Dwarf would make two outrageous demands before asking for the one thing he really wanted.

"*Bi üügeeree nyalkh khüükhedtei bolmoor baina,*" he said, his finger pointed at Gunhild. Horr splattered his ale and Eitri almost choked on his.

"What did he say?" Gunhild asked.

"He said—" the adviser replied with some hesitation. "He said he wants to make babies with you."

"What?!" Gunild barked as she hammered the table with her fist. "I'd rather die than sleep with this filthy piece of shit." Gunhild was never one to mince words or for diplomacy, but even for her, this was an extreme reaction, and I was afraid the old Dwarf might have understood the latter part.

"*Nadad taashaal khamaagüi,*" Fullangr said, "*Bi zügeer l tüüntei khamt khövgüüd khüsdeg. Ted gaikhaltai baikh bolno.*"

"He said he doesn't care about the pleasure of it. He just wants sons with you, for they would be amazing," the adviser translated.

"He isn't wrong," Rune said half-seriously.

"Oh, you shut up," Gunhild told the young man. "Drake, don't think for one second I will accept this."

I don't know why she said so to me; I wasn't the leader of our group. But I agreed with her. That Rune would become Skadi's toy for a night was one thing, but to let Gunhild be used this way was out of the question. Of course, Fullangr had expected this reaction, which is why he took no offense and barely reacted.

"And if he asks the same of Iona, I will shove his balls down his throat, you translate that," Gunhild said before she emptied the content of her cup angrily.

I guessed the adviser did translate accurately, for Fullangr giggled halfway through.

"*Ene tokhi,*" he said. "*Bi Tiriin garyg khüsch baina.*" This time, he nodded toward Tyr, and I truly hoped he had not just asked the same of the Æsir.

"Out of the question!" Huginn said, standing as if he had been insulted. I did not know he could understand their language.

"What is it?" I asked.

"He wants Tyr's second arm," Huginn replied, and

judging by his lack of reaction, Tyr had understood and expected something of the sort.

"*Bi Fyenrirtei tentsekh bolno,*" Fullangr said.

"Equal to Fenrir, my ass," Huginn whispered.

Tyr put his hand on the raven's arm, inviting him to calm down with a gentle shush.

"Of course, I refuse," Tyr said. "Now, Master Fullangr, tell us what you *really* want."

Fullangr flashed a malevolent grin. He, too, stood, dragging his chair backward in a long and painful wince.

"I want this," he said, pointing at my hip.

I had been right; all Fullangr had thought about since we had entered the room was Crimson.

The king frowned as he tried to look in the direction of his adviser's finger, as did the others, so I spared them. I unsheathed the sword and laid it flat on the table, pointing at myself.

"Ymir's balls," Eitri said. He left his chair and hurried toward us, his face paling with each step as if he were in the presence of a ghost, which turned out to be the case partially.

"*Id-shidgüi,*" he said when he shoved the old Dwarf away and picked up the blade. "Impossible."

Eitri's eyes scanned the sword up and down and up again, tracing the few lines of artwork on it with his finger. As if caressing a beautiful woman, the king took his time, letting the light from the torches embrace the metal and reveal its shape.

"Where did you get this?" Eitri asked me. There was no trace of the genial king in his voice. I had guessed Fullangr's will, but not this kind of reaction, and judging by his glances to the king, the old counselor was just as surprised.

"In Jötunheimr," I said, "at the center of Ironwood."

"So this is where he went," Eitri whispered.

"Forge-King?" I asked.

"This," he said, shaking the blade with its tip up, "is *Idshidgüi*, the last and greatest sword forged by Brokkr, my brother. Her name means *Without Magic*."

I guessed the rest of the story. Brokkr had poured his soul into this sword but had not managed to birth magic into it. Frustrated, he had left to accomplish a feat worthy of the legends and had chosen Fenrir as his mission. He failed, and Fenrir, Eggther, or something else killed the Dwarf, leaving his blade in the care of the Jötunn. A few hundred years later, the blade had found me and a way back home.

"What will you do with it?" the king asked as he handed the sword back to me.

"You do not ask for it?" I replied. This was his dead brother's masterpiece, and though I had come to adore it, Eitri had a blood claim to Crimson.

"Swords and Axes are above the law," Eitri said. "They choose their masters as much as we chose them."

I liked this idea, and it made me hesitant. I looked at the men and women around the table, wondering if Crimson was worth leaving three of them behind and which three. Among the eight of them, only Thrasir's value was unknown to me. The others, I knew, would be needed.

"Her name is Crimson," I told Fullangr as I reversed my grip and handed him the blade. "Her old name did not bring Brokkr luck."

"Crimson," the king repeated, "*Khürlaan*, a good name."

"*Khürlaan*," Fullangr said as he received his new treasure, stretching the last syllable with pleasure. As soon as his fingers curled around the hilt, I missed her.

"You hesitated," the king said. It didn't sound like a reproach, just an observation.

"This sword saved me," I said. "We formed a bond. And had I kept it, three of them would have survived for sure."

"Why didn't you then?" Eitri asked.

"I hate fate," I replied, "but I can't deny its power. It brought nine of us here, and it brought Crimson back to you through me. I will not fight fate, not when Odin's life is in the balance."

Eitri nodded and purred like an old cat.

"Come with me," he said. "As for you, my dear guests, you have earned passage across our bridge to Jötunheimr. Eat well, drink well, for you are going to a terrible place."

The king curled his finger as a request for me to follow him, and we left the guest room.

I had not realized until we passed the door, but the room was soundproof, and immediately, the world came back in a concert of metal hitting metal and bellows puffing air. We went farther inside Eitri's house, then down into a cellar of some sort. No one guarded its entrance, which was a simple trap door at the end of the main hallway.

Dust rose with each step we took on the staircase, itself barely visible, so dark was the place.

"This is my treasure room," the king said as he passed the fire of his torch above those hung on the walls. Soon, their light revealed a rather large room filled with heaps of items, mostly weapons, of course. Axes, swords, spears, shields, helmets, sickles, bows, knives, spades, hammers, something that resembled a pitchfork, and still more were gathered in a patchwork of metal and wood. Some blades were curved, others attached to their poles by chains. The heads of axes were mounted on spear shafts, some swords were single-edged, and I saw a helmet with horns on it. It was a place of wonder, a hoard worthy of a dragon.

"You made them," I said, recognizing a certain touch in

their crafts as I lost myself in the admiration of those beauties.

"Most of them," Eitri said with a hint of arrogance. "One is for you."

"You would give me one? Why?"

"If you need to ask, maybe you don't deserve it after all," Eitri answered, smiling like a father toying with his son.

"Because I brought Crimson back here," I said.

"And because you honored it," Eitri replied. "As a sign of my gratitude, you may choose whichever of those you like; it's yours."

"I am grateful, Forge-King." I had been right about Dwarves. They were wonderful people, straight in their boots and simpler. "You don't care about giving a treasure to a man fated to die soon?"

"You are?" he asked.

"Even if we rescue the All-Father and make it back to Asgard, Ragnarök is near."

Eitri sighed as if disappointed or tired. "You Asgardians are always rumbling about fate and the end of the world," he said. "And yet you fight like hunted beasts. Let me tell you, my friend, I know you don't want Ragnarök. I know a part of you believes it can be averted. This is why *I* believe it is not the end for you. Faith can overpower fate; we Dwarves know this. Not faith in the so-called gods; faith in yourself. And that, my friend, you have plenty of."

There was no word to reply; Eitri had said it all, and he had said it with panache.

I cannot say how long I stayed in the treasure room, but the king stayed with me and amused himself at my reactions. He answered when I asked about such and such blade, telling me how this one could conjure a flame or that one could freeze water. Some, he said, could cure poison.

Others could cut diamonds or find water anywhere. I held an axe made from a sky-rock and a shield that created a light of its own. I even unsheathed a sword that could speak in its owner's mind, but what it said about my mother I didn't like, so put it back in the scabbard.

"Doesn't look much," Eitri said, "but it keeps the lonely traveler sane in the head. So, my dear blade-lover, which one is yours?"

"This one," I said, retrieving a heavy sword from the heap it was buried in.

"That one?" the king asked, more surprised than if I had left with one of the torches.

"Yes, Forge-King, it has to be this one."

The sword I had chosen was by far the most luxurious blade I had ever seen. Its hilt was made of solid gold, with precious stones of many colors encrusted in the pommel and handle. Its guard was ridiculously decorated with runes in which rich copper had been melted, and the scabbard was even more richly made. *This is the flashiest, dandiest, and most useless sword in the nine realms*, I thought.

"Why on earth would you choose this piece of junk? This is not a warrior's blade," Eitri said, alarmed by my choice.

"It will serve its purpose," I replied as I examined the many details of the weapon.

"Not on Jötunheimr, it won't," he said. "This is a decorative blade for parades and such. I made it as a young Dwarf for Freyja, just before she spent a night with the three sons of Ivaldi. I cared little for her after that and kept the blade here. I beg you to choose another, my friend. It won't help against your enemies."

"Oh, I am confident it is as useful as wings on a swine," I replied. "But it is the one."

"Folks be crazy," the king said to himself. "All right, the choice is yours. Don't let your ghost seek vengeance, I warned you."

We went back to the guest room, where my comrades were deep in their cups and platters, mixing with the advisers as they relived the events of the day. I walked straight to Master Fullangr, who was admiring his new possession while tearing the meat from a chicken leg until I dropped my ridiculous and flashy blade flat on the table in front of him.

"This one against Crimson," I said. The whole room got quiet at once.

Master Fullangr was famously greedy, the king had said.

He looked at the golden blade, judging its worth with expert eyes, putting a price on each of the stones in the handle, and weighing the amount of ore used in its fabrication. He grunted an unpleasant sound, and my hopes melted. Fullangr was also an old warrior, and the greedy old man fought the veteran in his mind. Brokkr's blade was a rare treasure in itself. If Fullangr found value in its rarity more than in its preciosity, I was doomed to parade Jötunheimr with a blade fit for Freyja's walls.

The two swords lay next to each other. They could not be more different, and Fullangr's two lives collided in a difficult choice.

"*Zövkhön iriig av!*" the king spat at his old adviser.

Fullangr grunted once more, stopping his hand on top of Crimson for a second. He took it in his massive grip.

"Agree," he then said. He shoved Crimson in my hands, and nothing ever felt more right than tightening my fingers around her hilt.

The sounds resumed in the room as my friends cheered

and enjoyed the meal once more. Eitri came to me, a big grin on his face.

"So, this was your plan?"

"I hope you will take no offense, but—"

"—but none of my swords chose you." There was no anger in the king's voice.

"They are fit for gods and kings, but I am a simple man; I need a simple tool. And your brother has forged the *best* simple sword of all."

Eitri bit his bottom lip to fight the water accumulating in his eyes, and he nodded as he looked away. He had lost his brother for good that day, but he was proud of him and was glad someone else finally recognized Brokkr's talent.

A flaming sword would have come in handy against Jötunheimr's wolves. A light-shining shield could prove useful as well. But nothing would replace the sensation of Crimson in my hand.

"That went well," Bjorn said, licking his greasy fingers.

"As well as we could have hoped. But we need to go," I replied, though my heart was not in it. I would have loved to enjoy Eitri's hospitality a little while longer. Huginn must have heard me, for he asked a question of great importance to the king of the mountain.

"When did Odin leave?"

"A day ago, by your standard," Eitri replied, which meant we were still one day behind. It killed the joy of the meal for everyone. We needed to go now.

We had a god to save.

ᛦ

The bridge to Jötunheimr, a simple well of clear water, was on the other side of Sudri, past the pool of magma, past the red district of the town, and the entrance of a closed mine. It could only be crossed one way, which was why no one was guarding it. It also meant we had to find another way back to Asgard. It would probably have to be Eggther's hot spring. Sudri had other bridges to and from Jötunheimr, and Eitri pointed their locations on a rather vague map in case we needed to use another path out, but according to Tyr, they were all very far from Ironwood.

We were given flasks of ale and more dry meat, though we had just left Asgard, and our rations were still intact. Eitri also gave us a more valuable present, his friendship, which came in the form of handshakes and hugs.

The first adviser took one of the five items he had used for his riddle and blew in it. We heard no sound, but the bridge did, and a wave of colors passed on it in a ripple. Later, I realized that despite being the heart of his riddle, I never learned his name.

They were all great men, but Eitri was a one-of-a-kind leader. With a heavy heart, I gave a last goodbye to the Forge-King.

"Don't make this face," Eitri said as he slapped my shoulder. "You will come back here after Ragnarök." He winked, and I followed my comrades into the well. This was the first and last time I ever went to Nidavellir.

16

In many ways, crossing a bridge between realms was like performing a task that required no thinking, like splitting wood for the winter or cleaning a ship after a summer of raids. Thoughts of clarity appeared in a mind not ready for them; answers sought after for ages just popped in by themselves. I once told Heimdallr that maybe we could find a way out of Ragnarök if we could slow the passage through Bifröst. He had scoffed. But those thoughts, when we remembered them, could prove of great importance.

I had one of those thoughts just as I crossed the border between Nidavellir and Jötunheimr. The bridge we had just used had not been guarded because no one could cross it toward the Dwarf realm, but what if the other side was manned?

The sudden idea that maybe a group of Jötnar expected us on the other side got me into a state of panic. My heart started frantically beating when I saw the light at the end of the bridge. I could picture a hammer welcoming me and smashing my skull to pieces the moment I emerged.

So, when fingers grabbed me by the collar of my *brynja*, I

did not think for one second it was Bjorn and punched with all my might.

I got him in the chin.

"Fuck, Drake! What was that for?" he barked as I turned on my back, feeling the muddy earth under it.

"Sorry," I said, breathing hard as if I had been running for hours. "I thought—"

"Never a good idea," he interrupted me.

"I thought there might be guards."

I could see little of the place we had landed in and, at first, thought we might be in a grotto of some sort. Then I saw the stars. It was night in Jötunheimr.

"You thought right," Rune said as he offered his hand to help me up. "There were guards, but they can't do much anymore."

I was about to ask him what he meant, but the feeble light soon revealed a scene of carnage. Corpses littered the ground all around the pond. Those giant warriors had met a gruesome death. Right by my side rested a leg, cut clean mid-thigh, and on the water floated a head; its white eye reflected the moon as if looking at me.

"What on Midgard happened here?" Thrasir asked as he twisted his vest to remove the water.

"Odin happened," Arn replied, and he was right. This was Odin's work.

The All-Father had made quick work of the enemy. I could relive the fight in my mind's eye. Odin had crossed the bridge ready for battle, and his first action had been a mighty slash of his sword. The head in the pond came from it. Odin had given them no time to recover.

The Jötunn died with his eyes wide open and his mouth screaming in horror. They all died faster than they ever imagined they would, from a being smaller than any of them. And now, twenty of them offered their carcasses for the crows to feast on.

"Twenty-two," Iona confirmed. "He killed twenty-two of them by himself, just after crossing a bridge." She sounded both amazed and horrified.

"And without Gungnir," Gunhild said, a similar look on her face.

"Maybe he doesn't need us that much after all," Rune joked. A part of me was inclined to agree.

"How many could you take?" Iona asked me as I started searching for any sign of Odin being wounded.

"I would be lucky to have one," I replied, nudging a Jötunn's chin with my boot. "And only if that was a one-on-one."

Tyr stood from his crouching position farther down the line of bodies. "This way," he said, pointing at the dark line of the forest stretching across the night on the horizon.

The pond was, in fact, a spring flowing from a mountain's cliff. The water had eroded the rock for thousands of years until a small alcove had dug itself. It should have been an easy spot to defend, and those Jötnar probably thought themselves lucky in their assignment.

We were on the northern edge of Ironwood. Eggther's farm would be on the other side, with Fenrir's lair in between. From what the herder had told me of this land, we needed about three days to reach the beast from where we stood.

I entertained the thought of spending the night here. We would travel faster with the light, especially if we were fresh from a night of sleep. And we had crossed two bridges in less than a day, which was more exhausting than it sounded. But seeing Odin's work rekindled my energy, and I had yet to calm down from the panic of the crossing, so I said nothing about it. No one did, and we moved on.

There was no trace of the All-Father's passage after that. Snow covered the ground in a flat roll of white, stretching as far as the eye could see. The weather was calm, but it could change in an eye blink. The forest would keep us from any storm, and this was the only positive thing I could think of as we penetrated Ironwood. We walked as a pack, each of us carrying a weapon as if about to fight. Tyr walked in front, but the rest of us gathered in a tight group without proper form.

Huginn seemed to share my discomfort. I was about to pray to Odin for his Thought to remain sane while we crossed the forest, then remembered why we came here in the first place. Odin was the insane one, and he would not hear any prayer for the time being.

"What is it?" Bjorn asked, working his lower jaw to soothe the pain.

"I don't keep a great memory of the place."

"What's Fenrir like?" Rune asked. The hair on my arms stood when the young man spoke the beast's name. Why did he always have to say the worst thing possible?

"Are you trying to bring us some bad luck?" I spat.

"Be nice to the boy," Arn replied. I sighed. If he, of all people, warned me of my tone, I had to adjust it.

"Fenrir," I said, not liking the name from my mouth either, "is big as a mountain in his wolf shape. His eyes glow in the dark, and his fangs are long as a man. When he speaks, it's like his voice penetrates you and shakes your heart with fear."

I wondered what Rune had wanted to hear, but he did not ask for more, which, of course, meant I would keep speaking.

"But the Wolf King," I said, louder for Tyr's sake as well this time, "in his human shape, is somehow even more impressive. Savage and strong, as if all his bestial strength was stuck in a body too small for it. One look at him, and you can imagine your death, brutal and bloody. And it wouldn't be an easy one, for Fenrir is, even in that shape, an animal."

"I said to be nice with the boy," Arn said, "not to scare the shit out of us all."

The group giggled, but their hearts were not in it. Laughing while walking through Ironwood felt unnatural, as if we were proceeding to our funeral.

I expected Tyr to react. How, I do not know. I would have been satisfied to see him slowing his pace or even sigh. I wanted to witness some of the love he had felt for Fenrir, some kind of guilt for betraying him. So, I pushed further. I pushed too far.

"And yet, there is a part of Fenrir that is fragile, sad beyond measure, broken. If he wasn't our enemy, I would pity him as much as I feared him."

"Ridiculous," Gunhild said, using her wide sword to cut a bracken leaf from her path.

"Is it?" I asked. "Fenrir has been chained for four hundred years, and you know the story; he is as much a victim as he is a threat."

"Don't speak of what you don't know," Tyr said. Finally, some reaction.

"Am I wrong?" I asked. "Did Fenrir deserve his fate? From what the legend says, it seems the gods were afraid of him before he did any harm."

"Don't you always say that the legends are usually wrong?" Tyr replied.

"But not always," I replied.

"I remember a time," Tyr went on, "when you said that Loki was a victim too. You claimed that he had been unfairly treated. Do you still feel the same?"

"I do," I said, and I was partially honest. "Loki deserved his fate, but if the gods had treated him better, he would never have turned traitor."

"You speak of things you don't understand," the Æsir said. I wondered if anyone else could hear the growing impatience in his voice.

"Fenrir became an enemy when the gods tricked him, not before," I said as Tyr ducked under a branch. "They brought their fate by trying to avoid it."

"How ironic," Gunhild said, agreeing with me for once.

"It is," I said.

Tyr turned to face me all of a sudden. I was startled but remained strong as he planted himself a hand's length from me.

"Tell me, Drake, is this what you do when you lead your men? You sow doubts about us Æsir? You talk of us as if we are children or pathetic elders?"

"When you act like a bunch of assholes, yes," I replied, meeting him head-on. I was slightly taller than Tyr, but he used all his Æsir aura to drown me. Sadly for him, I had faced much worse over the last few weeks, and I was not impressed. Worse, the fire I had not felt since regaining my body was now sparking itself up in my chest again, rekindled by Tyr's ire.

"Be careful, Drake," Tyr said, which was weak of him.

"What I tell my men," I said as if he had not just threatened me, "is to own their mistakes, something your people are incapable of."

Tyr was so close to me that I could hear his teeth gritting. He was my friend, the only one among the Æsir now that Heimdallr was dead, but I was ready to tear our friendship apart for some acknowledgment. It was pointless; I had nothing to gain from it, but some things needed to be said, and I wanted to hear an Æsir showing some accountability.

"Drake—" he said. I assumed he was going to threaten me, but I did not let him.

"I know who Fenrir was to you," I whispered in his ear. When I looked back into his eyes, I saw a range of emotions stretching from frustration to sorrow. I regretted my words immediately.

"I wonder," Tyr said, "if you'll own your mistakes when the time comes."

He turned around once more and resumed his walk through the forest, his anger visible in his rushing gait.

I sighed. It had not felt as good as I had thought.

"See what happens when I'm nice to the boy," I said, pointing my sword toward Rune, the undeserving recipient of my wrath.

We progressed faster, in silence, but less focused over the next few hours.

Bjorn found the remains of a fire, and when he rummaged through it with his foot, some smoke rose. Odin had probably sparked it, though we could not be sure. If it was him, we were gaining ground. But it was dawn then, and many of us needed a rest.

ᚱ

For warriors, falling asleep is second nature. Bjorn was snoring before his head hit the ground, Arn followed soon, and I think Gunhild had been sleeping as we walked. As a pack leader to the Wolves, I had made a habit of being the last to sleep and only when I was sure those on watch would do their job.

On that Jötunheimr's dawn, however, I could not find sleep; it escaped me. Huginn and Tyr's voices, though barely whispers, were anchoring me to the real world. If I was honest with myself, guilt was also at work here. I had been too harsh with Tyr. What happened between him and Fenrir had nothing to do with me. I had drawn a parallel between the two of them, and Muninn and I, but those were two unrelated stories.

I stood, knowing that I was better off replacing Thrasir and letting the young man get some rest when I couldn't. The Æsir's voices stopped when I rose and resumed when I vanished behind the trees.

Thrasir sat motionless on a fallen trunk, the clouds from his breathing the only sign of his presence. He had not aged since the day I had ended his previous life and given him a new one, but his back seemed wider, his presence more grounded. I had never witnessed such rapid growth within an Einheri, not even with Rune.

He did not even flinch when I went around the improvised bench and sat on his left. I received one of his jolly smiles and felt warmer for it.

"Can't sleep?" he asked, his eyes never leaving the horizon, which was just an endless sea of trees and snow.

"Last time I slept in these woods, I woke up surrounded by wolves. And the time before, too."

"Good, now I won't sleep either."

"You should still try," I said. "Go get some rest."

"I'll stay a bit longer," Thrasir replied.

"Suit yourself," I said as I closed my cloak tighter around my chest. A squirrel ran up the nearest tree, chased by another. The forest was awakening. We would not stay long, and maybe it was better not to sleep at all.

"So," I clumsily said, "what did you do to gain my men's respect?" Arn had spoken well of him, Bjorn, too, and if those two men gave credit to a brother, I was bound to listen.

"No idea," he replied with a faint smile. "I did just as I did on Midgard. I trained, I fought, and I listened. The Wolves have been generous in their teaching."

I could imagine my men teasing the boy any chance they got, but he would indeed have learned much in their presence. "You won a square yet?"

"A few times the fifth, and once the fourth, though I was so battered that I almost fainted at the end," Thrasir said. There was no arrogance in his voice.

The fourth square, I thought, it had taken me nearly twenty years to get there. Thrasir had never seen or experienced the backside of Valhöll, which had preserved some of his kindness. "I heard you made more allies besides my men," I said.

Thrasir blushed. He knew what I meant. "Aye, well, I was lucky to meet Lif a few times," he said, fumbling on his choice of words. "I hope you don't mind."

"Why would I mind? If she's happy and if you treat her well, I couldn't agree more with your union. I would stay away from Ulf, though. He's just reconnected with his granddaughter. Not sure he'll take well that some wet-behind-the-ear pup has been churning butter with his precious girl."

"Churning butter?" he asked, confused. I mimicked the movements necessary to transform milk into butter, and Thrasir turned to another shade of red. "Oh, we never, well, we didn't—"

"Relax, young man. As I said, not my problem." I could

see how the teenager had made himself a welcome member of the Wolves. His timidity was refreshing. "And yes, you have," I said, knowing a lie when I saw one. "You want to marry her? Is that why you joined us?"

"Yes," he replied. "I will marry Lif, and there is no better way to make myself worthy than saving Odin."

"You mean that you are lucky Odin put himself in danger?"

"Gods, no!" he replied, louder than he should have. "This is *not* what I meant."

"I'm joking, Thrasir. I know what you meant. Since the eggs are broken, might as well make an omelet."

"Aye, exactly. Even if I could win the brawl, it wouldn't be enough. You might not know it, but Lif is already being courted by every single Vanir and Æsir in Asgard, including some who are not single. I need to do something amazing, unmatchable."

"Even if Ragnarök is right here?"

"Especially because Ragnarök is right here." My question must have shown on my face, for Thrasir explained himself without having to be asked. "Last time I was killed, I was about to get married. Who knows what happens next time I die? I'd better be already married to the one I love."

Thrasir amazed me. He was thinking beyond Ragnarök, while gods and men just dreaded it. The end of the world was maybe not the end after all. How many folks on Midgard had died not knowing about Valhöll, only to find themselves on its benches upon their death? Maybe there was something beyond the reign of the Æsir. Another realm where Thrasir and Lif's union would carry on. This was a beautiful idea.

"You don't need it," I said, "but if we survive this, you have my blessing."

"Thank you, Drake," the young man said, his pristine eyes reflecting the fresh light of a timid sun.

I prayed for Lif and Thrasir to survive Ragnarök, but while I liked his vision of an after-after world, I doubted it. So I prayed for the two of them to be among the very few survivors, and I would fight for it to happen.

"You know," he said, interrupting me mid-prayer, "there is someone else who needs your blessing."

"Who?" I asked.

"Rune," he said, and of course, he had meant Rune. The two of them had become inseparable.

"Rune wants to marry?" I asked. I could not recall him having a specific partner on Asgard, but a lot could have happened in three years.

"Rune, marrying?" Thrasir replied, snorting at the idea. "No, never. I meant that he just needs your blessing to... Well, to exist."

I shrugged, not getting his point.

"I've seen how you look at him, how you speak to him. You are a great leader, but with Rune, you behave like a Vanir, no offense," he said, holding his hands up as if it could make up for the insult.

"Offense taken," I replied. "I only treat him like that because he behaves without thinking. He always says the worst possible things at the worst possible times. Moods sour in a second when he opens his mouth, you've seen it. There was even a time I thought he might be an agent of Loki."

Thrasir giggled, clearly thinking that I was joking. His face hardened when he realized I wasn't. "Whose fault is it?" he asked. "No one has anything wrong to say about Rune but you."

He was right again; Rune had only supporters among

my men, and from what I had heard, he had even improved as a fighter.

"If Rune is clumsy, it's because of you, Drake. He cares so much about making a great impression when you're around that he stumbles and says the first thing that pops into his mind. Give him a bit of credit; he'll behave with you as he does with everyone else, and you'll see."

"Why would he care so much about my impression?" I asked. Thrasir looked at me as if I were the dumbest creature in the nine realms, and for a second, I was tempted to shove my blessing up his ass and let Ulf deal with him. Then, his eyes rounded up with surprise.

"Oh, you really don't know?"

"Don't know what?" I asked.

"Nothing," he said, shifting his gaze back to the sea of trees.

"Thrasir, what don't I know?" I asked, starting to feel vexed.

"I guess I'll go get some rest now," he said, standing up.

I stood as well, keeping my arm on his, for I was not about to let it go. "Tell me, boy," I said, putting a hint of threat in my voice.

"Drake, it's not my place to—"

Someone screamed by the fire. No, not just one scream, a multitude of them. Battle cries from voices that did not belong to our comrades.

ᛣ

They came from behind.

They came from the direction Rune had been guarding, and despite my previous comments, my bowels twisted at the thought of what might have happened to him.

Jötnar, thirty and some had thought to catch my men by surprise. They got something else coming. I could read the regret on their faces and hear the disappointment in their shouts. But Jötnar were nothing if not proud warriors, and they fought back, even when they came to face seven awakened and peerless fighters.

Only a couple were giants like Eggther and Skadi. The rest were a mix of males and females barely taller than us, with skins ranging from light blue to dark brown and with crude weapons of bones and wood. Had they known they would face us, they would have fetched reinforcement first.

Five or six lay motionless by the time Thrasir and I reached the battleground, just in time to backstab one of the two warriors locked with Arn. My friend reversed his grip on his spear to deal with the second when he saw Crimson through his opponent's belly. He gave me a nod, and I joined the center of the melee.

Tyr was giving a hard time to the two giants, who had been smart enough to team up against the Æsir. He dodged a hammer by a hair, letting it pass right above his head, and used his opponent's momentum to backslash at his thigh. He drew blood and got the giant to bellow like a beast. The second one meant to kick Tyr in the back, but the Æsir rolled on his shoulder and was out of harm's way. This had happened in less than five heartbeats. Two giants wouldn't be enough, and I left Tyr to his prey.

I searched for Iona, and when I saw her, my heart froze.

The spear of the man she faced came out of her back. I saw the moment it pierced through in one quick thrust. It went in as if she had been wearing nothing, and her name escaped my lips in a scream.

She then moved out of the spear. This was the best way to describe it. One second, she'd been hit by a lethal strike;

then she stood next to the spear, her elbow drawn backward to release an arrow. The Jötunn on the other side of the spear was as dumbfounded as I was and did not understand what just happened. He died not knowing, his brain annihilated by an arrow shot less than a spear-length away.

This was the first time I saw a warrior-Valkyrie fight, and it was a thing of beauty. Iona could shift to her ghost shape in an eye blink. Blades passed through her as if hitting air, and she dealt death the moment she reshaped. I was so enthralled with this graceful, fatal fighting style that I did not see the axe aimed at me.

A Jötunn had thrown a short axe from my right side, unbeknownst to me, but Bjorn parried it with his great axe, barking as he did.

"Snap out of it," he said right after the ring of metal on metal.

I obeyed.

Those eight comrades of mine could take care of themselves, so I did what I did best, I fought. My shield was on my left arm, Crimson in my right hand; what else could I possibly need?

I went after the axe thrower first, a dark Jötunn with long, thin arms. He meant to pick the knife at his belt, but I was on him faster and slashed with all my might. I split his chin and half of his face in two. His knees had not touched the ground before I was choosing my next victim, a female Jötunn who had made the mistake of picking a fight with Gunhild. She had been doing so with two of her companions, but one was already holding his bowels as I rushed to them. She saw me from the corner of her eye and came at me, sword above her head. Strong was this Jötunn, and my shield shook dangerously when she hammered it. But I was stronger, and the fire in my chest was getting hotter by the second. It wasn't just an impression; this time, I was sure of it.

I kicked her knee with all I had, heard the bones shatter, and simply raised the tip of Crimson, on which she impaled herself.

"Hey!" Gunhild spat, "she was mine." I don't know how she finished her opponent, but he had joined his brothers in death while I dealt with mine. And Gunhild now stood like a goddess of war, blood up to the elbow and not a single scratch on her.

"You're welcome," I replied.

The noises of the battle were dying down, but I had too much fury in me to stop and was graciously met by a young-looking Jötunn with something to prove. He did not yell and run; he just came at me, shield and sword in his hands. This was a strange sight, this quiet Jötunn with his blue, unmarked skin, in the middle of a battle. I knew from instinct that had we met in different circumstances, he would have been a great man to share ale and stories with. He knew they had failed, and he knew he would die. I could only respect his resolve and faced him as I would any honorable foe, with all my might.

He was skilled, too, and I thought he was probably some kind of noble's son, maybe the leader of this unfortunate lot.

Our swords clashed again and again. I even took pleasure in this duel. He could read some of my moves and replied in kind, receiving my blade on the edge of his shield and forcing me to use mine more often than I would have liked. But I was dancing with him, never giving him a step in my direction, always pushing him on his heels.

Then, the balance of the fight shifted.

It wasn't just experience; it was the power in me. The

same I had felt when in Loki's body. The fire, I now knew for sure, had not left me.

I received blows with less effort than I should have. My strikes damaged the young Jötunn's shield more rapidly than I could have in the past. Loki's power was showing in each piece of splintering wood and each moan of pain from my enemy. I was gaining control of the power as the duel went, and by the time my enemy stood breathless and battered, I was playing with the heat, shifting it from one hand to the next. I could decide where it went and how much of it I meant to use. It weakened as my anger gave place to a feeling of wonder, but it still made me strong. Too strong for the young Jötunn.

He threw his shield on the side, disgusted, and opened his arms, fire in his eyes. He said something that I didn't understand, but it must have been an invitation to end it. I would honor him.

"If there is something after Ragnarök," I said, "let's share some ale, you and I."

I made it quick.

The battle was all but over. Tyr finished his last opponent with a great slash of his arm-sword, decapitating the last giant in a wide spray of blood, and Bjorn was struggling to get his axe from a Jötunn's back.

The only one still fighting was Rune, surrounded by three Jötnar armed with hammers and axes. I was about to rush to his side, but Arn stopped me.

"Just you watch," my friend said, sweating. He'd been cut near the shoulder, but it looked shallow.

I did as he advised. We all did. A semicircle formed around the four warriors, and if anything, those Jötnar must have felt irritated at being observed like roosters fighting at the market. They knew they would die, but they would also not cross the bridge to the underworld without a tribute. Cornered beasts were dangerous, and despite Arn's attitude, I could not stop worrying. Rune was a great fighter, but he was surrounded by three Jötunn warriors.

But as I soon understood, Rune wasn't surrounded by those three. They were stuck with him.

The young wolf held his two axes low. The first of the three charged and was rewarded with the flat of an axe on the nose. I had barely seen Rune move. Blinded with pain, the Jötunn could not parry the second axe, which ended its course in his brain. Rune crouched to avoid a strike coming from behind, though how he had seen it coming, I did not know.

He stood again, a big grin on his face. He had been quick with the first; it was now two to one, and Rune was in the mood to play.

I thought of those years we had forbidden him from using two axes at the same time, claiming that he needed a shield. What a wasted time. Rune did not need a shield. Rune needed freedom and enemies to slaughter; that was all. The two Jötnar stood no chance, and it became clear to them as well.

They still tried.

The young Wolf met each strike with his blades or with a twist of his torso, turning the whole fight into a one-sided affair. Even when his opponents attempted a synchronized push, they were met by an effortless response.

And when their breath became heavier and their rage spent, Rune went for the offensive. He skipped from one foot to the next, as Sven Cross-Eyes sometimes did, and opened his arms as if to tell his opponents that he was just beginning.

"He spotted them in the forest," Arn told me, breaking

the trance Rune had put me in. "He came back and woke us up quietly. We were ready for them when they showed up, but they did not know."

I had guessed something of the sort had happened, but I must admit that I was impressed with Rune.

"Sounds like something you would have done," Bjorn said as he removed some gore stuck in his beard.

Thrasir, who had heard what Bjorn just said, looked at me with his most challenging smile. His right brow had been slashed open, and blood was running around his eye, but Thrasir, too, had done well, it seemed. I could almost hear his thoughts as he invited me to watch Rune. "Do you see it now?" he asked with his eyes.

I watched Rune, making an effort to remove any prejudice from my observation. Gathering the last of their energy, the two Jötnar charged Rune, but he did not back down. He took a step in their direction and then on the side just as a hammer came down. He slashed the arm of the hammer-wielder, forcing him to drop it. A spray of red formed an arch above the lot of them just as the second Jötunn tried to stab Rune with his long knife.

In an astonishing move, the Wolf let go of his right axe, twisted on his heels, caught the wrist of his opponent as the knife passed harmlessly by his hip, and sent his elbow into the Jötunn's nose. This was not the kind of technique that could be taught; it relied on pure instinct, and I knew of only one man who had dealt such a blow. Me.

Not letting go of the Jötunn's wrist, Rune forced him to his knee and knocked him out with the flat of his axe, breaking his skull in the process.

The last one, arm dangling by a bit of skin, would die as well from blood loss, if nothing else.

Rune stood behind him, face covered in blood, none of it

his, his grin incredibly white within the red. I watched him as if it were the first time, and never in my life have I felt more stupid. The truth about Rune was staring right at me. The awkwardness of his presence, his will to impress me, my constant reproval of his actions, all of it made sense, and none of it was his fault. What I was seeing wasn't just a peerless warrior who had toyed with his enemies like a cat with mice.

What I was seeing was me.

All of a sudden, Rune looked so much like me that I cursed myself for not seeing it sooner. The shape of his lips, the lobes of his ears, the length of his neck. No beard covered his chin, but it was the same as mine. The way he stood, the way he breathed, the way he stared at his victim. Even the way his fingers kept opening and closing on the handle of his axe reminded me of my bad habit.

Rune was my blood. Rune was what I used to be.

Even his name was nearly the same as mine, Sune.

I had left two daughters on Midgard. One of them had continued my line, until Rune. There was no doubt he was my descendant, and I had been blind and stupid.

He raised his axe, ready to end the last Jötunn's suffering.

"Wait!" I said.

I approached Rune, feeling the heat emanating from his body when I dropped my hand on his shoulder. We would talk, I told him in my nod. He lowered his axe.

"I have questions for you," I told the Jötunn, kneeling to his level.

He spat a series of words that must have been insults, so I grabbed his ruined arm and pressed on it until his scream turned to a whimper.

"I have questions, and you will answer. Otherwise, who knows, I might let the forest finish you slowly."

It took Tyr to translate, but the Jötunn spoke.

They discovered the bodies by the spring and followed our tracks, which meant they had not seen Odin. He said they had sent one of theirs for reinforcement, and more would come this way, but we would be gone by then. Being part of some remote garrison, he knew very little about his people's movements, but he had heard rumors of a great gathering. He then insulted our ancestors and died a quick death, as did all those who yet breathed.

Huginn came down from the tree he had been hiding in when the last of them expired, receiving a fair amount of judgmental eyes as he rejoined the group.

"What?" he asked. "I thought you would prefer not to risk my feathers."

He was right, and we left him alone.

We had won the fight with nothing more than a few cuts and bruises. If that was the best Ragnarök could throw at us, I thought, there was hope. But Ironwood and Fenrir had worse than unbloodied Jötnar to send at us. Much worse.

"Who knows what's gonna happen during the last great battle? Not even the Norns can know the fate of each fighting man and woman. Odin has bet on bravery; I bet on the greatness of individuals fighting as a group. The Einherjar have my faith. I just hope that when my times come, I will make them proud."

Heimdallr.

17

There was little sleep to be had over the next two days. The deeper we went into the forest, the more its presence kept us on our toes. I thought we would have encountered Fenrir's wolves by now, but we saw none. The rising suspicion among us was that any wolf scurrying this part of the wood would be after Odin, for the All-Father had not proceeded with caution. Even a child could follow the traces of his passage. Embers, chicken bones, spilled mead, apple cores, Odin had left a mess. So much so that Gunhild claimed he actually wanted to be found. I was inclined to agree with her despite Tyr's opinion. A part of Odin, I hoped, knew some ally would follow him, and he had left a trail for us. Each sign of his presence gave us a boost in energy and veiled our fatigue a little longer.

Huginn, on the second morning, suddenly claimed that he could sense Odin's presence, though it was far and feeble. Every once in a while, he would tell us how much stronger he could feel his father ahead. I don't know if he spoke honestly or if he was motivating our progress, but it worked. We moved faster and more carelessly. He could not share thoughts with Odin, but he was there, just ahead.

We were gaining ground, but Odin was never in sight. The volcano, however, was, and with it, the limits of our hopes.

Its summit appeared through the trees all afternoon long during our second day in Ironwood, and I could hear fate laugh. It was bringing me back to Fenrir's lair, and no matter what happened, I knew it would end within the volcano. Bjorn joked that dying on Angrboda's Tit wasn't the worst thing in the world. May the gods bless Bjorn for his untamable capacity to see the light through the clouds.

Two days of walking without sleep had drained his fat quite miraculously, and the man who stood by my side was now close to the champion I had known for a couple of centuries. Sadly, it meant the end of the fat jokes.

"So," he said out of the blue just after he finished the last of his water, "you and Freyja, huh?" It took me by surprise, and for some reason, I felt the heat coming to my face.

"Not what you think," I stupidly replied. "Huginn told you?"

"I didn't," Huginn replied de facto.

"Ulf did," Bjorn said, and of course, it had been Ulf.

"Sorry, brother," I replied, for a night with Freyja was the only thing Bjorn had ever wished for. I would have preferred not to pursue the point, for Iona's sake, if nothing else, but Bjorn was bored and envious.

"No need to be sorry," he said. "It's not like you knew I have longed for her for more than two hundred years." I had nothing to reply and did not. "Did you at least enjoy it? Did she?"

I nodded in the direction of Iona, walking a few steps ahead, inviting him to realize that my silence was not born out of timidity but out of concern for the Valkyrie who worshipped Freyja.

"She sounded like she did," Iona then said, surprising all of us and killing any chance I had of stopping this conversation. "Repeatedly," she added, smugness in her voice. It was so unexpected that the whole group laughed. A peculiar and rare sound within Ironwood.

"You got to tell me how you convinced her," Bjorn said when the giggles died down.

"That's the thing, brother," I said, "if you try to convince her, you've already failed."

"Huh?" he asked, giving me his oafiest glare.

"As all great skalds will tell you," Arn said, "it works better if you show instead of tell." I was surprised to hear such wisdom in the art of courting from Arn but knew it would be lost on Bjorn.

"So you mean I should just show her my—"

"No, that's not what he meant," I said. "Just don't ask her, as you've been doing for ages. The gods know I didn't."

"No, we don't," Tyr joked. It was his first humorous trait of the trip, and I got to give it to Bjorn; he even had the most sullen of our gods wrapped in his mood.

"She might just kill me for trying," Bjorn said.

"Yeah, remember how she toyed with Thor at the *thing?*" Rune asked, whistling as he mimicked Freyja throwing the god of thunder as if he were a puppet.

"Remember?" Bjorn puffed. "I'll never forget. I was scared and aroused in equal measures."

"So was I," Gunhild said, which got another round of guffaw.

"Believe me, brother, she won't hurt you for trying or just the way you'd like."

"How do you know?" he asked.

I hesitated in telling him the truth, but Iona's corner smile told me I could. She knew her mistress better than I.

"Because she told me." I had never heard Bjorn gasp as he did.

"She did?" he asked. I nodded. "Couldn't you have said so before I agreed to come here?"

"Would you have come?" I asked.

"Hel no," he said. "I would have spent every last minute till Ragnarök in her bedsheets."

"Exactly," I said. "But don't worry, we'll get back to Asgard. You'll have your chance."

I believed those words; I had faith in them. Which was why I had not spoken with Rune yet. For now, that he knew that I knew was enough. I never had a son, but this was how I now regarded him. Looking at him was a stab in the stomach, my guilt being a very sharp blade. I would make it up, I kept telling myself, somehow I would make it up. I gave him a nod, which is all I seemed to be able to do with him. Things were growing awkward between us, but just as he replied in kind, Iona shushed all of us.

She crouched and dropped her hand flat toward the ground. We imitated her and hid behind the closest trees.

"What is it?" Tyr asked in a whisper.

She put her finger on her lips and joined her two hands to make a wolf face, then raised one finger. Silently, she picked an arrow from the quiver on her back, then drew her arm.

I saw nothing, heard nothing, not even the bowstring as she worked it to extreme tension, but I trusted her Valkyrie skills, and after a time stretching to a few breaths, she released the arrow.

It thumped into something before I registered it had left

the bow, then there was a short-lived whimper. Iona rushed after her shaft, and we followed.

A brown and gray wolf of Fenrir, a juvenile, judging by its size, lay motionless on its side. Iona drew her knife and slit his throat for good measure, but the arrow lodged in his ear had already done the work.

"Cover it with snow," she said as she proceeded to do so herself. "It will mask the scent for a little while."

"This thing is huge," Thrasir said as he shoved snow on top of the carcass.

"That's a small one," Huginn replied.

"We're close," I said, remembering the hundreds of pups sheltered in the flanks of the crater. The trees were thinning, and the volcano looked immense. Even the atmosphere felt different, thicker, and dangerous. All it had taken was a young wolf for us to remember where we were.

"Just five minutes that way," Iona said. "It's just as Drake described. Small packs of wolves roam the empty space between here and the volcano. But there are many Jötnar, too."

That was new but not surprising. If Ragnarök was about to start, every army of Jötunheimr, Múspellsheimr, and Hel would gather and depart for Asgard.

"Any trace of Father?" Tyr asked.

"None," she replied, "everything is quiet."

Iona, alone, had scouted the rest of the path.

"You sure he's that way?" I asked Huginn.

"Yes," he claimed with certainty. "Odin is over there, not far." His finger pointed in the direction Iona had come back from, toward the volcano.

"Could he sneak in?" Gunhild asked.

"Who knows with him," Tyr replied. "He might try to pass for a Jötunn; he is half one, after all."

"How do we go then?" Bjorn asked. We could not sneak in unnoticed, at least not all of us. And I knew of only one way in, which was from the other side of the volcano as well.

"That's the way Odin will have taken," Tyr said when I mentioned the narrow corridor. "And that's the path we will use as well."

We designed a plan, and I disliked it from the beginning. But none better came to mind, and I was forced to accept it.

Five of us were to circle the plain and get as close as possible to the crack in the volcano. I thought it would take about two hours and said so. The other four were to stay and create the greatest diversion possible for the appointed time.

"If it's big enough, it will empty the plain, and then we can sneak in," Tyr said.

"And then you run," I told those in charge of the diversion. "You don't wait to see if it worked. You run and do not wait for us. Huginn will get you to Eggther's farm."

"I'll try," Huginn said, though he had repeatedly mentioned that he wasn't certain of the way.

I would have preferred Huginn to stay with the first group. Maybe he could reach Odin, being his thoughts and all. But Huginn was the only one, besides Tyr and I, who knew of Eggther's farm, and it wouldn't harm to have an Æsir in each group.

"And if something happens inside the volcano before we get to Father," Tyr said, "forget the plan and rush to Odin's help."

If it comes to that, I thought, *we're all dead.*

And so we left, five of us, while Huginn, Iona, Thrasir, and Arn remained.

If we had the chance to encounter some Jötnar, we would take their garments from their dead bodies and try to pass for some of them, as Odin probably planned to do. Iona, even with our best efforts, would never pass for one. Thrasir, I had yet to know of his value and preferred to leave him behind. As for Arn, the cut on his arm had started to get infected and the smell would be an issue if we passed by wolves. Plus, I felt better knowing he was with them.

"See you at the farm," he said as we clasped arms.

"If he gives you trouble, tell Eggther that he still owes me one for the rooster," I said. Arn's puzzled look was a thing of beauty. "He'll understand."

Thrasir complained, and Iona was furious at being left behind, but since Gunhild herself agreed with the plan, the Valkyrie remained to guard our backs as we disappeared westward.

We first went back deeper into the forest, then veered to the west, keeping the volcano in our sight through the thickness of the trees. Each step was a choice between speed and stealth, and I'm afraid we chose the first more often than not.

Unencumbered with any thought of silence, the wolves and Jötnar drowned the plain. They were an army. Tension was palpable among their ranks, and more than once on this arduous journey, I heard a clash of swords. They were waiting. Waiting for the great battle of our time. It was but an axe throw from them, a few days away at best, and it took all they had to keep their feet on the ground.

How they planned to access Asgard was unknown to me, but it twisted my bowels to think this was but a portion of what awaited us on the final day.

The forest filled with visions of Jötnar wielding enormous spears and the shadows of bloodthirsty wolves roaming the vicinity of my imagination. The fatigue of the voyage was taking its toll. My eyes blinked more and more often. Titus had once told me that the rush we feel before the fight is like a power contained inside our human bodies to make us stronger. But such a power should not last longer than a few seconds, for it drains our energy away faster than anything else. How long could I keep going before I lost complete control of my focus?

Rune's hand on my shoulder startled me. He was pointing at the edge of the forest.

"Is that it?" he whispered.

Yes, it was, I said in a nod. The crack in the rock, the path to Fenrir. It slit the volcano, ground to summit, like a bad scar from a thunderbolt, just as I remembered. We still had some forest to cross if we wanted to be right in front of it, but we were almost there.

From here to there, we halted twice. Once, to let a single wolf walk back to the plain, and a second time, as a group of four Jötnar penetrated the forest, apparently in search of a lost comrade.

They were four giants and I did not like our chances of finishing them quietly, so we just waited for them to disappear and went our way. We had lost time, and I wondered if it had been two hours already. Huginn and the others could not know it any better than us, and they might pull the diversion earlier than intended. The more it went, the less I liked this plan.

With the south on our right shoulder, we made a stop and turned to face the crack in the mountain. We came as close as caution allowed to the edge of Ironwood, close enough to smell the mixture of sweat and fur from the plain's roamers. Crouching through a thorny bush, I peered into the mass of them, searching for any sign of an old Æsir on the loose. But it was so quiet and packed that I would have been lucky to spot anything resembling Odin.

Bjorn was breathing hard, his forehead gleaming with pearls of sweat. The others fared no better, even Tyr, whose eyes scanned the plain with a growing sense of apprehension. We must have looked odd, the five of us hiding behind some overgrown thorny bushes, facing an army of several hundred. A Jötunn with a bit of cleverness could sneak on us and finish us in one big swoop of his axe. This is the thought that hit me when I heard a twig snap right behind me.

I turned and raised my shield, sure to find myself in front of some monstrous axe or flat hammer. Instead, a sword welcomed me. Its tip pierced through the planks of my shield as if it were made of wool and only stopped an inch from my throat. Wielding the sword was an old man with a face caked in fresh blood and wild eyes filled with fury. They softened as soon as he recognized me.

"Drake!" Odin said.

"Odin?" I called as I invited him to lower himself.

"Father," Tyr said. His eyes did not know which part of Odin to focus on, for the All-Father was far from his grand self.

I could guess his last meals from his beard, his last bath from his smell, and his last kill from the blood-smeared from blade to boots. The four Jötnar and their missing comrades would never resurface. The bag under Odin's eye was darker than Eggther's skin, and the unfocused way he blinked showed how tired or mad he was.

"You brought Tyr," he said, whispering. "I knew you'd

come, my boy." He put his left hand on my shoulder, patting me as he would Frekki.

Even his grin, white and wide, failed to reassure.

"That wasn't me, Odin," I said, dropping my hand over his. "That was Loki. He looked like me, but he is the one who told you to come here."

"Don't you think I would recognize the trickster?" he asked, feigning to be vexed.

"He speaks the truth, Father," Tyr said. The Æsir removed his scarf and passed it over Odin's face to wipe some of the blood. Odin did not even flinch as his son washed him. "Loki has tricked us, but he's dead now."

"Oh," Odin said, humming the sound for a long time, "if you think Loki's dead, it means he's tricked you more than me."

"No, father, this time he's dead," Tyr said. "Heimdallr killed him, just like in the prophecy."

"Heimdallr did? That's a good son of mine. Did I tell you, Drake, how I created him?"

"You did, All-Father," I replied, using all the patience I could muster to speak.

"That was a wild night with his nine mothers, let me tell you that," he said, making a nine with his fingers and turning to Rune, who replied with a shy smile. "Hey, you brought your son, Drake. Good for you."

"He's my descendant, not my son," I said, wondering if absolutely everyone on Asgard but me knew of Rune.

"Descendant, son, Logi, Loki," Odin replied as if it was just a detail. "You raise him well, all right? You hear me, Drake? You raise him well, and one day he'll make you proud. Like Heimdallr made me proud by killing that son of a poodle of Loki. Wait," Odin said, straightening, his face getting pale. "Does that mean?"

263

"Yes, Father, Heimdallr is dead too," Tyr said.

Odin's eye remained open and dumb for a few seconds, locked in Tyr's as if waiting for his son to say that he was joking. But Tyr wasn't, and Odin knew. Tears broke without restraint. A line of blood ran from under his patch. He brought his shaking hand to his face and sobbed like a child.

Gunhild turned her eyes on me and waved her first finger by her ear in a small circle. She was right; Odin's mind was not in the right place.

"Odin," I said, dropping my hand on his knee. "Huginn is on the other side of the mountain with some others. They are about to make a diversion, and all those wolves and Jötnar will chase them. You need to talk to him in your thoughts. Tell him you're fine, and tell him not to follow the plan."

"You found Huginn?" Odin asked, shifting from sorrow to joy in a split second. He wiped the tears with the back of his hand, spraying blood over his nose.

"I did," I replied, getting frustrated. We needed Odin to snap out of it and focus, but he seemed incapable of it. I remembered an old man from my village when I was a child, whose brain had departed his body long before his death. To my shame, with my friends, as children, we had made great fun of the poor man. Odin behaved just the same, but I wasn't laughing this time. "I did. Talk to him, you'll see."

"I'm so glad you found him," Odin said, squeezing my shoulder a little too hard. "He and his sister are troublesome, but they're good kids. You know, I think she has a thing for you." His cunning old self came back for the time of a wink.

"Yes, All-Father, I know. But right now, she's in a cell, and she needs you. We need to go back home. Can you tell Huginn, please?"

"Muninn, in a cell? Why on Midgard would she be?"

This was getting nowhere. "She's erased your memory and made a mess of things," I replied.

"Nonsense!" he said, waving his hand as if to say that I was talking through my ass. "She didn't erase my memory; I asked her to."

"You knew?" Tyr asked before I did.

"Well, yes, right now I do. I just remembered."

"Odin," Gunhild called. For a second, I worried she might simply shove her hand in his face. But Gunhild surprised me and found the only thing that could get Odin's attention. "We are going home through Eggther's bridge. You know what it means, right?" She gave him what could pass as an impish smile.

"Freyja's bath!" he replied, his eye lighting up like a fire at Yule. Lust, of course, *that* would work.

"Exactly," Gunhild said. "You just need to tell Huginn, and then we're on our way, all right?"

"That's a good plan," he said, winking at the shield-maiden. "Where is my raven-son you said?"

And just as I pointed toward the other side of the volcano, hope vanished.

An arrow flew to the sky, wrapped in a bright flame, right above the Tit. And when it peaked, there was a splash of red, exploding like a plum against a wall, and as it did, we heard a long and strong note from a horn. We were too late; Huginn and the others had done their part, and they had done it well.

The commotion that followed as hundreds of Jötnar and wolves turned in the direction of the horn created an uproar worthy of the sagas.

"Well, at least that's working," Bjorn said, not bothering to lower his voice.

"Odin, tell Huginn to get the fuck away from here," I said. Odin did not react; his eye lost itself on the horizon. I shook him by the shoulder again. "Odin!"

"I'm here," he said. "I'm here."

"Tell Huginn, and let's go then."

"I came here to face Fenrir," he said in all seriousness.

"Father, no," Tyr said. "That was Loki tricking you."

"Well, he was right," Odin said. "We've let fear lead us for too long. Especially me."

"All-Father," I said, "Loki and Heimdallr killed each other, Ragnarök has begun. If you face Fenrir, you know what it means." I challenged him with my stare, and he met it without any sign of weakness. I was facing our lord.

"Drake," he said, "I piss on the prophecy."

It was so unexpected that I snorted a laugh, as did Bjorn and Rune.

"So, we're going there?" Gunhild asked, thumb pointed at the volcano.

"None of you has to," Odin said as he stood and pulled his helmet over his head. One of the metal wings had been chopped in half, but it still looked formidable. "But I welcome the help. And if not to help this old fool, at least you will save our friends there."

"How?" Rune asked as he, last among us, stood.

"Let's make more noise than they did," Odin replied.

One second later, he slashed the bush in half and rushed toward Fenrir and his fate.

All of us followed.

18

The way I viewed the gods had changed over the years, reaching its lowest point after Heimdallr's death. But I had forgotten how strong and formidable they could be and the miracles they could muster. Odin reminded me of it that day. He reminded me why we worshipped them and why they were feared.

The plain was packed with Jötnar and wolves wondering what to do about this strange signal in the sky. The most boorish of their kind had left right away, but those who stayed formed a merciless barrier between us and Fenrir.

Those are the ones who died.

Odin drew blood from the moment he left the cover of the forest, slashing his great sword at the first leg and moving on without interrupting his gait. The Jötunn screamed and died by my sword. The All-Father carved a path of red and gore, cutting through the enemy as if they were a field of wheat. The five of us behind Odin had little to do besides ending their torment. At least, at first.

Chaos sprayed like a wildfire, and fights erupted around us as we walked toward the crack. In a matter of seconds, we went from a jog to a run, avoiding axes, hammers, and fangs as the improvised battle increased in intensity. Odin must have used a charm, for few of them even looked at us. We were smaller than most Jötnar, but they barely noticed our presence as we cut and slashed. Some did, and they were dealt with right away. Tyr ran right behind Odin, with Bjorn on the other side, and whatever our lord left alive, they took care of. All those Jötnar and wolves had turned the plain into a snow soup that was more brown than white. It was slippery and mushy.

A Jötunn fell between Gunhild and me, and he saw us. His face widened, and he yelled something right before my sword pierced his throat. I hadn't been fast enough, and the tide of the chaos changed.

Those around us interrupted their struggles and noticed us, too. There was a moment of hesitation. My heart ached as Odin's voice boomed over the sudden quiet.

A flash of blue light and a hot wind passed through me. The wave of *seidr*, benign to me, was like a hammer to our enemies. They fell backward, shocked by Odin's power.

"Run!" Odin yelled.

So far we had been protected by our size and the density of the crowd. Now, we were the center of attention. And for the second time in my life, I ran toward the crack in the volcano. We wasted no more time on killing.

"They're coming," I shouted.

The crack was right in front of us, just a few seconds away, but a small group of five Jötnar had gathered by its entrance, probably guessing it was our destination. We would have to fight our way through, I thought, then Odin once again proved me wrong.

He leaped, and it was a jump worthy of a young Æsir. The All-Father seemed to hang in the air, blade high above his head and voice echoing through the plain. It astonished those Jötnar, and only one of them had the brains to raise his shield. A pointless act, anyway. Odin's sword sliced through the air, a spear-length before he should have hit them, but a wide splash of red welcomed him as he landed. Five heads rolled by our feet as we penetrated the volcano, leaving a scene of carnage and a good hundred confused enemies in our wake.

"That was madness," Rune said as we struggled through the narrow path. He was barely sweating; I was drowning in it.

"Didn't need us at all," Gunhild said, closing the march. She and Bjorn had more troubles than the rest, their bellies and thick armor proving cumbersome.

"No fat jokes, all right?" Bjorn said as he pushed himself between two sharp rocks.

"Not feeling like joking," I said.

Fenrir would be at the end of the path, along with his sons and daughters. Odin was powerful, but Fenrir's *seidr* was dark and heavy. And between those two supernatural beings, I didn't think I would leave the volcano alive. Even if, by some miracle, Fenrir was killed, how were we to escape? I shook my head. What was the point of thinking beyond Fenrir? Each wolf I took down would be one less for my brothers at Ragnarök. This was my purpose. Fight, kill, make my kind proud, and die.

"They're coming from behind," Gunhild said.

On my last visit here, I had only faced wolves. But today, they had Jötnar with them, and some were small enough to follow us. I had not thought about it.

"Move," Odin yelled from the front as if we had been idle so far.

I heard them swearing and puffing behind us. We moved

faster, scratching our skins and bumping our knees on the walls, but their voices were getting closer.

"Drake," Gunhild said, "your shield."

"Why?" I asked.

"There's a smudge on it," she replied. "What d'you think, you idiot? I need it!"

Uncerimoniously, she shoved it behind her, sticking it across the wall so that it formed an improvised obstacle. Then she took a stance behind the shield, her own tightly gripped against her chest.

"Go!" she said.

We had no time to argue, so I left Gunhild to protect our backs. She was a Wolf, and I wouldn't have hesitated with another of them. I owed her my trust.

We passed a turn in the corridor right after I heard Gunhild insulting some Jötunn's mother.

"Don't worry," Rune said over his shoulder. "It turns out a shield isn't so important."

In a way, he was right; shields against wolves would be as useful as horns on a chicken. And at least I could use both my blades at the same time. I drew Wedge from my back, feeling much better with her weight in my hand. Crimson was already red. Blessed be Brokkr for his craft.

I bumped into my surrogate son; we had halted.

"What's happening?" I asked.

Bjorn shrugged, but I guessed Odin had stopped moving. He had arrogantly challenged the prophecy earlier, but as he approached his fate, even Odin would hesitate.

He'd been alive for thousands of years. There may even have been times when he was tired of it and wished for an end. But it waited now a few steps away. A rumble of barks and howls called for us. It was sinister and maddening, but maybe Odin heard more in it. The call from death, the horn of destiny, the end of his saga. Who knows what the All-Father saw in his all-wise mind as we reached Fenrir's lair?

Tyr dropped a hand on his father's shoulder. Odin nodded.

Fenrir had been expecting me last time, but on that day, the lair offered a different sight. Wolves of all sizes and colors had gathered in a dense mass around Fenrir, who stood giant and dark at the center of the volcano. It reminded me of the gods' gathering, where I had boldly claimed I would save Odin.

"Thor's balls," Rune said, his mouth agape as he noticed the bestial shape of Fenrir. The Wolf King stood on all fours, snarling. He was in a mood today.

There was no smart approach to be made here. If Fenrir didn't know about our presence, he soon would. And as Odin said, we had to make more noise than our comrades in the woods. So we did.

Odin's voice shook the earth and my chest as he bellowed his challenge, and for the time of a breath, everything became quiet. It changed when the five of us charged.

I immediately lost sight of Bjorn on our far right. He hammered his great axe at the closest beast before it understood that they were under attack.

Wolves, while being lethal and cunning, aren't the bravest creatures by nature, and when suddenly faced with an angry Æsir, their first reflex was to back away. It was all the space we needed.

Tyr got his arm-sword wet as he shouldered the closest beast. He aimed for the heart, and the wolf died before it toppled to the ground. His blade came out with no difficulty, and Tyr moved to his next victim with the dexterity of a swallow in flight.

Odin was less precise and didn't need to be. His sword

cut the air, claiming blood from a distance, leaving only a line of dying beasts ten meters deep. More took their spots, and after the second slash, a few dared to come closer, realizing this was their only chance. Rune and I took care of those.

He threw one of his axes at the closest beast, and I swore inside, for you just don't discard one of your blades like that, but the wolf fell at Rune's feet. He had just enough time to pluck his weapon from the beast's skull before jumping away from the next.

The third wolf came at me. It was a gray beast, thin and aggressive, with eyes of fire and yellow fangs made for the kill. I had seen it crouching when Odin had last used his *seidr*. It had been smart then, but not so much for picking me.

I took a step back when the wolf jumped for my throat and raised Crimson to welcome the beast. It didn't die right away, but I could see my blade in its maw as it tried, again and again, to close it on me. Life vanished from its eyes as I lay its massive head on the ground.

Odin's *seidr* passed through me again, and more of the beasts died in front of my eyes, cut down by a wave of magic. It was unfair, but fairness and war don't belong together.

And we needed to make noise.

I don't know what we expected from such a direct approach, but it worked. They were hesitant, kept on their paws by Odin, and punished for their bravery by the rest of us. Each life we claimed got us closer to Fenrir, who watched, quiet and helpless, his chain stretched to its maximum.

"This is fun," Bjorn said as he regained his spot by my side. He looked savage, his whole chest marred in red and his hair hanging widely around his generous face.

"No, it ain't," I said. We had done the easiest part. The real ordeal had yet to come.

As we moved farther, we exposed our backs. Worse, the wolves regained their senses. We had used the element of surprise. They backed away all at once, and judging by Odin's crisping face, they had measured the reach of his attack. Bjorn and Tyr moved to the back of our small band so that we formed a square around Odin. I thought that maybe Fenrir had ordered his soldiers down and was inviting us to come to him, close enough for his fangs and claws to matter. But this wasn't his plan.

They had regrouped and attacked all at once, and my blood froze.

There was another wave of Odin's *seidr,* which sprayed enough blood to form a curtain of red in front of us. More wolves ran through it. We welcomed them. They would swarm us in no time, but I wouldn't make it easy for them.

Wedge and Crimson were hard at work, the first keeping them at a distance, the second piercing through skin, bone, and flesh. This wasn't time for fine work; it was time to butcher the bastards. One wolf died with Wedge lodged in its eye, and I almost lost the knife, but a second bumped his dead brother away, and I managed to keep hold of the blade. I shoved it into the newcomer's maw, feeling the heat of his breathing on my face and the iron smell as it tried to bite my arm off. Energy vanished from the beast, but its fangs still damaged my skin and drew some blood. I fell with the wolf and swung Crimson widely to scare my next opponent while I recovered my footing.

My arms grew warm and tired, my breathing difficult, and my mouth turned so dry that I welcomed my sweat in it. But the fire was there, taking root in my chest, vibrant and intoxicating. I did not think twice about what it meant and unleashed it through a jab when the next beast climbed his dead sibling.

Teeth flew from its lower maw, which completely unhinged itself and hung pitifully as the beast looked at me, eyes filled with terror. It wanted to flee; I could see it in its pleading stare, but I was filled with this powerful fury and stabbed Crimson through its brain.

I thought for a moment, dazed by my own strength, that we could manage. As if somehow, by myself, I could take on the entire lair.

But we were losing.

When I turned to check the situation, I saw Bjorn, his right arm dripping with blood. He was using Tyr for support, but the Æsir fared little better. His shield was nowhere to be seen, and the blade from his arm-sword had broken in half.

Odin's eye was closed. I assumed he was gathering his magic for the next slash, for my chest felt suddenly heavy. Part of me wanted to scream at him for not taking a more active part in the action. But Odin was the only reason we yet lived.

A scream took me back to my side of the fight, just in time to see Rune hard at work with two white wolves. His axes moved slower than before. With some extreme luck, he landed a blow on the nose of the closest one, which did not kill it but sent it back into the pack. The second, however, got its jaws on Rune's leg.

He looked at me with sorry eyes as the pain suddenly penetrated him, and just as he started screaming, Rune vanished from my sight. The wolf who had caught my son went back, pulling Rune to be torn apart. The fire turned to ice as the youngest of my men was swallowed by the pack of wolves.

"Drake!" Odin yelled right before he attacked again.

This wave of *seidr* passed through me, but this time I felt pain. Odin had put more of his power in it. The howls whimpered all around us as the wolves died.

"Get him," the All-Father said, his voice weak and coarse. He even dropped to one knee.

I rushed to the pile of bodies where I assumed Rune would be found, slipping on bowels as I knelt. Fenrir howled a sound that chilled me to the bones, but I had no time to check him or the others. I was more afraid than ever and counted on Odin to keep any of the animals away while I searched for Rune.

A hand sprouted between two carcasses, curled like a dead spider. I gripped it. My breath came back when the grip was returned.

"Don't move," I stupidly said as I pushed the upper wolf a little, just enough to see Rune's face, red and pale.

"I'm all right," he said, though he looked anything but.

A shadow lurked over the carcass I meant to push farther, and I wondered which of us had come to help. Its form suggested a thin man, which could have been Tyr, but I saw two hands, both holding a sword. The shadow raised his right hand, and I looked up just in time to parry the real deal with the flat of Crimson.

Fenrir was capable of shifting from wolf to man; so were some of his sons and daughters, it seemed. The man facing me was as close to a wolf as a man could be. Naked, save for the two blades, his body was athletic, carved from a life of hunting. His hairy chest and the hair hanging low in locks spoke of a wild man, while his long canines and deadly little eyes belonged to a killer. He swung his sword again, not with the dexterity of a man but with a greater force. It shook my arm to its core when I parried again. The man-wolf yelled and hacked, not leaving me a second to stand or gain a better position.

He barked and smiled a horrendous grin until Rune's hand found his ankle. I thought he would cut it, but this second of inattention was all I needed, and Crimson plunged into his belly before he could react.

Killing a wolf is a tricky business. You never knew what you hit or if it was going to be enough, but men, that I knew. I stood, using the traction of my sword in his abdomen to pull myself up. The man-wolf seemed confused, then his eyes rolled inside his head, and he joined his siblings in death.

The more regular wolves had backed away, forming a large circle around us again, but through their ranks appeared more of those men-beasts. A good dozen of them. They formed a crude shield wall, then came to us. I pulled Rune out of the meat trap and took us back to the All-Father.

"I'm all right," he kept saying as I dragged him through the corpses and puddles of blood.

"I know," was all I could reply.

"You took your time," Odin said.

I was about to tell him where he could shove his impatience, but one look at my lord was enough to shut my mouth. Heat was evaporating from him in a continuous wave of undulating air. He was drained. We had covered nearly half of the distance from the crack to Fenrir, but Odin was wasted while the Wolf King remained fresh and ready.

Fenrir flashed his deadly fangs in a smile. He was sending us his best sons and daughters, and even if that failed, he still had hundreds of soldiers willing to sacrifice themselves. They would inevitably swarm us.

Bjorn's face had turned the color of sour milk, his eyes

lost in the distance, and if nothing was done, he would die before he would be killed. Tyr sat him down, using his leg as a support for my champion. I dropped Rune behind him so that they could support each other.

"Keep him awake," I told both and received two feeble nods in reply.

I had not seen her coming back, but Gunhild was now standing by Tyr's side, Bjorn's axe in hand. She had lost a finger on her left hand, and blood was pouring from her scalp, but she fared better than most of us. She must have been right on our heels, though I had failed to notice her.

"They had very long spears," she told me in what could pass for an apology.

And just as she spoke, Jötnar emerged from the crack. Few of them, and on the short side, but they were enough to keep us from escaping. The two shield walls approached from both sides. We had lost.

"I'm sorry your time with us has been so short," I told Gunhild.

"Whose fault is that?" she sarcastically asked. Even at a time like this, Gunhild could spit her bitterness in my face. "It's an honor nonetheless," she said.

"Father," Tyr said.

"Give me some time," Odin spat. "Drake, get me some time."

He had spoken as if I could fetch him a few minutes from the pantry, but it showed how weak Odin was that he needed an Einheri to stall our enemy. Time would not help much, I thought, but Odin had an idea, and since I had none, I obeyed.

"Is this what you want?" I shouted from the bottom of my lungs. "Fenrir, is this what you want? You'd let your pups kill Odin and Tyr?"

"Drake, what are you doing?" Tyr asked.

"Getting us some time," I answered.

"Why should I care how they die, as long as they do, human?" Fenrir replied, his big wolf voice bouncing throughout the lair.

"Because I know what they did to you," I replied. "They betrayed you, and nothing will feel right if you don't end them yourself. Am I wrong?"

Fenrir woofed, and his sons halted their march just a few paces from us. The Jötnar followed their examples.

"Do you recognize me?" I asked, stepping forward and jolting Crimson in the air. "Do you recognize this?"

Fenrir squinted, sniffed the air, and snarled his wolfish smile. "Drake?" he asked. "I am glad to see you again, though you make a bad habit of killing my children. So, this is your real form?"

"It is, Wolf King." *Good*, I thought, *let's keep chatting*.

"My father?" he asked.

"Dead, as promised."

"How did he die?"

"Faster than intended," I said. Fenrir growled. "Heimdallr crushed his throat; it was painful, at least."

"Ah," Fenrir barked. "Loki died voiceless; how appropriate."

I let Fenrir decide what would be said next. His shield wall was so close to me that I could admire the designs of the few shields they carried. A wolf, of course, howling to the sun, carved inside the metal itself with great dexterity. It was made by Dwarves, and I wondered which of their clans had been working with the Jötnar. I counted twelve men and women beasts in the wall, all naked and armed with swords, spears, and shields.

"You had your vengeance, my friend," Fenrir said, "now it's time I have mine."

"Not from where you stand, you won't," I replied. "You want your fangs at Odin's throat, don't you? You want to drink Tyr's blood yourself. I know because this is what I would want. I promise you, Fenrir, if you let them be killed by one of your pups, you will spend the rest of your life regretting it. You will feel hollow, incomplete. It will gnaw at your spirit until you turn mad with bitterness."

"Break my bonds," Fenrir said, "break it, and I will come to you."

"I don't have this power," I said. "And even if I did, I would not free you, Fenrir; you're too much of a threat."

"That's what your *gods* made me," he barked. "I was no threat." He took a step to the side, making his chain rattle on the ground. "I was their ally; I even loved some of them." The last bit, I knew, was meant for Tyr.

"I know," I said, observing Fenrir in his back-and-forth pacing. "But now you are a threat to my kind. We can't change that."

The man-wolf facing me at no more than a sword length growled with impatience. He was a lord of his people, one of Fenrir's chosen sons, but he was an animal, and his lust for my flesh was stressing him to the limits of his patience. The woman next to him had an even harder time. Her tongue passed over her lips, and she could not stop staring at the jugular vein pulsing blood along my throat.

"And you will die here today," Fenrir said, "and we can't change that. So what do you want from me, Drake? Another chicken?"

"You know the prophecy as well as I do," I said. "You are to kill Odin, but his son will avenge him. Well, Odin's only son here is Tyr. I offer a *holmsgang* between you and Tyr. If you win, you get to keep sending your children at us until we all die, knowing that no matter what, none of us here can kill you. If Tyr wins, we go free."

A look over my shoulder allowed me to see Tyr nodding. He approved of my request. But he could not know that Fenrir would refuse. The king of the beasts hated Tyr more than any other being in the nine realms. They had loved each other deeply, and Tyr had betrayed Fenrir. A part of him lusted after Tyr's death and suffering.

But another part still loved him, maybe even tried to understand Tyr's act, and would want nothing more than to forgive him. I knew because I had loved and hated Muninn. Three years or four hundred years would change nothing. I would be incapable of hating her, just as Fenrir could not stop loving Tyr, even if a little.

"I see," Fenrir said, stretching the last syllable in a very snake-like fashion. "It seems, my friend, that you do not yet understand the prophecy."

"What do you mean?" I asked.

"I'm afraid you will die not knowing," Fenrir said. "You offer me nothing, Drake. In fact, I believe you are just stalling."

"It was worth trying," I said, smiling at the king because he, too, I could not hate.

"You did well. Odin has probably rested a little. Let us see if it will be enough. Go back to your men. This is the last time I grant you a favor, Drake."

I saluted Fenrir with my sword, offering the sight of its gory blade to the men facing me.

In truth, I would have loved to exchange more words with Fenrir. Not to stall for Odin, but just because he was a being I could understand and who could understand me.

Those were few in the nine realms, and it pained me that one of us would die today.

"All I could do," I told Odin as I regained my spot.

"I wasn't resting," Odin replied.

"I know, All-Father, I know," I said, patting him on the shoulder as I would any other man. Rune's eyes were open and alive; he was not in immediate danger, but the same could not be said of Bjorn. His blood had finally interrupted its flow, stopped by a flimsy bandage, but his breath was shallow and uneven.

"A shame he refused," Tyr said.

"He'd never have accepted," I replied, just as the two shield walls reformed their ranks.

"Drake, those shields?"

"Dwarvish," I replied.

Odin's tongue clicked angrily in his mouth. "Damn those dirt-eaters," he said. "My *seidr* can't pass through those things."

Both Jötnar and men-wolves resumed their slow approach and knowing that half of them would have to be faced the regular way wasn't a pleasant perspective. Even worse, among us, only Gunhild had a shield.

"I will take care of those bastards behind," Odin said, "then *we* take care of those in front. Just make sure they don't backstab me before I'm done here—Wait!" He closed his eye, and a discreet smile found his lips. I thought for a moment that we had lost Odin again, that his madness had returned and would leave us in an even worse situation. The men-wolves were ten paces away, and if anything, at least it would be over soon. I would curse fate from Hel.

Dozens of thoughts passed through my brain as I stared at death. I thought of Muninn, who would join me in the underworld. Lif and her grandfather, who I would never see again. I sent my apologies to Eitri, for his brother's blade would most likely never see Nidavellir again. I cursed for having learned of Rune's place in my world just to have him taken away from it a day later.

"All right, listen," Odin said, eye open again. "Form a line. Tyr on the left, Drake on the right, and—"

"Gunhild," she said without anger.

"Gunhild in the middle. You don't attack until the very last moment. Drake, don't go for the one in front of you; take the ugly one to his left. Hear me?"

"Yes," I said, wondering if Odin had somehow seen the future. This wasn't a power I knew he had, but with the lord of lords, you just didn't know what he was capable of. So I shifted my gaze to the shields facing us, six men, two lines deep. The one in front of me was the one I had faced earlier during my exchange with Fenrir, but Odin had told me to leave him, so I checked the one on his left.

If there was a wolfish version of Thor, it was this one. Wide shoulders, brown and red hair in a bush of a beard, and a chest to rival Bjorn's, this would be my victim. The details of his face appeared clearer. The missing tooth in his grin, the small twitching of his right eye, the scar at the bottom of his left ear, I saw all of him.

Three steps before they came into striking distance, Odin used his power and grunted as a wave of *seidr* reduced the back wall to a pile of corpses. They had no shields to protect them, and by the sound of it, they died viciously. Odin dropped to his knee right after, cursing into his beard. If this was all he could do, we were lost. The Jötnar's death did not slow the wolves.

I sucked my breath in and kept my blades low, steady, until the very last moment, just as Odin had said.

It came like a bolt. The blink of an eye during which a

warrior raises his weapon and gives you a small, careless opportunity. I stabbed Wedge into the big man-wolf's throat, feeling all the tissues and nerves binding the head to the body, leaving me completely exposed to his neighbor's blade.

Odin's future then shined on me.

The one who should have killed me died right in front of my eyes. He died, an arrow sprouting from the top of his head.

Odin had not seen the future; he had made it happen.

Yes, he had not been resting. This old, cunning bastard of an Æsir had called for reinforcements, and they came from the sky.

Two black wings covered the battle with their shadows. Huginn had come, and not alone. Tucked in his arms, facing forward, hung Iona, her bow already pulling a second arrow. Just as I did, some of Fenrir's children checked this surprising appearance, but I recovered faster and shortened the wall on my right with one less of them. The she-wolf died holding the wide cut I had traced across her throat, and as she gargled, I managed to pick the heavy shield from my first victim's cold hands.

Huginn landed heavily behind our thin line, and a couple of seconds later, Iona stood on my right. I blocked a blow coming at her from the second line of our opponents. Iona did not, in fact, need my protection, for she could shift from woman to ghost at will. Something the wolf-man facing her found out the hard way.

"No, take them," I heard Odin say.

"I can't take two," Huginn replied.

"Fuck, son, do something," Odin barked.

The circle of beasts seemed to tighten around us as their best warriors died at our hands. Gunhild was struggling, but her curses remained strong, while Tyr, I knew, would be facing the brunt of their attack. They had six dead, while two more warriors joined us. But it only excited the wolves along the circle. Who knew how long they would keep their ground before charging again?

"Grab him," Huginn said.

I felt a whoosh of wind on my back, and a mere second later, Huginn was in the sky again, Rune in his arms. The young warrior held Bjorn by the belt, leaving my champion's arms and legs to dangle as the raven struggled to a greater height.

Huginn chose his direction poorly and was about to pass right above Fenrir, who was crouching low. My heart sank as Fenrir leaped, jaws wide open. It all happened slowly in my mind. The king had timed it perfectly. His fangs would close on the three of them just as he would peak. Rune's name escaped me in a scream.

Fenrir's jaws shut, but Gleipnir reached its limits. The chain binding the Wolf King dragged him back to the ground with a vengeance. The earth shook as Fenrir landed on his side, and Huginn flew away unharmed.

Rune was safe. I could fight again.

I would die on that day. Wolves would feed on my flesh, drink my blood, and fight for scraps of me. All I could do was avenge myself first.

I punched the shield into my next victim's nose and followed with a stab through his mouth. His face recovered some of its canine form as he died, but I was already on the next. I pushed through and cracked their wall. They went from outnumbering us to having me at their backs.

I was furious, not caring for my life. I stabbed and slashed, pierced one's back as he was locked with Gunhild, then freed one from Tyr. He was more agile and managed to block my thrust. But just as he meant a riposte, Odin's sword came out of his chest.

There was still more fight in me, but no one left to kill.

Huginn landed by our side once more, this time properly since he was alone. It didn't stop him from kneeling. He shook and struggled back to his feet. The old raven had been created to carry thoughts, not people.

"Is that the best you got, you ugly mutt?" Odin yelled. "Why don't you lie down and wait for me to end your miserable, rabid life, huh?"

Fenrir's hair stood on his body, making him look even bigger and threatening. He was pissed, and his snarl was the stuff of nightmares. He roared like a bear, or more like a hundred bears, and immediately, the neat circle of wolves disbanded, and they came rushing.

Iona's next arrow landed straight into some gray wolf's shoulder, which did not stop it. She picked the next arrow, but it would be the last. The wolves would reach us before the third.

"Take Gunhild and Iona," I told Huginn, who had probably guessed my thoughts, for his hands were already on Gunhild's belt.

"Drake, no," Iona said, but before she knew it, Gunhild hugged her. Her arrows rained down harmlessly from her quiver as they took off.

Odin bellowed. Tyr and I imitated him, and we charged.

Nowhere was safe, so we went straight toward Fenrir.

The All-Father stabbed his sword ahead and instead of a wave of *seidr,* it became a spear thrust of it. It carved a corridor of flesh through the ranks of beasts. Fenrir was right ahead, the only living thing facing us.

The shock of Odin's thrust quickly faded, and the wolves closed on us again. They formed a new fence between us and their father. One I was willing to shatter. Bringing the shield against my chest, I charged without any thought. I just wanted to open the way for Odin. All that mattered was for the All-Father to kill the beast. We could end Ragnarök right here, right now. I only had to burst through whatever stood in our way.

I put my shoulder into it, I put my life into it, I put all the fire burning in my chest into this charge. I yelled like never before, letting the heat of battle completely take me over. Head low, I could not see what I would hit, but when I did, I felt its bones break and heard its whimper of panic. Then that of those behind it. I pushed the heat, shoving its power from my body to the shield, then farther ahead, and still kept charging.

Until, all of a sudden, there was no more resistance.

I fell face-first, taken by my own momentum.

I opened my eyes in panic, only to see Fenrir ahead and above. I thought he was smiling, but when I recovered from my fall, I realized that he was snarling, and I was now within his reach.

Odin leaped over me, his blade dripping and his chipped helmet shining like the Bifröst. Fenrir brought his paw down on him, but the All-Father skipped away and gave a wide cut at the wolf's leg.

"Drake!" Tyr called. He, too, had taken one of the Dwarvish shields, and this is what I grabbed so he could help me up. I did so just in time to welcome the charge of a more daring beast. Tyr took care of it while I simply raised my shield against its claws. That's when I realized how depleted of energy I was. I could not raise the shield longer than needed and let my arm fall with exhaustion.

The others hesitated, if not because of us, at least because we stood in Fenrir's range, and nothing was safe from their father as he fought a duel of legend with the leader of the Æsir.

Odin was on top of Fenrir's skull, right between the ears, about to bring the tip of his great sword down, but the king shook his head violently, and Odin was thrown off balance. He landed flat on the ground and coughed some blood.

Fenrir's paw pinned him down, almost entirely covering his body. Tyr and I watched, dumbstruck, as Fenrir brought his maw by Odin's head.

"Fenrir!" Tyr yelled. "Wait."

The king obeyed. His blood-filled eye shifted to us, but he kept his fangs so close to Odin's neck that he could end it whenever he chose.

Tyr dropped his shield and worked on the laces of his arm-sword. He removed it with a grunt, leaving his bloody stump exposed. Then, he drove the blade to the tip of his wounded arm and cut a deep line.

"What are you doing?" I asked, mortified at seeing my friend hurting himself so badly. Fenrir's whole body shook with rage. Tyr dropped the sword, which fell with a heavy clunk, then shoved his fingers into the wound. When he took them out, red and slick, they held a piece of dark metal.

"You want this," Tyr said to Fenrir as the king removed his deathtrap from Odin's face.

Tyr held a key. The key to Gleipnir, I understood. The only way for the beast to escape its chains.

Huginn landed once more by our side, and he seemed to understand the situation right away, for he did not even ask.

"You let Father go, and those two," Tyr said, "and this is yours."

The king growled at the sight of something he wanted more than vengeance, freedom. His gigantic head swayed from Tyr to Odin and back to Tyr, calculating how he could get both. He could not, especially with Huginn here.

"How can I trust you?" Fenrir asked.

"Look," Tyr said, keeping his hands high, the key in evidence, "no trick this time."

He took a step forward, but I could not let him go. I grabbed his arm, the one with the key.

"What are you doing?" I asked.

"Atoning for my mistakes," Tyr said, "as you suggested."

"That's not what I meant," I replied, not liking the implied accusation.

"But you were right. We wronged Fenrir and brought this situation on us. Me, more than anyone. I am the keeper of justice; one arm isn't enough of a price for my betrayal. Let me do this, for Father at least." He gently shook my hand off and took another few steps. "Hand us Father," he then asked Fenrir.

The king removed his paw from our lord and took a step back. Odin coughed again, but his eye remained closed. He was alive but not with us.

"Drake," Tyr called, inviting me to get Odin back.

I passed by him, not looking at his face. His decision was my fault; I had pushed him to face his guilt, and he would pay the price for my harshness.

Odin was out for good. I picked him up as I would a sleeping child, for it was clear from his deformed armor that he had a bunch of broken ribs and probably more. Fenrir's shadow on my back was threatening, and the heat from his breath made my bowels twist on themselves.

"You survive another of our encounters," Fenrir said. "Next time will be different."

"Oh, one of us will die next time, I guarantee it," I said,

looking over my shoulder. "But don't you commit the same mistake your father did. Don't underestimate me."

"See you soon, my friend," Fenrir said.

I could not avoid Tyr's eyes as I passed by his side again, and I would lie if I said he looked heroic, but he was resolute.

"You still have my rune," he said, looking at the back of my hand. Three years ago, right before I left on my last mission as Odin's Drake, he had blessed me with a rune of power. I thought it was a mere symbol to give me some confidence. "Next time you see him," Tyr said with a nod toward Fenrir, "use it."

"Asgard will know what you did today," I said, and from the moment the words left my mouth, I felt their weakness.

I joined Huginn, who had the decency to say nothing for once. He stretched his wings as wide as possible and flexed them back, ready to take his flight.

"You were wrong, by the way," Tyr said, turning to face us as Huginn hugged me from behind. I tightened my grip on Odin, hoping that I wasn't making anything worse. Fenrir, looming like a mountain behind my friend, slowly vanished into thin air, and the shape of the handsome wild man took his place. He stepped closer to Tyr. "Earlier, when you told Fenrir I was Odin's only son here, you were wrong." I did not understand the meaning of his words, and it must have shown on my face. "Ask him about that when he wakes up."

Tyr's smile, as we rose, was the saddest and warmest ever given to me. He was but a speck, walking toward his former lover, when he vanished from my sight. The last I saw of him, he was alive, so close to Fenrir that they looked as if embracing. And this is the image I choose to keep of Tyr, as Huginn's wings flapped painfully through Jötunheimr's sky.

EPILOGUE

I told Huginn that he didn't need to check from the sky; they would not follow us. But he would not listen. Every so often, he would open his wings and spend the next minute scanning the horizon in search of any sign of threat. Every time, he would come down shaking his head. Fenrir would not pursue us, I knew. He had a sense of honor most of us ignored.

And if he wanted to catch us, we were not hard to track.

Bjorn and Odin lay on two makeshift stretchers, weighing our steps down and turning our progress into a slow procession. Bjorn woke up once in a while, and his face had regained some color. He was far from being out of the woods, literally and figuratively, but he had survived. Heat and rest would make him as good as new.

Odin's state, on the other hand, was worrisome. We did not stop to check him in detail, but bones had indeed been broken in several places. And what damage had not been done by Fenrir, he had done it to himself by abusing his power to the very last drop.

I ordered the group to a halt a few times, for I had not

seen his chest rise in a long time, but it would ultimately bloat again, and we, too, breathed easier.

Arn and Thrasir carried Bjorn, who was heavier. They were fresher than any of us, having missed all the fun, as Thrasir had poorly commented. But they, too, had been hard at work.

After their diversion, which had taken them to obtain a massive horn from a Jötunn, the four of them had done as planned and ran through the forest. But after a time, just as they realized the number of pursuers had decreased, Huginn heard Odin's voice in his head, and the raven rushed to our help, carrying Iona. The two Einherjar had been left to flee from wolves and Jötnar without the precious help of the Æsir or the Valkyrie.

"Never ran for so long and so fast," Arn had declared.

Gunhild and I carried Odin, though Huginn would replace one of us once in a while. Iona had her hands full with Rune, who needed her support for walking. The longer we went, the paler he became, and if I hadn't known how far we needed to go, I would have called for more halts. But we were close. Close enough that the unmistakable smell of poultry, pigs, and cattle called our attention.

The fence and gates of Eggther's farm appeared through the trees, and if nothing, our gait quickened. Heads filled with images of a hot meal and fresh ale, and they regained some energy. But Huginn and I could guess that something was wrong.

Something was missing, something big, the noise.

The place was quiet, quieter than the forest itself.

"Wait here," I said as Crimson found my hand.

The gate creaked as I pushed it open with the tip of my sword, and on the other side was a great nothing. Feathers in the thousands, piles of dung shaped like footprints, lines from wheels in the ground. An army had passed here and left with enough food for a siege.

Nothing remained, though it had not been long since the Jötnar had claimed the fruit of Eggther's herding.

"We need to hurry," Arn said as he stepped by my side.

"Aye, if it's not too late," I replied.

We moved to the hot spring. Its water was flowing freely and noisily amid the silence of the place, and there we found two things.

The first was Eggther's harp, dropped carefully against a tree. Eggther was absent, but for some reason, he had left the key to the bridge, and only then I realized how screwed we would have been if he hadn't.

The second was pinned to the same tree through its beak.

The crimson rooster, dead and missing a leg, like a bad omen for anyone coming to the farm, hung against the old fir. The message was clear; the rooster had served its purpose. It had crowed. The beasts of Jötunheimr had been warned.

Ragnarök had officially started.

To be continued in

Vengeance of Asgard.

AFTERWORD

Beasts of Jötunheimr was my favorite of the trilogy to write. Drake has moved from being a victim and is now acting out of pure anger, something that came at a cost. This second book is a transformation for him between what he was and what he will need to be in the final stage of this saga. Let's say it was his cocoon stage, and it was not fun for him. Well, you know, except for the part in Sessrúmnir...

This book was also a chance for female characters to shine more strongly than in Blood of Midgard, which wasn't difficult because there weren't many of them. Freyja, Gunhild, Iona, Lif, and Muninn shaped the second half of this book. For obvious reasons, I was looking forward to Freyja's stronger presence in this book, and the truth about Muninn's motives and her exchanges with Drake was also an interesting piece to write. Iona was a bit of a surprise character, but she is one of my favorites in this saga. And Gunhild happens to be a spin-off character, taken from the novel I mentioned in the last book's author notes, Sword-Maidens. In that one, she is a central character, and if one day I publish it, you'll find some easter eggs in the Army of One trilogy.

The saddest part of *Beasts* is the absence of the Wolves as a group. It was a necessary moment in the story for Drake to act without them, but I do love this group and can safely say that the third volume is really about them.

Again, don't try to find too much historical/lore accuracy in this book. I drew inspiration from all the "original" texts mentioning Ragnarök and Norse mythology, but it was less research-heavy than my historical fiction novels. I did my best to stay true to the Norse spirit, and I hope it was enough for you all to enjoy this saga. I look forward to its conclusion.

Skål

ACKNOWLEDGMENTS

Gratitude to any and all of the people who one day pissed me off. Your presence in my life inspired Drake in this book. You did help, after all.

A more sincere thank you to Lara Simpson, my kind-hearted editor. This is our second book together, and I enjoy the process all the more.

And an undying love to my wife, my very own goddess, who I worship with hundreds of hours of writing in her name that she will most likely never read.